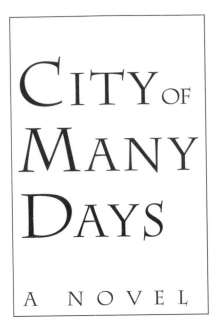

CITY OF MANY DAYS

A NOVEL

SHULAMITH HAREVEN

TRANSLATED BY HILLEL HALKIN WITH THE AUTHOR

MERCURY HOUSE
San Francisco, California

Published in the United States by
Mercury House
San Francisco, California

United States Constitution, First Amendment: Congress shall make no law respecting an establishment of religion, or prohibiting the free exercise thereof; or abridging the freedom of speech, or of the press; or the right of the people peaceably to assemble, and to petition the Government for a redress of grievances.

Mercury House and colophon are registered trademarks
of Mercury House, Incorporated

Printed on acid-free paper
Manufactured in the United States of America

Library of Congress Cataloging-in-Publication Data
Hareven, Shulamith.
    ['Ir yamim rabim. English]
    City of many days: a novel / Shulamith Hareven; revised ed.; translated by Hillel Halkin with the author.
        p.   cm.
    ISBN 1-56279-050-1
    1. Jerusalem—Fiction.   I. Title.
PJ5054.H292I713   1993
892.4'36—dc20   93-12726
                                                        CIP

5   4   3   2   1

CITY OF MANY DAYS

CHAPTER ONE

SARA'S FATHER, never having met Morality, had perhaps been exempted from it. Even in Jerusalem of the early century, which was a warm-hearted city of warm-hearted quarters, Don Isaac Amarillo was considered an exceptionally warm-hearted man, unable to resist the general sweetness of things, such as the pure breeze that blew down the oboes of the alleyways when the day's heat suddenly broke, driving before it sun-bronzed women, all colors of children, smells of jasmine crying out loud in Arab courtyards from an abundance of evening, a dusty shepherd returning from the fields of Nikophoria with a new lamb on his arm, a fragrance of arak, thyme, and repose. At such times his defenses were down, tears of utter helplessness flooded his good-natured, near-sighted eyes, any baby could bowl him over; he was capable of giving away all he possessed, his own soul, had anyone requested it, tying it in his not always immaculate handkerchief, and bestowing. One might compare him then to a big, kind Gulliver with a horde of children perched on his hat brim, tweaking his ears to make him run and stamping their feet on his forehead for the fun of it. And when summertime came, bringing the wild red rut of watermelons piled high in the market by the Jaffa Gate, along the path that led down to Hebron Road from the Old City wall, he was at the mercy of the first woman who came along.

Perhaps it was just such a time, at the break of a heat wave, when life began to flow again through the narrow streets as though blown out of a bellows, that saw him dry the tears of Hanna, a young socialist pioneer from Russia who had come to live in Jerusalem, in the new part of Bet Yisrael. As her weeping proved too much for him, he came back again and again, until she bore him a son whom she named Tanhum. Don Isaac Amarillo promptly acknowledged his paternity. Indeed, he might have acknowledged it if he hadn't been the father, too, for how was a man like him to abandon an unclaimed baby, and a little boy at that? Proud and penitent, a white tropical hat on his head, he stood in the doorway of Hanna's room, holding a bouquet of flowers. For a while he felt obliged to live with her in Bet Yisrael, so as to stand by her when taunted by the neighbors over the shameful consequences of his own too-fond heart. But the neighbors were young socialists too: they went about unkempt, wore tattered Russian blouses, worked at their printing press until all hours of the night, and couldn't have cared less about the precise origins and ancestry of Hanna's squalling child.

Three months after Hanna gave birth to Tanhum, Don Isaac was summoned home, where his wife, Gracia, had given birth too, to a second daughter named Ofra. Once again he stood proud and penitent in a doorway with a bouquet in one hand. This time it was his own wife's tears that proved too much for him. He moved back home.

Eventually Hanna took Tanhum and went to live in a village near the coast, where she taught school for a living—whereupon Don Isaac's tortuous escapades might have come to an end, had not a strange young woman turned up in Jerusalem several years later. A small, slender thing surrounded by bundles and suitcases, she arrived in a gigantic hat that resembled a cart wheel, and a white muslin dress, chattering away in loud French. Rumor had it she was the daughter of a French count and countess. Since Don Isaac was one of the heads of the Jewish community, she appeared before him in his office one morning like a starched hornet, with a roll of pictures under one arm. The story she told was a strange one. The pictures, she said, were painted by her late mother, and her one desire was for Don Isaac to help her *arranger une exposition,* that is, a public showing, in Jerusalem. Dipping her lips in a little coffee, she explained, seated opposite him, that she was the daughter of a French count and countess who traveled to Lebanon and lived there for a while, until, compelled one day to return to France on family business, they left her behind with their Arab servant and his wife. The count and countess tragically perished at sea and she became an orphan.

Don Isaac was so overcome with compassion that his tongue clucked unconsciously in his mouth. The more it clucked, the less he was able to stop it, for the tale went from bad to worse. The servant and his wife brought the girl up, but they were vulgar, common people with whom it was impossible for her to live any longer. Not only that, it was just her luck that as she matured—and her benefactor, Don Isaac, could see for himself that she wasn't exactly unattractive—her servant-guardian began making advances to her until she didn't have a moment's peace. She packed up a few of her belongings, just a smattering of what she owned, took her mother's paintings, which were her most precious possessions, and fled.

Don Isaac wiped his eyes. He would be only too happy, he declared, to come to her aid as best he could, even arrange *une exposition* of her mother's paintings in Jerusalem, though in fact no one in the neighborhood knew what *une exposition* was, or how it might be arranged. In this and all other possible ways he could think of, he would help her raise the money to trace her legal kin in France. He was so carried away by his desire to be of assistance that he hardly bothered to listen to the rest of her story, which included such things as stock companies in Panama, diamonds her guardian had made off with, and various other financial details that could make a man's head spin round and round.

The exposition never was held. On one occasion the countess wasn't feeling well; on another she feared that there weren't enough paintings for a proper show; on still another she canceled because not enough guests were invited, or because they weren't the right sort of people. Finally, when a hall had been rented and Don Isaac had taken care of everything down to the smallest detail, guaranteeing the presence of just the right number of just the right sort of guests, people who keep their promises, she sent him a messenger the morning of the opening with a note to inform him that the paintings had been stolen the night before. And that was the last of them.

Don Isaac Amarillo was not one to abandon a countess in distress. He himself was a man of some means, and he spared no effort to see that she was properly looked after with lawyers for her stocks, pawnbrokers for her jewelry, doctors for the mysterious attacks of illness that periodically befell her, and maids from Silwan for ironing her dresses. Eventually he became her slave. She sent him messages over every little thing, until he found himself devoting half his time to her and her affairs, and ultimately the whole of it. Before five months were out Don Isaac disappeared from Jerusalem one summer day along with the Countess Claudine—who, it was rumored, was not really a countess at all, and was perhaps only an allegory of Don Isaac's intimity to begin with.

Sara was seven at the time. "An evil beast hath devoured Zaki," her grandfather declared. The members of the family didn't officially go into seven days' mourning; but they did nonetheless mourn Zaki, that is, Don Isaac, their pride and their joy, of whom it was difficult to say whether he had cast them out of his life, or himself out of theirs. One way or another, he had suddenly ceased to be a husband, son-in-law, father, and son, and had become as good as dead.

Sara was sick with a fever that week, covered all over with the chicken pox, which itched and itched, and she simply couldn't believe that her father could desert her at such a time. He had always been so nice to his daughters whenever they chanced to join that invisible ballet of which his days were composed. Why, just the other evening, standing by her bedside after returning from his day's affairs, he'd gently wiped her moist brow and promised that if she didn't scratch the blisters and pockmark her face for life, he'd invite the Turkish army band to serenade her beneath her window on Saturday night. He'd promised in so many words—and now he was gone for good. In Jerusalem he was never seen again. It was said that he was in Panama. Or perhaps, like Elijah in his chariot, he was carried off in a storm, to Brazil. Sara's mother kept a stiff upper lip and never mentioned his name. In all likelihood she had hated him down all the years, with a dark and ponderous hatred, for his stupid, compassionate heart. Indeed, now that he was gone it was remarked on in Jerusalem that somehow one's contacts with Don Isaac Amarillo had always ended in disappointment. This feeling was well put by a local porch-sitter named Nissim Mizrachi, slyly translated by the sarcastic city into Miracolo Orientale because of his dandyish ways. "It's as though," said Miracolo, a thin slip of a man who drove the burial society wagon, "Zaki were always promising to take you to heaven in a speeding coach, and you trusted him so much that you didn't even look where you were going, and then suddenly, wham-bang, he reins in the horses and out of the wagon you fall."

In practical terms, nothing changed very much. The role of Sara's grandfather, Elder Amarillo, became even more clearly defined as that of paterfamilias. The family continued to live in one house with him and Sara's grandmother, a mean woman who spent all her days bedridden in her tiny alcove, from where she issued orders to the household. Grandfather Amarillo was a strong and taciturn man, strict and pious in his habits; he never patted the cheeks of the children and always met his obligations. He considered it his duty to look after Tanhum, whose grandsire he'd been made by his idiot son Zaki—nor was Sara unaware of the fact that he frequently sent money to a certain village near the coast, much to her mother's displeasure.

One day Sara met Tanhum. Hanna came with him to Jerusalem. A dry, bespectacled woman, she immediately shut herself up with grandfather in his office, with its big, black, intricately carved safe. It was shortly after the Turks had left the country, and Hanna had come on hard times. Gracia retired at once to her room, whose blinds were drawn and well tied, and lay there groaning with a headache, a handkerchief soaked in eau de cologne on her forehead, muttering *tranquil, tranquil* to herself as though it were a magic charm. Bukas, the cook, made a tomato omelet for Tanhum, who sat silently in the kitchen and refused to eat.

Sara saw him when she entered the room: he was only a little shorter than herself, thin and intense, with electric, strong hair. She sat without a word by his side and cut up everything on his plate into little bites, though he was at least nine years old and could have done it himself; yet he took the food from her hands and ate. "Eat, Tanhum, eat," she urged him on quietly, a lump forming in her throat. He didn't shy away when she stroked his wiry hair. His arm was black-and-blue all over, because, Bukas said, that *pisgada* of a pioneer was always pinching it. The two of them sat on the windowsill, swinging their legs; though they didn't talk, they were friends. Afterward, Sara wasn't sure whether they really hadn't exchanged a word that day. She would have given anything to remember, for within the year they found out that Tanhum was dead of diphtheria. If Don Isaac Amarillo had any sons left, they could only be growing up in Panama, watered daily by his contrition. And if he hadn't, there were only the two daughters.

Grandfather Amarillo prayed hard all week long; Bukas wiped her eyes in the corners of the house; and even Sara's mother was heard to remark, "*Pobro chico,* to think that such a good-looking boy could come from such an ugly thing!" The day of her unbearable migraine, it appeared, she had sneaked a good look at the two of them through a crack in the blinds.

Hanna moved soon after to a kibbutz, several of whose members she knew from her old neighborhood in Jerusalem. In time she married a pioneer from Germany, a fanatical socialist who was bald and loved sports. Grandfather Amarillo stopped sending her money and even gifts for the holidays. The family lost touch with her.

The holidays were the worst times of all. The first night of each of them her mother's quarrels with her grandfather invariably came to a boil, frothing up like one of Bukas's pots, which were always seething and simmering crossly, like the cook herself. Gracia wanted a divorce in order to be able to remarry. Grandfather Amarillo wouldn't hear of it. "Some day," he would say, "Zaki will come back. What will become of you then? Shall we make a harlot out of you?" "Then find him for me so that he can divorce me himself," Gracia would scream in a desperate, drawn-out, up-and-down wail. "You have no pity!"

She knew perfectly well that Don Isaac was not to be found. There wasn't an agency through which Elder Amarillo hadn't tried to trace him; he had even turned to the British government, whose tentacles were all over the world. Privately, he was of the opinion that Zaki was no longer alive. "The boy is crazy," he admitted, "that's true. And he's weak, that's true too. But it's still inconceivable that he would leave his wife and family in such a fix, just like that. If he could write, he would write. Chances are that he's dead."

Sometimes Grandfather Amarillo was brought lists by Captain Tony Crowther of His Majesty's Army. In them were the names of all sorts of men whose bodies had been found, murdered perhaps in some violent brawl in one of the port cities of the world, under smoky, flickering lights, amid the smells of cheap alcohol, fish, seaweed, and salt; astride rotting, slippery planks, on docks and piers licked by the ocean tides, in the shadows of moldy warehouses greasy with gas and tar. There were lists of the dead in railway accidents too, descriptions of men missing, of curious fatalities in India and Abyssinia, Turkey and British Guiana, circumcised corpses of whom nothing else was known. Lord, how many weird, anonymous, footloose Jews were on the run in your world!

None of the descriptions fit. The names on the lists were strange, even comical, each a joke in itself. Sara and Ofra would sit in a corner and repeat them one by one, roaring with laughter. Their lives were permeated with the names and fragments of names of the anonymous dead. Men put on and took off names like clothing, changed them; the name became a rag, came to life again in some office in Jerusalem like a balloon blown gloriously up for a minute, for the sake of some document, clarification, identification, only to be punctured again and discarded like old scrap. None of them was Don Isaac, neither the official Isaac ben Rabbi Moses Amarillo of the record books, nor the Zaki whom everyone knew. One day Captain Crowther brought a faded, yellowed photograph of a man in a white hat, dressed in a white tropical suit and white shoes. Sporting a thin mustache, he stood leaning on a column in the patio of some villa against a background of palms. It was hard to say whether the villa was real, or a painted backdrop in some photographer's studio. Elder Amarillo, his daughter-in-law, his children and grandchildren inspected this snapshot for three or four days with a magnifying glass, until they returned it to the captain with a mixture of heartbreak and relief: no, it wasn't he. The Englishman, who happened to be in dress uniform with a diagonal belt on his chest and a swagger stick under one arm, sipped his arak on ice, the cloudy complexion of which may have reminded him of London fog, and said: "Pity!" He looked intensely as he spoke at Sara's mother, who seemed the most romantic-looking woman he had seen in his life.

That evening Gracia stayed up sobbing till midnight:

"I can't stand it any longer! May God strike me dead! All the wicked live, let Him kill me instead!"

Sara and Ofra stopped their ears in their room and put their dolls to sleep with a lullaby:

> *Daddy's work is far away*
> *He'll come back at close of day*
> *He'll bring games for us to pla-a-y.*

In the course of time Gracia's suffering became ritualized. With the approach of every holiday or feast, the family braced itself for her screams, her migraines, her vehement slamming of doors, her drawn-out wails that faded away in the end to an incantatory *tranquil, tranquil,* her appeals to God in Hebrew, French, and Ladino. Glancing up at the grandfather clock that stood in the kitchen, where she was busy straining egg-folded wheat to make grits, her sleeves pushed back and her arms caked with flour, Bukas would grumble:

"Look how late it is! Why hasn't she started yet?"

The whole neighborhood awaited Gracia's screams: they gave everyone the chance to say *miskenika,* poor little one, allowed the women to despise their husbands and remind them of all their sins, and the men to congratulate themselves, despite their peccadilloes, for not acting like that fool of a Zaki, who left his wife high and dry. At such times a kind of communal atonement took place, a ritual of purification that reaffirmed what mattered in life and made everyone feel his self-worth. The important thing, the neighborhood held, was what went on behind a family's doors, not in front of them—and so strengthened in their convictions, all sat down to eat, penitents if not perfect angels, poured the children a drop of wine, and made sure that they drank no more.

Once when Sara was sitting in the kitchen with Bukas, kneading a small ball of dough which she had plucked from the bowl, she inquired:

"Bukas, why doesn't Grandfather let my mother get married again?"

"Who said she wants to get married?" said Bukas crossly. "Much screaming does not make a single truth."

Sara jumped up and hit her. Grandmother Amarillo banged with her cane on the floor of her room to make them stop. Bukas went to complain. It ended with angry tears.

"Don't you ever dare tell me again my mother's a liar!"

"She's not only a liar, she's cross-eyed too," said Bukas as she left the room.

Little by little, however, Sara began to think that perhaps Bukas was right. There was something put on about her mother's holiday tantrums. Once Sara went up to her mother's room before the Passover seder and saw her burning a piece of cork in order to blacken the already dark circles beneath her eyes. Sara and Ofra stopped paying attention to Gracia's attacks. Only Grandfather Amarillo still paced back and forth in his room, troubled and ill at ease: back and forth, while his daughter-in-law wailed downstairs, until, spying Sara in the doorway, he would motion her inside and hand her a bill from the safe.

"Go buy yourself something, *miskenika.*"

There was an air of trumpery in Grandmother's room: ancient, cunning trumpery, brazen and improperly concealed. Grandmother was full of a malicious energy. She rambled querulously on and on, whether to herself or someone else no one knew:

"I'm sixty years old. That's a fact. Of all the neighbors only Luna Cordoso *no tiene* any shame, she says I'm seventy-two. What a lie, what a lie! God strike me dead if there's a word of truth in what she says. They've all become liars, *kazzabeen.* It's impossible to live with them. That Bukas is the biggest liar of all. *Mentirosa.* She told me she paid four mils for my handkerchiefs, but I saw it say five on the label with my own eyes. Why does she lie to an old woman? What for? When I don't get out of bed, nobody knows I suffer. Everyone cheats me to my face. Gracia's a liar *también.*"

The matter of prices was anything but simple. Grandmother Amarillo refused to believe a word about prices going up. The merchants, she insisted, were cheats, and the family was stupid enough to be cheated. To placate her, it became a household rule never to tell her the real price of anything. Even this didn't satisfy her, though, and she would begin to mutter to herself, chewing the price with her ancient teeth. The family had been deceiving her in this way for years, doing everything to avoid her wrath, until one day she decided that it wasn't enough for prices to stay the same: the family deserved a discount. Propped up in all her trumpish magnificence in her huge bed, which resembled a taut-sailed schooner that never raised anchor, she demanded a discount. The family obliged her and knocked prices down even further. In Grandmother's room bread now cost a quarter of what it did in the market. But Grandmother Amarillo still didn't believe them. Playing a cunning game of her own, she secretly sent

Sara or Ofra to ask what things really cost. In their innocence the girls did as they were told. "Grandmother, he said half a piastre a rotel. He said a piastre and a half a bottle, Grandmother." The old woman nearly had a stroke each time. Stubborn, senile, stinking of pee, she would scream at Bukas until she was red in the face:

"You're a liar! A cheat! There's no God in your heart! God, there's no God there!"

It would end with her groaning:

"It was never like this when I was *en mi cama matrimonial.*"

She meant her big double bed. Ever since she had left it for her alcove kingdom full of chamberpots, trumpery, pistachio nuts, muslin nightgowns, shawls, and Arab loucoum sweets, the world had never been the same.

Grandmother Amarillo played cards with the girls and cheated with a straight face. They played rummy in her room, which always smelled of medicine and urine, the cards scattered over her bed. Grandmother Amarillo ate candy while she played. She refused to offer any to the girls and boastingly won every hand. Sara caught her cheating once or twice, but got a box in the face when she mentioned it. Ofra, on the other hand, either didn't or pretended not to notice, for the only way to get one of grandmother's sweets was to lose.

"How well you play, Grandmother," twittered Ofra, looking up with her baby blue eyes, while Sara whispered venomously in her ear:

"Asslicker."

One time Grandmother Amarillo cheated so openly that it was impossible not to react. Sara screamed. Grandmother Amarillo screamed too. Grandfather Amarillo came to the room.

"*¿Que se pasa aqui?*"

Grandmother Amarillo said that Sara was a snake: that's right, a snake, whose head should be smashed before it bit everyone. Grandfather Amarillo took one look at the cards, gathered them up, and threw them out the window.

"Sodom and Gomorrah!" he said out loud, and left the room.

Ofra picked up the cards in the street and returned them to her grandmother.

Gracia sits on the terrace with a friend while Sara does homework inside. Though she cannot see her mother, she sees her long brown taffeta dress hanging down to the splendid floor tiles, the black tassels that dangle from it, and above them, a black knitted shawl. She sees her mother's hand too, holding a purple Japanese paper fan, and the railing of the terrace, which had been beautifully worked into a pattern of lilies, acanthus, and horse-drawn carriages, all held together by long, formal ropes of ivy that too were black grillwork. In the spaces between the bars the smith had made a kind of anchor that hung suspended in air, over nothing.

"For giving them money, I forgave him," Gracia says to her friend. "What he did *con su cuerpo,* with his body, I forgave him too. Everything I forgave him, except what he whispered in their ears. I could have torn his eyes out for that."

"Yes," says her friend. "You're right about that, Gracia. They can be forgiven everything except the whispers."

One day a pleasant-looking Arab arrived in the lane and asked for Elder Amarillo. It was the last house on the corner; beyond lay an empty field and then the great unknown. The Arab entered the house and shut himself up with Grandfather Amarillo in his office. He spoke Arabic with a Lebanese accent.

He was, it turned out, the father of the countess. He lived in a village not far from Beirut and was a fez cleaner by trade. In his shop, he related with modest pride, he had a special steam press: Elder Amarillo would scarcely believe what pleasure he got from adjusting a wrinkled fez on the machine and seeing how clean, smooth, and ready to wear it came out, its tassels newly sparkling and springy. He had ten children, of whom one, his daughter Claudine, was never quite right in the head. The paintings for the exposition that she claimed were her mother's were actually her own, while the jewels, begging Elder Amarillo's pardon, were all stolen. This wasn't the first time she had run away from home or found some man to fall for her story. He was genuinely sorry that she had done such a thing to the Amarillos. The news had come as far as his own village when he had already given up all hope of finding her. He had simply come to the Elder, as he put it, to help him shoulder the misfortune. Her madness had struck both their families, not just one of them, he said. Should Elder Amarillo ever visit Lebanon, he and his family must be sure to stay with them. As for Don Isaac Amarillo's children, he considered them his own.

Elder Amarillo insisted that the visitor stay for a while. They dined together, conversed till late in the night, and parted on friendly terms.

That evening Ofra asked with perfect nonchalance:

"What happened, have they found Father?"

"They haven't and they never will," said Bukas. And Gracia added: "One lie has met another."

Sara and Ofra broke into wild laughter in their room. They jumped on their beds, threw pillows at each other, and shouted at the top of their lungs:

"No Panama! No Nicaragua! No India! No England!"

And when the family tried to quiet them, with cajoling and threats, they screamed till they were hoarse:

"No father! No mother! No grandfather! No grandmother! No anyone!"

In the end a pillow broke open and feathers flooded the room. Sara started to bite them. Ofra fell on the bed and hurt her hand. Imperceptibly they passed from shrill laughter to tears. Bukas refused to sweep up until morning. They fell asleep among the feathers, exhausted by the sensation of a bitter and all-knowing victory.

CHAPTER TWO

CACHEZ-VOUS, CACHEZ-VOUS!
GARDEZ-VOUS, GARDEZ-VOUS!

A game of hide-and-seek in the alley. Colorful voices slip like busy birds through the window bars of the houses, bearing news of summer on the large stones. A boy plays; a man walks; a woman does the wash. No need to prove anything. Growing up in Jerusalem is an identity all one's own.

Like Tía Victoria: big, rumpled, laughing. No one knew exactly what she did. She liked best just to sit at home. Victoria's home was an oasis in the great family desert to which one could escape for a while from Gracia's worries, Grandmother's smells, and Ofra's self-indulgences. Lately Ofra had become a real crybaby, and Sara picked on her. Once when Ofra swatted a bee on the windowpane of her room, Sara told her that all the bees in the world were in league with each other and that forty swarms of them would come to punish her at night and sting her to death for the murder of their friend. Ofra came down with a fever from all the nightmares, but Sara wasn't sorry in the least.

14

"Serves her right. That jerk."

In general, Sara had become a bully ever since the Arab from Lebanon's visit. Or as Grandmother Amarillo put it: a snake. Passing by the baby poplars that had sprung up outside their house, she beheaded them by striking each as hard as she could with a stick: die! She mocked her family, school, teachers, friends. The neighborhood became too crowded for her, as though its stones lay piled on her chest at night and kept her from breathing. She liked to think she was bad.

The school: named after its philanthropical founder, a German nobleman; a luxuriant caper plant, its flowers wedding-white, blooming spectacularly on its high wall. Vizu and Nitzhia, Adina and Linda, Alis and Shoshi: squirrel-eyed, mustache-traced on the upper lip, hair pulled back with rubber bands, lithe-bodied and sharp-tongued. Nothing spoiled about any of them. In each was coiled the strength to carry many baskets, many children in her arms. Sara was the tallest of them, kinky-haired like Topsy, braided and sarcastic.

They were all frightened that year of their Hebrew teacher, a short, adamant man who never gave anyone better than a "fair." "Excellent," he liked to say, was for God; "very good" for the poet Bialik; "good" for himself; and "fair," sometimes, for the girls. They used to see him shopping after school, carrying a rope bag in which there was often a kerosene stove. No one knew why he so very often carried the stove around. Perhaps it really broke down all the time, or perhaps he took it to some poor relative's house to share in the cooking. He was a lonely old man, a tight Eastern European Jew who never felt comfortable with all the Sephardic girls in his class, so he kept at a scrupulous and uncharitable distance. People thought him a miser.

Once Sara bet the rest of her class on a dare that she would visit him at home. Everyone knew that he never had guests. Sara, who was editor of the school journal that appeared at the end of each year for the benefit of the school's charitable supporters, simply informed him that she was coming one afternoon on business. He was too taken aback to protest.

She came and saw bereftness. Stacks of undusted books stood in the corners; a saucepan of milk lay on the windowsill; the faded plush bedspread, which had once been either red or brown, gave off a suffocating smell. The teacher sat in the middle of all this. She handed him the article she had come to discuss and sat opposite him while he bent over it, looking at his tiny, unexpectedly finely shaped ear, around which a thick cover of white hair sprouted from the ivory skin. A wave of compassion for him welled up inside her. In another minute, if she didn't control herself, her hand would reach out of its own accord to touch the lock of hair at his temple, or the creased nape of his neck, which suddenly seemed to her terribly brave, wise, and grown-up. What would happen to her if it did?

Just then, however, he finished reading and looked up. "I see no reason not to accept this, Amarillo."

"Then I can print it?"

"You can print it. Here or there a word may need to be changed, but that's a small matter."

He rose and walked her to the door. As they stood there, he fumbled in his pocket and produced an old sucking candy, wrapped in wrinkled paper.

"I haven't been a very good host to you, Amarillo. I live here all alone, as you see, and I haven't a housekeeper to remind me of my obligations. Here, this is for you."

She blushed all over and stuck it in her pocket. Outside she found half her class lying in wait for her behind the wild oleander bush on the street. They fell on her with a whoop, demanding to know what had happened.

She shrugged:

"Nothing special."

"Did he at least give you anything to eat? A piece of chocolate?"

"A candy from Bialystok."

The next day it happened: for the first time in the history of the school a student in Hebrew class—a girl named Sara Amarillo—received a "good" in composition.

"He's fallen in love with you, that's it!"

Though Sara made a rude gesture of contempt, her heart pounded.

Little did they know that she slept with the candy under her pillow in its wrapping at night, brushing it occasionally with open lips, haunted by a softly stirring, pitying feeling for the old, bent, oblivious head, the head of an unloved man.

The more secrets she had, the stronger she got. Always the same old lack, stuck in her throat like a long, sharp spit on which she had been turning for years. She grew and grew as though soaring toward some limitless height. She became bossy. Neither family, school, nor street claimed her allegiance anymore. She couldn't wait to be independent of them all. Meanwhile, she took to pitying at random, in sudden awakenings that came and went, frightening her as they did. On Jaffa Road a shop had been opened for orthopedic shoes with a manikin in the window: its dark hair neatly combed, its face agonizingly contorted, it sat there holding its aching foot while a hidden machine swung its head back and forth with an expression of eternal pain. Sara could never pass by the window without getting tears in her eyes. It wasn't the suffering itself that overwhelmed her, it was the fact that it never stopped. Day and night, while the rest of the world ate, slept, enjoyed itself, and went about its business, the poor manikin sat suffering in the window, on and on. Even when it was dark out. Even when nobody saw it, and the last bus, cart, donkey, and man had ceased moving down Jaffa Road, it kept shaking its head from the pain, unable to utter a sound because the mechanic who gave it its twisted, rather English face, its neatly combed hair and very red mouth, hadn't given it the power to cry. Somehow, for Sara, this was the height of indecency. She was sure that if only the manikin could whimper, someone in the shop would remember to shut off the machine that propelled it, at least for the night, so that it might get a little rest.

She had a brother, of course. He changed names with the times. For a while he was Robert, a world-famous surgeon in Canada. Later he became André, the Monte Carlan ski champion. During the long, dreary winter nights, while orange peels charred slowly on top of the kerosene stove where they had been put for the aroma, she saw him shooting down the slopes of a distant land through the painfully bright, whiter-than-white snow. Down, down he went, red-shirted and electric-haired, gracefully swooping from unparalleled heights, down tens of kilometers of slopes like fresh sheets, saved on the way from a thousand dreadful perils of which she was the only one to know. And when he crossed the finish line to the cheers of crowds of Monte Carlans, who for some reason had slanted, oriental eyes, though they shouted in biblical Aramaic as they tossed their embroidered Bukharan caps in the air, while two beautiful movie stars fell on him with kisses, he pushed them all aside with an imperious movement and demanded: "Where is my sister?" Then up to him stepped she, Sara, a bit shy of the great multitude, Gentiles, Philistines, while he embraced her and declared: "To you I owe my victory."

Still later her ruggedly handsome brother Captain Donald Nelson put down an uprising of doped-up, murderous savages in the jungle; her tall, pale brother Dr. Peter discovered a new wonder drug against the ultracoccus; and her brother Aminadav, a judge and commander in Israel, standing suntanned in a light-blue-and-white robe, an armlet on one arm, ordered the British to depart from the country. She saw him raise his right hand, Jewish law and authority behind him, and the British troop hangdoggedly away, submissive to the justice of his verdict. Among them, a diagonal belt on his uniform, was Captain Tony Crowther, who had become a regular visitor to their home, calmly chatting with her family over a glass of mint tea on the terrace facing the street.

The more stories she told herself, the more she admired her brothers. Slowly she was feeling her way toward the possibility of love. Had she chanced to meet one of them, she would have been ready to abandon her sarcastic, superior aloofness and hug him really and truly, kissing the soft of his palm, or brushing her lips against the good, warm place where his neck met his jaw. He was exactly that much taller than she.

Meanwhile, she remained in her tower. She read a lot. A closed garden.

I am a rose of Jerusalem and my halo is dust, a lily of the Valley of the
Cross strewn with garbage, a queen in weary Zion reeking of cabbage,
breathing the breath of the stones.

All words are dirty, impossible. Only the stone before dawn is clean
and clear. Absolute.

Who didn't try to civilize them. Once their class was visited by a dele-
gation of religious old ladies from England, most of them hobbling on
canes because of the gout, who came to see how they studied the
Scriptures. They were in the middle of Ezekiel that day, and the
blushing teacher quickly skipped the chapter of the two whoring sisters, Oholah and Oholibah, so as not to embarrass the ladies. There
were visits from American philanthropists, too, who came to see them
doing exercises in the small yard, their baggy sweatshirts making
them look like the inmates of an institution for pregnant orphans. One
bitter winter day, when heavy gusts of wind trod visibly in the pale
lemon-and-black light through the thistly field nearby, a guest of
honor arrived from the Foundation of French Culture, or perhaps it
was of French Friendship. A short man with ugly, glittering eyes, he
wore an immaculate suit and spoke French with a carefully cultivated
voice that was perhaps the one attractive thing about him. He stood
before them with the look of a man who has eavesdropped on life and
not liked what he has heard. Their principal, rubbing his hands, in-
troduced him as Monsieur Gaston. In a French like rattling peas,
the Culture Director, or perhaps it was the Friendship Director, proceeded to deliver a speech about the greatness of the Encyclopédistes,
whom he, Monsieur Gaston, would now tell them about in Jerusalem.
Grandeur. Gloire. The light of human reason. Enlightenment. The
kerosene heater was on the blink that day and they were all nearly poisoned by the smoke. The girls sat looking gloomily at the fists of rain
hammering on the melancholy windowpane, until a dark hail began
to fall and drown out the speaker entirely. Monsieur Gaston whipped
out a giant umbrella and disappeared like an evil dwarf.

   Even their French teacher, fat old Monsieur Schnur of the Franco-
fied Schnur family, disapproved of the lecturer. Perhaps Monsieur

Gaston of Paris had slighted old Schnur, the patient torchbearer of the Encyclopédistes in the Holy City, but a few lessons afterward he declaimed to them in a sarcastic simper:

"In Paris, the city of light, the center of the great French culture, of which I, Monsieur Schnur, am about to tell you in Jerusalem, there is a museum. The name of this museum is le Louvre. And in the museum of le Louvre in the city of light stands a statue. This statue is nude. Do any of you know why this statue is nude? This statue is nude because the sculptor who made it was poor and had no money to buy it any clothes."

All the old man's chins trembled with laughter. The girls liked him. He had deserted the Friendship Director and gone over to them.

They were being civilized with penmanship, embroidery, and prayer. No longer did they pray for the health of Sultan Abd-el-Hamid, but they still thanked the Lord for their souls every morning. In music class they sang:

> *In valley deep and mountainside*
> *God His bounty doth provide.*

They were quizzed in science too.

"Amarillo, how does light travel from place to place?"

"On the waves of the ether."

"Saporta, what is the smallest part of matter which is indivisible?"

"The atom."

"Laniado, why does water go up a siphon?"

"Because it's scared of the vacuum."

The city kept growing on them. The British built a thousand and one wonders: the YMCA, its tower resembling a tall erection, its interior decorated with Persian carpets, inlaid Damascus tables, Hellenistic mosaics, and English hunting scenes. They built the massive post office to look like one of Queen Victoria's railway stations, done up inside in strange, imported green marble. Dirt paths and wagon trails turned into paved roads, by the sides of which cypresses stood straight as sentries, drawing back from the dust of the horses. The Jews and the Arabs went on building as they always had, with flesh colored

Jerusalem stone and red roof tiles from Motsa. They draped grape-vines on trellises, sat in courtyards under fig trees, and cured olives in soldered tin cans. The more educated among them went to browse in the British libraries. When Sara grew older, she began to borrow books from the YMCA. Once she went there on His Majesty's birth-day and found it closed. The doorman, a black Sudanese dressed in a shiny white robe, a shiny red fez, and sneakers on his sockless feet, didn't open the heavy, European-wood door for her as usual. Instead he jigged up and down with joyous abandon:

"No mees, no mees, no libarry, no libarry, beeg day for you, beeg day for me, long leev de Keeng."

The air in the neighborhood: vibrant, familiar, smelling of stone that is lived in, used. She fell asleep at night to the high voices of the cistern cleaners returning from work, cradled by the sharp metallic bang of the shutter bolts, which Grandfather Amarillo always inspected shut-ter by shutter in case of thieves. Then came the cranking of the pulley-chain of the grandfather clock, which he set every evening. Cats rustling and yowling among the wild olive shoots. The kitchen clock chiming slowly. It was half a tone lower and then seconds faster than the other: soon the grandfather clock would chime too. A long, starry, oboelike breeze.

Early in the morning she was brought back to the light by the braying of Mahmoud, Shabu's donkey, and the gurgly clink of the bottles of red wine from Mr. Hankes's store that blistered in the sacks on his back. A pinkering light in the stone. A window yawning open. *I thank Thee my God, King everlasting, Who restoreth to me my soul,* all washed and shiny. Followed by the litany of the vegetable man from Bet Suhur who arrived every morning with dawn: *Yallah,* orrranges! *Yallah,* frresh orrranges! Tomat, tomat, tomat! The muezzin from the mosque. The church bells and the goat bells. White parachutes of shivering sheep cluster cold on the fog-snagged hill. Back to work come the cistern cleaners in their clothes that stink to high heaven so that the waters of Jerusalem might be clean.

The sounds of a small city. As small as a man's palm.

Bukas the cook, Bukas the belly-filler, spends one or two days with her family at the far end of the village of Shiloah and sleeps at the Amarillos' the rest of the week. She brings back with her by the basketful real country olives, as wrinkled and sharp as a shrewd old peasant, definitely not for the timid; hunks of cheese still smelling of goat and flecked with the straw they were wrapped in; a jug of water from the village spring, its cavernous chill undispelled, for Grandfather Amarillo, who considers it the best water in the world; heads of long, thin Arab lettuce; clumps of radishes and coriander; wicker bowls of full-blown, almost overripe figs that open at the touch of the mouth and taste like a sweet mouth themselves; hard Arab dough-rings which she makes herself in the oven of the village baker, whose trays, she claims, have a flavor all their own—hard-muscled, nut-brown, manly rings sprinkled with thyme and sesame, of which one could never eat one's fill.

Bukas has a little vegetable plot somewhere above the King's Gardens, the same green oasis that has existed since Solomon's time, if not earlier, at the point where the downwash of three water beds renews the soil of the valley each year, and the age of the figs is long forgotten. Under their branches, deep in the garden, in a dappled green light, wetness all around, the king's well runs clear to this day. Donkeys squish in the moist, richer-than-rich earth, busily bray, the tin water cans rattle on their backs. Bare feet in the mud, belly-deep-down. The plenty of earth's bottom. Across the valley the bare Ophel outside the Old City, shoulder of the Jebusite. The walled town above it, mountaining higher. No need to dig here to go back in time: the valley itself lives time-lower, underneath the city, underneath the Ophel, in a fierce dappled green that cannot be found anymore, for there were then few men in the world, the king's park was forbidden, and the mitred, all-honored figs robed in light were still very young.

It is from there that Bukas brings back her baskets, quarreling with the coachmen who always take on too many passengers by the copse of

Saint Peter Gallicantu, and curls up with her wares in a huge knitted shawl. Under it she sits with them, a silent, suspicious mass of certainty that she had been overcharged for her ticket again. It is with a sigh of relief that she gets off at the Amarillos' corner and continues on her heavily laden way, giving voluble thanks to be delivered from the hands of the coachmen, scoundrels, highway robbers, the worst thieves in the city. Her own bony hands, tattooed in Arab style, are stronger than a man's. She is never satisfied. The reason for this, she once explained, was that she had been born prematurely, a twisted little baby. To keep her warm and alive she was placed in a spice box inside a fur hat on the ledge of a stove. She lived all right, but she never untwisted. It is a good thing she has strong hands.

The arched transoms of the Amarillos' windows are made of stained glass, so that at any given hour of the day the light plays somewhere on the floor tiles of the house in red, green, blue, violet, or an ochrous lion-yellow like the hills of the Judaean wilderness at dusk. Only one side of the house never gets any sun, not only because of its northern exposure, but because it faces out on a high, blind wall of Sa'ada's whore-house. Sa'ada's girls wear heavy makeup and have red purses that swing at their sides. She has procurers working for her too, sallow, stupid young men whose job it is to shout "Hello, George, hello, George" at every passing man. Once, when Zaki Amarillo was still a proper husband and father, a sudden gust of wind blew some sheets that were drying on the Amarillos' roof into Sa'ada's courtyard. It happened to be a day when Bukas was off. The family debated who could be sent to fetch them. Not Gracia, who mustn't be seen in the courtyard; not Zaki either, because there might be gossip; Elder Amarillo was certainly out of the question; while Sara, when she volunteered out of pure curiosity, got a spanking for her pains.

"Couldn't you get along without them?" Zaki asked Gracia.

But Gracia refused.

"The plain ones, I don't care about, but the *broderie anglaise* ones, I got them from my grandmother."

The whole family went below and called "Sa'ada, Sa'ada" in a chorus. Sa'ada didn't hear them, but the whole neighborhood did and laughed. So did Sa'ada's young panderers, who stood there shouting in a high falsetto: "Sa'ada, Sa'ada, where are you, *ya* Sa'ada?"

In the end Tía Victoria came to the rescue. "Why the hell should I care," she said.

She went over to Sa'ada's, a cigarette in the corner of her mouth, and came out a while later with the pile of sheets in her arms.

"Bravo, Victoria!" the curiosity-seekers congratulated her.

"What's the matter with you?" answered Victoria with a look of disdain. "She's all right, that Sa'ada. She would have brought the sheets over herself in another minute if she didn't feel so embarrassed."

Like most old Kurdish Jews, Shabu the porter mispronounced his Hebrew words. He called Rosa Rasu, said Shashu instead of Shoshi, and shouted "Baddu boyds, baddu boyds!" at the children who teased his donkey, Mahmoud. Sometimes, after work, he gave the children a royal, tumultuous ride on Mahmoud's back. Nobody knew where he lived, who his family was, or whether he even had one; nobody knew where he came from every morning or went off to every evening. Even Mr. Hankes, the Ashkenazi owner of the wine store, knew nothing about Shabu, though he had worked for Mr. Hankes for years without missing a day. Shabu and his donkey arrived in the neighborhood every morning; Shabu stacked sacks, crates, and wine bottles on Mahmoud's back, and the two of them went about transporting their load until evening. Sometimes Shabu sat by Mahmoud's side on a donkey-colored blanket to eat flat Arab bread and raw vegetables, munching them slowly and handing his beast an occasional cucumber or tomato. On Sabbaths and holidays he always appeared with a fine old green Tyrolean hunting hat on his head, beaming with pride as he led behind him Mahmoud, bedecked with colored paper and small flags. One of the flags was the Union Jack; another was the rising sun of Japan, which no one knew where Shabu got. In outsized pantomime he would proceed to do a takeoff of fat Mr. Hankes, or of Elder Cordoso's son Leon the busybody who lived above the alley and got into everyone's hair. Once he even imitated Captain Crowther, who came to visit the Amarillos: thrusting a broomstick under one arm, he

puffed out his chest and tripped mincingly along, every inch the officer and gentleman, saluting Mahmoud on his way.

It was the beginning of spring. The almond tree in the empty, gar-
bage-strewn lot had been in bloom for several days. Hayyim, Leon
Cordoso's son, climbed the tree and announced:
"I'm commander of the tree."
He broke off some branches and judiciously handed them out.
"Here's for Yossi. Here's for Shoshana. Here's for Mas'uda. Hey,
you there, come here."
Sara wasn't sure that Hayyim would break off a branch for her too,
since his grandfather, Elder Cordoso, and Elder Amarillo had a running feud. Grandfather Amarillo never referred to his neighbor as
"Elder" at all; he called him Señor Cordoso instead, and even that
behind his back, as the two of them never addressed each other. But
Hayyim gave her a branch. She looked at it. Its little buds were
clenched like a baby's fists, as though some crystallized essence of
spring had stuck to the bare wood in clusters amid the unfulfilled
promise of green leaves. A giddy happiness, or perhaps the mere inti-
mation of happiness, swept over them all. They sat chattering on the
steps of the alleyway that led to Mr. Hankes's store, each with his
branch in his hand. Mahmoud stood near them hitched to his iron
post, while Shabu lay half dozing on a sack as always when the store
was closed. There was no way of telling where Shabu ended and the
sack began. A smile seemed to flit over his swarthy face, but perhaps
he had only grimaced against the sun. The world was bursting, giddy-
golden, with the first days of spring.

They sat with their almond wands and vied in making up stories,
surely, expertly, as though time had flipped suddenly over and the
future already gone by. In the end it was evening. A moon as red as a
balloon rose up the canyon of the alley. It was time for Shabu to loose
his donkey's bridle and trudge home after him. But he didn't budge.
"Hey," someone said. "It's time to wake up Shabu."
"Leave him alone, he's deaf anyway."
"No, he isn't. He can't talk so good but he hears."

"No, he doesn't."

They took bets. Cans were collected from all over the neighborhood, rusty, riddled tin cans to which bits of food and old labels still clung, brown, anonymous cans that had lived through the winter; rope and pieces of rope were brought too; and the whole was tied to Mahmoud's tail. The donkey dragged his train screeching over the ground, braying pathetically, but Shabu still didn't move.

"What's the matter, he dead or something?"

They went closer to him and cried, "Shabu, Shabu!"—but he still gave no sign of life. The bolder children took their almond branches and brushed them over his face.

"Get up, Shabu, get up!"

Shabu lay where he was.

They began to hit him, flogging him and the sack with their branches until both dark masses were covered with a blossomy white plume. Shabu didn't move. It was then that Sara bent over and laid her hand on his exposed cheek.

"*Ya,* she touched him! Sara touched Shabu!"

Sara stood up.

"Shut up," she said, "Shabu's dead."

Now they were frightened. "How do you know?"

"I know."

"Dead as a schnitzel," said Mr. Hankes's son with satisfaction.

They ran to get their parents. Leon Cordoso, whose brother was a policeman, arrived and began to shout:

"Break it up! Break it up!"

Someone went to call the police and someone else for a horse-and-wagon. The Jewish coachman refused to transport the corpse, because, so he argued, it might contaminate his wagon for descendants of the *kohanim,* the priestly class. They bargained with him, even tried telling him that Shabu was still half-alive, but he refused to give in. In the end Miracolo Orientale came along with his burial cart and took Shabu straight to Dr. Wallach's freezer.

Meanwhile Mr. Hankes appeared on the scene, all flushed and sweating, and on his heels two policemen, one of whom asked questions while the other wrote down the answers. Leon Cordoso tried giving a speech, but had nothing to say except that his brother was a policeman too and that he himself would be only too happy to help the Law and the British Crown if he could.

"What was the name of the deceased?" the policeman asked Mr. Hankes.

"Shabu, I think," said Mr. Hankes, perspiring.

"That's not so, no one knew!" shouted the children, who proceeded to explain the precise nature of Shabu's speech impediment to the policemen. His real name might have been Shova or Shavna. There was no telling. He even called Shoshi Shashu.

"Known as Shabu," dictated the first policeman to the second. "Where did he live?"

"I don't know," said Mr. Hankes.

"Did he have a family?"

"I don't know," said Mr. Hankes.

"How long did he work here?"

"Sixteen . . . no, seventeen years."

Tía Victoria, who had come downstairs in the meantime, stared at Mr. Hankes and whispered loud like a bashful trumpet:

"A man works for him for seventeen years and he doesn't even know his name or if he has a family. Did you ever hear of such a thing?"

"Excuse me, Madame Victoria," said Mr. Hankes, mopping his brow. "I'm not a bad man. I'd certainly be happy if they could find his family. I'd give them a whole month's salary, right to the thirty-first, even though the month isn't up yet. I won't touch a penny of it myself. I'd like to help out."

"He won't help anyone out," said Tía Victoria, a cigarette dangling from her mouth. "Now he's talking, tomorrow morning he'll be sorry he talked too much."

"Quiet, please!" ordered the policeman. He consulted with his companion in a whisper and the two of them drove off in their car. Leon Cordoso began to clap his hands rhythmically:

"Everybody home! Everybody home! Everybody home! Everybody home!"

Someone took a broom from Mr. Hankes's store and swept the alleyway of Mahmoud's turds, Shabu's rags, and what remained of the almond branches.

Subsequently Mr. Hankes rented an old truck and took on an unruly young boy named Matti Zakkai to deliver his sacks, crates, and bottles. Mahmoud disappeared from the neighborhood.

Matti was all brown: he had brown hair, a brown jacket in winter, nicotine-brown fingers, even a brown smell. His funny eyes were brown too, walnuts in a burnished wood bowl half in and half out of the sunlight. He took good care of his truck, puttering about in its insides whenever it broke down from sheer weariness, and singing in a cracking, adolescent voice:

> *Comrades, comrades, please find me a job*
> *Before I have to go out and rob,*
> *The boss hires the Arab and fires the Jew*
> *What can a poor Jewish workingman do?*

"*Miskeniko,*" said Victoria. "His mother's a tile-layer and his father's dead."

For a year, two years, they baited each other.

"Sari, Sari, quite contrary, your legs are hairy, your face is scary."

"Snotty Matti, I'm collecting for poor bridegrooms, maybe you've got something to give?"

"Beat it, Sarika, in a second I'll catch you, and then you'll be sorry."

They became the madcaps of the neighborhood. In their wild pursuit of one another they dashed down alleyways, leaped over peddlers' carts, shoved women carrying vegetables out of the way. "They're loco," everyone said of them, "really loco. A straitjacket is what they need. Cuckoo in the head. Wildness, that's what they have."

Late September afternoons the windows of the houses on the hilltops burn red in the sunset as though many conflagrations were burning inside them with a cold flame from which nobody has to be saved. An old gray cat squats over the city. In the rain-washed windows, in the waning light, another, nonexistent city is reflected, image within image within image. A great, mountainous ridge of clouds rises behind the houses like a second horizon. To do homework or read Sara has taken to escaping from home to beyond where the sewer pipe runs, to a place of abundant white squills and a huge acorn tree whose branches cover the hill. Ofra and Gracia always bothered her when she read, as though it weren't a serious occupation. One evening when she had gathered her books and was about to head back, she heard the honk of a horn from a nearby street: Matti and his truck. She ran toward him with a happiness that is like none other: to meet a friend on an autumn day.

"Get in."

Something began to fall that could have been dew or rain. Their sweaters smelled of wet wool. The wiper cleared a fan-shaped, dimly glittering world for them on the dusty windshield. The road was wet. There was no telling where the city's lights ended and where the first stars began. Sara furtively inhaled the smell of Matti's cigarette and noticed how he slightly wet the tip of it in his mouth.

"Give me a puff."

"It's wet," he warned.

"So what?"

She drew on it and handed it back.

"Enough?"

"Enough."

He groped above the dashboard, found a large sandwich, and handed it to her.

"Here, this is better for you than all that smoke."

She bit into it hungrily.

"What are you staring at?"

"It's like this, see: when you can't stand someone, then you can't stand to see how they eat, either."

She nodded. Recently she had begun to find her family's table manners unbearable. Grandfather Amarillo chewing his food deliberately, methodically, working his horsey teeth in long, monotonous strokes. Gracia cutting hers daintily, slipping it sideways into her mouth so as not to seem gross, her little finger stretched out. Ofra would bolt hers quietly, secretively, like a fox.

"Here we are," he said when she'd finished the sandwich. "If you were bigger I'd ask you to pay for the ride. But you're still a little girl, you'd be scared."

"I am not scared."

"Show me."

She put her two hands on his shoulders and pulled herself toward him. He kissed her once and again, his mouth strong.

"Now scram before I really get the hots."

"I am not scared."

"That's what you all say, but afterward it's 'mommy!' We'd better not."

"Then it's you who's scared."

He grabbed her more strongly than she'd counted on. At first she let him, but when she felt his body pressing on hers, on what was private, she pulled violently away. Too much.

"Damn you!" he panted half-jokingly. She opened the door and got out. It was important for her to keep calm.

"Thanks for the ride," she said.

That same day the Amarillos had a visit from the one person whom Sara had been petrified of all through her childhood: Tío Yosef, her grandfather's brother, who was known as "The-Messiah-Is-Coming" because of the way he glowingly greeted everyone. Otherwise he seemed normal, but Sara and Ofra were sure he was out of his mind. He made fruit wines and brought them as gifts, sweet, underaged wine that unripely puckered the mouth.

"The Messiah is coming, Sara," he welcomed her with a friendly smile. "He's on his way." She stood there in the doorway, shaking like a bird.

"Kiss Tío Yosef's hand," said Gracia.

She bent and quickly kissed it. It was wrinkled and smelled of fruit, or perhaps of frankincense, like a priest's, the opposite of that too-strong, impatient, sane hand that had embraced her a moment ago.

"Sara's nearly grown up," said Tío Yosef. "Soon she'll shower us with blessings."

"Some blessings," said Gracia. "Two daughters and not one son."

"Each will open seven households for you," promised Tío Yosef.

"Over my dead body," said Sara.

"Tfu, tfu, *no tienes* any shame! Ask God for forgiveness, *pronto,* so that He doesn't hold it against you."

There was no one to ask for advice but Tía Victoria.

When Sara walked in, Victoria was sitting on the sofa, wearing a flowery kimono cut low over her ample bosom, surrounded by scraps and long triangles of fabric. The seamstress had come for a fitting. Cigarette ashes were scattered all over the floor wherever the fabric left room.

"*¡Pustema grande!*" Victoria said to the seamstress. "I swear, you have to be a *pustema* to make it so tight. You must have forgotten who you're sewing for. Who do you think I am, Mae West? I've got good meat on me, sweetheart, just look what a *pata!*" She whacked herself on her massive bottom as she spoke.

"Sarika, come in, *chica*. I'll be done trying on in a minute, and then we'll have tea. Your mother dropped in this morning, did you know? She pokes around and around and then starts her Victoria, don't smoke so much, Victoria, you drink too much coffee, Victoria, you have to go on a diet. She kills me."

"Why let it bother you?"

"Look, here I am drinking tea instead of coffee. It gets to you. I know just what the neighbors say about me. Those Cordosos. 'This morning a blond dropped by with some bread; at lunchtime a dark-haired fellow with meat; for dinner two brown-haired boys to fry eggs; and tomorrow morning she'll have a redhead over for beans. Where will it all end?' Tell me, Sara, isn't that how they talk about me?"

"*Chapachula,*" said the seamstress, wiping tears of laughter from her eyes. "What a mess! Here, try on the top."

Victoria stood before the mirror, turning this way and that, while the seamstress knelt beside her with a mouthful of pins. Sara's aunt shook her huge frame like jelly and roared, imitating the street vendor below:

"A penny, a penny, get it all for a penny, the owner's gone to the loony bin!"

"Pipe down," begged the seamstress. "In a minute I'll swallow a pin."

Victoria lifted her two great breasts in her hands with a look of perfect contempt:

"Two for a penny, two for a penny, they're not so new anymore!"

They finally finished the fitting. The seamstress retired to the next room to drone away on her sewing machine.

"Now have some tea and tell me what's troubling you. Your mother giving you a hard time? Your grandmother?"

"Look here, Victoria, my mother says that once a woman starts with a man she can't stop. Is that true or not?"

Victoria puffed on her cigarette and thought before saying:

"What is it, Sara, are you involved in something?"

Sara didn't answer.

"All right, forget that I asked. Look, Sarika, how do you expect me to give you advice? If I tell you to follow your heart, you'll end up like your father who broke everyone else's. If I tell you, God forbid you should do anything, you'll be like your mother, who couldn't stand to let Zaki near her even before he started up with his countess, Mademoiselle de la Merde. Once it was her finger that hurt her, another time her hair ached, he should just close the door and leave her alone, *tranquil, tranquil*. So what should I tell you, that you should be God forbid like Victoria?"

Sara drank some tea and asked:

"So it's true that in the end you can't stop?"

But Victoria was through philosophizing and in a clownish mood again. She grabbed a large piece of fabric from the floor, took hold of Sara, and began to sing an Arab *debka*, twirling the cloth around her finger like the handkerchief used in the dance:

"Ta-la-la-la, never stop, never stop! Ta-la-la-la, never stop, never stop, no! Ta-la-la-la, never stop!"

The seamstress stuck her head through the door and yelled:

"I don't care if you pay me a thousand pounds, this is the last time I do anything for you!"

She and Matti clung to each other in out-of-the-way places for a whole year, he more frightened than she. She stuck to him, wouldn't let him go, with a persistence that puzzled even her. She knew nothing about him and didn't want to know, but the same choking, doomed tenderness came over them each time they embraced. It was hard for them to talk. There was something almost sorrowful about the way he caressed her, big and angular though she was, the storm raging within them, stroking her head like that of a child who doesn't yet know that he's in for a major operation.

"Sari, if you don't keep away from me there's going to be trouble."

"Coward."

"Sarika, I'm throwing you out, fast."

Until one day in Mr. Hankes's cellar, among the barrels of wine, to which she'd descended after him, by the damp wall, amid the heavy red smell, he couldn't hold himself in any longer.

"Don't be afraid, Sari," he panted as soon as he could. "Nothing's happened to you. You're still a virgin."

Matti, you silly, the thought went through her head, do you really think that's what's worrying me?

She kept after him.

Meanwhile out in the alleyway, already deep in evening shadow:

"Vizu, Nitzhia, Dvora, Joya, *cachez-vous!*"

And Leon Cordoso in baggy pyjamas to all his children:

"Everybody home! Everybody home! Everybody home! Everybody home!

Mr. Hankes sold the store. Matti and his truck vanished from the neighborhood. Gracia came to a decision.

"Ofra, you're small and pretty, like my side of the family. You'll stay home and take care of your looks. You, Sara, you're too big. Like Victoria. *Como todos los* Amarillos. You'd better go find yourself a job."

CHAPTER THREE

DR. HEINZ BARZEL came to Jerusalem roundaboutly. Having heard in his native town of Frankfurt am Main that the *palästinisches Klimat* was a hot and rigorous *Klimat,* and being of a scientific turn of mind, he decided first to accustom himself to great heat. Where was such heat to be found? The young doctor made inquiries and was told that the hottest place on earth where he might condition and adjust his Organismus was the Persian Gulf.

Dr. Heinz Barzel set out for Bandar Abbas, where he lived in a hotel room with a ceiling covered by a gigantic fan whose blades stretched from wall to wall. Even this, however, didn't help very much, so that he found himself showering approximately every quarter of an hour in dust-colored, rust-flavored water. The first time he went to the marketplace, he noticed that the merchants of Bandar Abbas spent the hottest part of the day seated in barrels of water, from which they emerged only to wait on customers. The heat wasn't heat anymore: it was the spiteful protest of city, stone, sky, Gulf, oil wells, everything, against the presence of the invader from Frankfurt am Main with carrot-red hair and a violin in an aluminum case. Everything conspired against him. Slipping easily under the netting that he hung up at night, the mosquitoes mockingly informed him of his imminent eviction.

Scientist that he was, Dr. Barzel wrote home of his impressions:

"I wish to inform you that I have discovered in Bandar Abbas the probable source of the legend of Ali Baba and his forty thieves who hid in barrels. The tale undoubtedly derives from local folklore, since the merchants here hide in barrels from the heat. I should especially like to call the attention of my friend Professor Reichenbach to this fact. As for my violin, the aluminum case was apparently a serious miscalculation, for the strings have all snapped, the bridge is now warped, and the wood looks rather parboiled. My Organismus is still not entirely adjusted, but as of last Thursday the intervals between my showers have increased from one quarter to one half of every hour."

From Bandar Abbas he proceeded to Abadan and from there to Kuwait. One way or another, the emirs and sheikhs of the Gulf found out that the famous man of learning, Dr. Barzel, was among them, and began to request his services. Oil had yet to be discovered along the west side of the Gulf, and the Arab coast especially was remote, godforsaken, the end of the world. The young doctor was summoned to harems throughout the region, where the local sheikh's mother, wives, daughters, aunts, and female cousins stood waiting in line with veiled faces. For the most part they refused to undress and insisted on being examined by the application of a magnifying glass to their palms: this, it transpired, had been the method used by a certain Yugoslavian, who had circulated about the Gulf, in the guise of a physician, some seven years before. There was no way of proving that more patients had died from this system than from others, but the women agreed, after many whispered consultations, that Dr. Barzel might examine them by his own technique, which he explained was from Heidelberg, though only through their clothes. The young doctor had no choice but to accept, although in at least one case, that of a woman covered with pustulating boils that had been unsuccessfully treated with camel dung, the husband of the patient, the local sheikh, allowed her to disrobe. The woman was put in a room with her body inside and her face sticking out of the room through a bead screen, so that Dr. Barzel would never know who she was. Her companions from the harem sat outside by her head, wiping her brow with handkerchiefs, while by her body sat its lawful owner the sheikh, the local *kadi,* and an old woman who chewed kif and spat the juices on the floor.

"You simply can't be a bad doctor in the Gulf," Dr. Barzel wrote to a physician friend. "Without any medical care eighty percent of the sick die here, so that even if you're a terrible doctor and kill seventy percent of your patients, you're still ten percent ahead."

Most remarkable of all Dr. Barzel's cases in the Gulf was one that involved the sixteen-year-old wife of a local emir, pregnant with twins, who had been told by the midwife that she could not give birth because the infants were upside down inside her. At the time Doctor Barzel was on board the train from Zahran to Riyadh. The emir sent a band of armed horsemen who stopped the train, removed Dr. Barzel from it, sat him on a great steed with a canopy rigged to the saddle to shield him from the sun, and escorted him at spear point to the patient. She was frightened but curious, even gay, and not scared enough to permit Dr. Barzel to treat her as he would have liked. The emir too put his foot down: his wife, he said, was too young for such things. In the end Dr. Barzel had to perform the operation for which he afterward became famous in Jerusalem: he reversed the breech babies through their mother's dress.

"I had no choice," he explained, his willowy body shaking with laughter. "*Also,* I pressed and pressed until the fetuses had no choice either."

After five months in the Persian Gulf and Saudi Arabia, Dr. Barzel took note of the fact that his Organismus, however debilitated, was still alive, and decided that it was time to move on. He got off the train in Damascus and bought a horse, on which he proceeded to cross Transjordan, stopping to cure several people of what ailed them on the way, and to arrive in Jerusalem via Jericho on Yom Kippur eve. When after a leisurely ascent from the wasteland of Judea he spied the spires of Augusta Victoria and the Church of the Transfiguration on the Mount of Olives, he dismounted with emotion and continued slowly on foot, leading his horse by the reins. Near the village of Abu Dis he caught sight of the entire wet, gray, sullenly beclouded city straight ahead, the churches in the Kidron Valley glistening with a tinny sheen, the houses of Bethany on the hilltop like a flight of gulls, their fierce, cold whiteness frozen in black cloud. Directly before him stood the darkly dripping ramparts of the Old City. Then Jerusalem broke into detail, no longer an encompassable whole. The city for which he had suffered so many months in the wilderness now spat cold rain over his face and clothes.

Upon arriving at his hotel on Jaffa Road, Doctor Barzel was forced to conclude that his Organismus had become unable to take the cold of a Jerusalem winter. His first week in the city was spent in bed with pneumonia. "Dear friends," he wrote ruefully home, "I've already learned two things here. The first is, always approach Jerusalem from the desert. The second is, whatever you think of this city, it will always surprise you in the end."

His first year in Jerusalem was a hard one. The orthodox Jews of the city were hostile to his free ways. They too, of course, didn't hesitate to call him when ill even on Sabbaths and holidays, but though they looked the other way when he entered a patient's house, they more than once shouted insults at him, even hurled stones, when he left. His violin was repaired: the expert who fixed it was named Alfred von Kluck, a stranded Prussian whose two great passions in life were fiddle making and bulldogs. Next Dr. Barzel built himself a truly fine-looking house in the new neighborhood of Rehavia. An Arab gardener planted jasmine and rose bushes, orange bignonia, and ink-blue delphinium, and Dr. Barzel wrote away for a cedar of Lebanon to put in his garden: a cedar, it seemed to him, was the right sort of thing to go with a new home one had built in Jerusalem. Precisely this reen-try into the forms of civilization, however, from which five months in the Persian Gulf had unmoored him completely, made him fiercely nostalgic for home. His mother sent him all the furnishings of his old room in Frankfurt in a neatly packed lift, including his old black desk, his Biedermeier table, his black, round-seated chairs with their antique yellow upholstery, his heavy Persian rug whose fine weave and soft colors he only now had learned to appreciate, and, most important of all, his Bluethner piano. Sometimes, on late afternoons, when the heat had died down, the air was full of the fragrance of flowers, and the next-door neighbors could be heard conversing softly in German on the other side of the fence, he wasn't sure whether he was here or there. He played his violin for hours on end, solo, hitting the wrong notes, consumed by longing. It was always his opinion that the cedar failed to take root because he himself hadn't struck any yet.

One evening, while he was still struggling to learn Hebrew, he sat down and wrote a story in it, the gist of which was as follows:

Once, when the Israelites were wandering in the desert, a certain man named Reuel was placed on trial before Moses. This Reuel was a poet, a musician, and a seducer of hearts. During the long desert nights around the campfire he sought to sway the people to return to Egypt, telling them of the wonders they had left there. Those old enough to remember grew homesick unto death.

Everyone was sure that Moses would make short shrift of Reuel: sooner rather than later, undoubtedly, the earth would swallow him up. Yet to the astonishment of all, the two lingered on and on in Moses' tent. Reuel was asked by the leader to sing about Egypt, its great palaces and fertile river. "Why, you're homesick, too," he exclaimed. "Anyone with a little culture has to be. What do you have here—sand and promises?" To which Moses replied: "True enough, but I consciously prefer that which is in the process of creation to that which is finished and known." Forthwith he summoned Eviatar, the captain of the guard, a young product of the desert whose men had just taken prisoner a caravan of Ishmaelites that had passed nearby. He bade him free the wayfarers with all their goods, and ordered them to escort Reuel back to Egypt under penalty of death should any harm befall him. The bare-footed Eviatar, to whom the fuss made by the old people over Reuel was incomprehensible to begin with, nodded and did as he was told. Moses personally accompanied the departing caravan to the limits of the encampment. "Have a good trip," he said to Reuel.

"Frankly, I'm afraid you'll come to no good end in the opium dens of Ramses, but in the meantime, give my regards to the opera house in Memphis, whose tower I still see, golden in the sunrise, at least once a week in my dreams."

Dr. Barzel never published this story, which he filed away in the drawer of his big black desk. His sense of Hebrew, he told himself, was not yet good enough to write in it. It was a language that had no green lawns between its words. Besides which, he knew nothing about Sinai, his descriptions of which were almost certainly inaccurate. To his mother he wrote:

"I don't deny that I sometimes feel homesick, but I'm not budging from here. I've always been in search of the absolute, and Jerusalem is a very absolute place, though it could stand to be a bit cleaner."

His second year in Jerusalem was marked by two events. First of all he married Hulda Friedmann, a suburban princess from Bet Hakerem, who was fifteen years younger than he; secondly he discovered a music partner, a certain Captain Tony Crowther. Now his meals were decently prepared, his collars were freed from the hated starch that the laundress had refused to leave out of his shirts, and his evenings were spent with Captain Crowther, who accompanied him on the piano, sonata after sonata, while his voice carried happily down the fragrant Rehavia street:

"La, sol, la-flat, ugh, *kvatch!*"

Hulda, fifteen years younger, who loves him very much, laughs in the next room whenever he hits a wrong note. Her laugh is like slivers of sunlight.

Nobody in Jerusalem called him Doctor Barzel. At first he was known, because of his red hair, as Doctor Ginger, which was shortened to Doctor Gingi, which eventually was corrupted to Doctor Bimbi. People forgot he had any other name. Everyone called him Bimbi, even Hulda, her twin brother, Amatsia, and their whole madcap family. Even he, when he had to introduce himself to a stranger, would say, "My name is Dr. Barzel, alias Doctor Bimbi."

Amatsia, lazy cat-eyes and a Philistine profile with a nose that descends in a straight line from his forehead, comes every afternoon to the Barzels' house in Rehavia to tell Hulda about his latest conquests. Here and there he even exaggerates perhaps for her listening enjoyment. Face flushed, eyes nervously flashing, she suddenly peals with laughter or claps her hands sharply with covert satisfaction.

"Amatsia, no! I swear, you didn't!"

Her long, thin hands almost pluck at his shoulders; her face is feverish, flushed.

"Amatsia," she whispers, bending over him. "Tell the truth. Did the two of you *really?*"

"No."

"I don't believe you. She's always falling all over you."

"Let her fall."

"You're so handsome." She lightly bites his earlobe from behind. "By God, you're handsome. What a pity you're my brother."

"You might say I wouldn't throw out your shoes if I found them under my bed, either."

They talk, as though to rid their systems of an ancient desire. Next to her, his mirror image, but a woman, he feels his own blustering masculinity even more strongly, the difference, inescapable, between his twinness and hers. They had grown up together, curled around one another in the same amniotic fluid, their fingernails tiny, coeval, their two heads like half-empty sacks on the fragile stems of their necks, their mouths as though painted on their faces, flesh of each other's flesh. And back further: a pair of bloated stomachs side by side, primitive beasts from the Pleistocene, an amoeba still unsplit.

Once, when they were three years old, Amatsia took sick with something contagious. Hulda was moved out of their bedroom to keep her from catching it. Immediately both came down with an itchy eczema that did not go away until Hulda was returned to the room. Naturally, she was infected. They lay happily together, babbling past midnight. The eczema was gone in two hours. No one tried to separate them again.

"Hulda," Doctor Barzel once says to her, glancing at her in the penetrating manner that she refers to as his educational look, "you shouldn't encourage Amatsia's wild side so much."

"Do I?" she regards him wonderingly. "But he doesn't come to me for advice, he just tells me about it afterward. He's lucky I'm not a jealous sister."

"You're a very jealous sister. It's just that you feel safe as long as he has twenty girlfriends instead of one." As though to soften the severity, but not the seriousness, of his tone, he lifts her triangular, sorceress's chin with his freckled hand and goes on: "He'll get married one day, you know, and even if your sister-in-law is a saint, you won't be able to stand her."

Her eyes twinkle:

"But he's not married yet, Bimbi, is he? And I'm still his best friend, aren't I?"

"You're married, though."

"I'm allowed and he isn't. I'm not permitted to sow my wild oats for the sake of my Organismus. All I could do was get legally married. Amatsia knows I had no choice. It would have been different if I were a man. It's all in the Organismus, you see."

"At least now I know why you married me."

"To have redheaded children, Doctor Bimbi."

"How you'll ever give birth to them with those narrow hips of yours is beyond me," he says fondly.

"You know what? Let's try and see."

He holds her, towering over her, her flared foal's nose twitching finely, pressed to his chest until it almost hurts. A treasure house. Her lovely contralto laughter in the rooms. That delicately vibrating nervousness, a flower at the brink. She is all flower, all brinks, all of which are imaginary: the brinks of a fairy-tale princess, which exist because she does.

In the end it was Tony Crowther who brought Sara to Dr. Barzel's hospital. After first convincing the doctor, he had to struggle to persuade Gracia, who didn't think that hospital work was class. Sara herself was far from excited about it, but she agreed to give it a try.

She arrived with Tony Crowther, who waited smiling in a corner of the room like the cat who has brought in a valuable find.

"When you were a little girl," asked Doctor Barzel, "did you or did you not climb trees?"

"I did."

"That's good. That's very good. The best women are those who competed with the boys when they were small girls. If you're already a little lady when you're ten, that is not so good afterward. Everybody suffers. Do you like to learn?"

"Yes."

"Are you scared of dead people and ones that don't look so nice?"

She thought of Shabu covered with almond blossoms.

"No."

She got the job. Tony Crowther asked his friend what he thought of her. "*Eine* Topsy," he said, "but I think she's got heart." By the end of the month she had become indispensable to him. She came every morning, as fresh as though life were just starting: youth come into the fortress. The hospital had massive walls, enormous casement windowsills, high ceilings, rooms that opened on rooms that opened on rooms. Sara found a new world in each.

Once they brought in a drugged young Arab who had overdosed. Dr. Barzel was unhappy with the way the intern on duty was treating him. He put on an apron and took over himself. Sara assisted. They pumped the Arab's stomach. He gagged, teared, fought, rolled his half-seeing eyes.

"Here you have a young man who did not take responsibility for himself," said Dr. Barzel while working. "A young man like this can no longer be easily set straight. He doesn't have what it takes, *moralisch*. No important values."

"He just wanted a good time," said Sara. "Is that forbidden?"

Dr. Barzel straightened up:

"No, young lady, it's not forbidden to want a good time. It's just very, very vulgar."

Another time he lectured at an autopsy:

"I admit that death is hard, but that is the price that the human race pays for its individuality. When life in this world was nothing but amoebae and primitive plankton, death did not exist. The Organismus just went on dividing and dividing, ad infinitum. Even if the original amoeba died, in other words, it didn't matter, because it still existed in all its other halves. Such an existence is in effect immortal. We pay the price of mortality for not being amoebae. Death has given us individual worth, fear, love, humor, the knowledge of good and evil, values. Without death nothing would be worthwhile."

They listened in silence. On their way out Dr. Nahum, a short, stocky intern with puppy-haired skin, standing next to her said:

"Fine, that's all very nice, but what was he teaching today, medicine or philosophy?"

"How do you know where the dividing line is?" Sara asked.

"I know where it is. And I'm here to study medicine."

Many came to the hospital who were poor and homeless, beggars and emissaries who went all over the world collecting for Jewish causes and organizations. They were a sort of circulatory system of the nation, always coming back again to Jerusalem, which was the heart, and going forth reinvigorated once more to the farthest, outermost limbs: back and forth, back and forth, with their stories, foreign currency, and diseases. Dr. Bimbi used to sit and listen to them. He liked hearing about faraway Jews he didn't even know existed. Most of these patients, however, didn't remember very much besides the prices of goods and flophouses. The map of their world was an atlas of prices and deceptions.

There is an old woman from the Caucasus on the ward. She is toothless, bodiless, with legs like broken matchsticks enclosing a diamond-like space; in her dreams she sees the snowy peaks of Georgia, embroidered sheepskin coats, fur hats, brides bedecked with apple blossoms; the high mountain dialect she squeaks in is comprehensible to no one. Into her body goes a stream of blood and medicines, while she curses herself yellow, the world black around her, her face a hard knot of dark, thin threads. No one comes to visit her. It is hard to even think of her as a human being. A hallucinating spleen.

"Has she been given anything today?" asks Dr. Nahum by her bed. He is sterilizing his hand, which she has just bitten. At times she is really in pain; at others she just hates the world.

One morning Dr. Barzel insists that she be made to get up and walk a few steps in the corridor. Sara volunteers to see to it. Passing back a while later, he sees her supporting the old woman, who could barely keep on her feet, and singing straight-facedly in a nasal voice like Miracolo Orientale's at funerals:

The voice of the groom,
The voice of the bride
The voice of the merrymakers
Happy at their side—

With everyone on the floor clapping hands in time to the wedding tune. A woman begins to ululate. The old Georgian beams with toothless mouth.

"Sara will be our best nurse," Dr. Barzel tells Hulda, pleased with himself. "Local talent, I've always said to Mrs. Szold. We must use local talent."

Rather than take meals in the hospital cafeteria with its unpleasant smells, the younger medical staff was in the habit of eating at a nearby dairy co-op run by two sisters, Firochka and Lidochka Auerbuch. Both had mustaches, though Lida was somewhat the softer and quieter of the two. There were many such old spinsters in Jerusalem: all were tall, bony, hard-bitten, as though Adam's rib had never taken on flesh in them, and all spoke Hebrew with a heavy Russian accent and called whomever they didn't like a svoloch, which meant a scoundrel. A customer who smiled too much could be a svoloch; so, certainly, was the Kurdish vegetable man; so, indeed, was anyone not an Auerbuch. The world was not to be trusted. Whatever had cast them in the first place on these shores, with their reefs of eggplant and banks of yoghurt, among so many svoloches?

They served coarse bread, yoghurt, olives, eggs, salad without pepper or oil, blintzes, and coffee from which all the coffeeness had been wrung. Firochka, that is, Esther, which in Russian was Esfira, was the boss. She waited on tables and kept the books, slamming down the food like a fait accompli that had better taste good or else. Lidochka, that is, Lida, was in charge of crumbing up after meals and keeping the restaurant clean, though the young doctors and nurses who ate there didn't leave many crumbs in those days. They liked the place because it was sterile, neutral, like the food of old people who are afraid to taste anymore: it had nothing of the zing or crackle of life, nothing to remind them of the body, its long decay, and that other, cloying smell they had just escaped from for a while.

One day Firochka came up to the table where Sara was sitting with Dr. Nahum, Dr. Tidhar, and several nurses and said in a low voice so that Lidochka couldn't hear:

"I'd like to ask something of you. I happen to know, it's of no importance how, that Lidochka is soon going to be very, incurably ill. What I'm asking you is, in the first place, give her a good room and good care. And second, let me know in time before she dies, so that I can have some proper notices run off at the press. Those svoloches over there always do such sloppy work and then blame it on having to rush. So I'm asking you to tell me in time, so that I can get nice notices run off for Lidochka and not put the family to shame."

"How do you know she's going to be ill?" asked Dr. Nahum.

She frowned evasively. "It just so happens that I know. Do I have your word?"

"Do you always make sure to organize everything even before it's happened?" Dr. Nahum persisted.

"Why, if somebody didn't organize things, the world would be one holy mess."

She went to order three sugar blintzes, leaving the staff at the table convinced that she was about to poison Lida: strychnine in an innocent tomato, digitalis with mayonnaise on an eggplant. They waited for it as though for a curtain to rise, but far from looking poisoned, Lida was actually getting more color in her cheeks. One day word spread that she was marrying an illiterate widower, the Kurdish vegetable man. Firochka stopped talking to her. A roughneck like that in a respectable family? No, no, no, and no again. Between quarrels the blintzes were burned sour, the cucumbers went unpeeled, the milk for the coffee turned sour, and the dishes made their rounds without being washed anymore. Nahum, Sara, and their friends developed the habit of washing them in the sink of the WC, but things clearly couldn't go on like this much longer. One morning they arrived hungry for a late breakfast from the hospital to discover that the co-op had been closed without any date for reopening.

Dr. Tidhar was not well liked. He had a mustache like a pair of quotation marks and hair drenched in brilliantine, which he covered with a black net at night to keep from getting mussed. When he walked, he glided with long steps as though dancing, his hips hyperactive, sprinting straight to the mirror hanging over the wash basin to attend to his shaving nicks, or squeeze the pimples on his chin, before saying good morning to his patients or even glancing at their charts. The patients learned to wait.

His best friend in the hospital was Husni, the youngest son of Subhi Bey and his wife Faiza, a prominent Arab couple who had close ties with most of the better-known Jewish families in town. Husni was a male nurse, which meant that he changed dressings, gave injections, and looked soulfully at every female patient from the age of six to sixty as though he lived for her alone. After work he assumed a second self: now he was the romantic crooner Steve Harold, whose great desire was to become a world-famous singer. He was by no means inhibited, and sometimes, on request from the staff or the patients on the ward, he put a white panama on his head, reached for a walking stick, and sang:

Swaneeee,
How I love you,

How I love you,
My dear old Swaneeeee.

He stood like a star, mindful to bow his head despondently when the last bar was done, modestly letting a boyish curl tumble over his forehead as the applause rippled forth.

Both Tidhar and Husni were bon vivants. More than one young lady, to her own surprise, had found herself bestowing her favors on Husni for no other reason than his talent for gratitude. "One kiss from you," he would say in his Steve Harold voice, "brings heaven to earth for me." Happiness. Bliss. The lost Eden. Eventually, it was discovered that Husni's paradise was strictly graded, and that in a small black notebook he kept an alphabetical list of Jerusalem's females with well-researched observations on each. A scandal ensued but it didn't last long. Husni simply changed his approach. "You," he now said to the girl he was with, "aren't notebook material at all. With you it's pure feeling. Here, feel how my heart is pounding." And everything went on as before.

Since several nurses, all local talent, had finished the hospital course and were awaiting their diplomas, Dr. Bimbi decided to hold a ceremony. Professor Marcus, the dean of the medical staff, was supposed to preside; but as he wasn't feeling well that day, Dr. Bimbi, who was about to be made a professor himself, did the honors instead. Sara and the other girls sat on a bench, knees primly touching, excited.

"Girls," he said, very concentrated, his eyes floating above them in space, "my dear girls. You are now officially part of the war that all of us are waging in this place. It is a war in which there are never any absolute victories. Death is still stronger than all of us. The most we can manage to do here is to delay a man's death a few years. Nothing more."

There was a stir among them. All through their studies no one had talked to them like this. They had been talked to in terms of accomplishments, victories.

"You will have to share the load with us knowing full well that all our victories are at best partial, incomplete, without illusions. It won't always be easy for you. I expect there will be moments of weariness and despair. There have to be. And so I want to ask every one of you now, right here, before you receive your diploma, to consider carefully whether you have the strength to spend all your working time with us here, perhaps your whole lives, winning victories that are always partial and uncertain even when they are occasionally great. Nothing you do here will last forever. If you're looking for a taste of eternity, go home and raise children. Not here. And if any of you, or all of you, feel that you are not cut out for such a life, you'd best speak up now."

No one moved. Most of them didn't know what he was talking about. Dr. Barzel sighed and handed out the diplomas. They drank a toast.

The girls were furious.

"Bimbi has no call letting out his German despair on us at a time like this," one of them said. "I want to feel happy, and he has to ask me all kinds of questions that don't even have any answers."

Dr. Nahum, who walks Sara home afterward, agrees. They turn down the alleyway, which is now a frocky, baskety, hung-up-to-dry gold in the soul-colored sunset. They pass a dusty old cypress tree, which looks in the first fading light like a dusky candle drowning in its own dripping wax.

"What would you have said, Nahum?"

"I'd have said: 'Congratulations on your graduation, girls. If any of you thought it's been difficult until now, just wait till you see what's ahead. And now get cracking, the bedpans in surgery haven't been emptied for two whole hours.'"

She laughs and takes a dancelike step, her rolled-up diploma tied by a ribbon to her wrist. She isn't really pretty, Nahum thinks, but she has what it takes to be woman. Or a mare: long hair, long legs, a long neck.

"You see, Sara," he continues, "Bimbi is an excellent doctor—for his generation. I look at both life and medicine differently. And Bimbi's mistakes are as big as his soul. I'm not at all sure that I need Schubert and all that in order to be a good doctor."

"Have you had a fight with him?"

"Naturally. This morning he called me a rationalist. He said that I had the ultimate vulgarity of all rationalists."

"Why are you men so competitive?"

"Why are you women so inquisitive?"

He kisses her good night. She is taller than he and is surprised by his intensity. A puppy dog, full of self-importance, hot-skinned and ambitious.

Now that Sara was a nurse, she and Grandfather Amarillo became friends. "You're the only one in the whole family," he said, "who is doing something for others, *por los otros.*" He liked to talk with her, to go for long twilight walks. Sometimes Ofra came too. Gracia made her sit at home all day long with nothing to do.

The three of them are strolling from the railroad station to AbuTor.

"Once we lived in the Old City," he tells them. "Everybody did, inside the walls. I can't tell you how crowded it was. My father was one of the first to move out, to Mishkenot. Suddenly there was room. My mother couldn't get used to all that space, she hardly ever left the house. I remember how Father used to come on his donkey from Abu Tor on Sabbath eves bringing guests—Jews, Arabs, Turks. He'd stand just where we are now and shout across the valley: 'A good Sabbath, Behora, a good Sabbath!' She'd hear him on the opposite hill and get ready."

"Did she comb her hair?" Ofra wants to know. "Was it pretty?"

"Maybe she combed it. I don't remember it so well. It was always covered. She wore a nice kerchief on it. She used to grind her own coffee by hand. We ground everything then by hand, with millstones, or pestles. It's not like today when you buy it all ready-made."

"Look how Jerusalem's grown," Sara says softly. "I remember when there were hardly any houses here."

"The rabbis compare Jerusalem to a fig tree. Just as the fig has a short, stout trunk but spreads very wide, so Jerusalem first grows strong within walls and then spreads all over the hills."

"Him and his rabbis!" snorts Ofra under her breath to Sara. "Nothing matters to him unless it's written in some old book."

"Why do you care?"

"It annoys me. It's time he turned off the holy tap."

"If I had my whole life to start over," says Elder Amarillo, "I'd be a farmer. What I like to read best to this day is the part about growing things in the book of Hemdat Yamim."

Ofra, fed up with caring for her good looks at home, goes to work for the electric company. Now she wears suits and heavy makeup and sits typing all day in an office in Omariyya. Her small, dovelike knees rouse the compassion of the men. One night she comes to Sara's room.

"Tell me, Sara, are you still a virgin?"

"No," Sara says.

Ofra puffs nervously on a cigarette. "So is it true what mother says, that once you start with a man you can't stop?"

Like Victoria that day with the seamstress, Sara doesn't know what to say.

"Why worry about it?"

"There's this treasurer at the office. He just walked me home. I tell him that I don't want him to be a treasurer by day and a wolf by night, but what really is a person to do?"

Sara, tired after a day at the hospital, is in no mood to preach.

"Do what seems right to you."

Ofra is offended. She feels Sara is being condescending.

"Well," she says spitefully, "you have to because you're too big. I don't. I'll get married a virgin, in a white gown." She stalks out, taking her scent of tobacco and her perfume that Sara cannot stand. With all her affectations, her purple cartwheel hats that she wears on Sabbaths, her aloof airs, she is getting to be more and more like Gracia. She too, in a sense, is a portrait of captive refinement, but she is more captive than refined. Her tiny body perfumed and irritable, she rubs against the bars of her cage.

For the first time since Zaki Amarillo's disappearance, something is beginning to stir in the house. There are many visitors with whom

Grandfather Amarillo spends long hours. Captain Tony Crowther keeps coming back. He is enchanted with Gracia, the uncertified widow, and no less with Elder Amarillo, whom he calls Dr. Amarillo, since a doctor of divinity was the closest thing to an elder he could think of.

"Dr. Amarillo," he asks one evening as they are sitting around the table, "how do you explain the fact that the Jews fought so many wars even after they received the Bible on Mount Sinai with the commandment not to kill?"

"The Hebrew Bible, Tony, doesn't say 'Thou shalt not kill.' It says, 'Thou shalt not murder.'"

"Oh. I see. Our Bible isn't translated correctly."

Another time he asks:

"Dr. Amarillo, what in your opinion is the mission of Jerusalem?"

"Mission?" ponders Grandfather Amarillo. "Jerusalem is its own mission. Whatever God wills will happen to it."

After the Englishman leaves, he remarks to the women: "It would take a Gentile to think of it. What is Jerusalem lacking right now? My own father used to say to God: 'If, God forbid, You should ever decide to remove Your presence from this city, please don't let it worry You, because we're staying put, come what may.'"

Cracking sunflower seeds between her teeth one Saturday night, Victoria says:

"Did you hear the latest about Leon Cordoso? When Solomon Cordoso comes to visit him the other day, he turns off all the lights: after all, he says, we're brothers, why waste electricity? So yesterday, Leon comes to see Solomon and finds him sitting there without pants. What's the matter, Leon, he says, after all, we're brothers, why wear them out?"

"Don't be a badmouth, Victoria," Grandfather Amarillo cautions, but he too joins in the laughter, wagging his beard and baring his perfectly yellowed teeth.

"Tell us another one, Victoria," Ofra and Sara beg.

"That's enough. I'm all out of badness for today."

Waves of light in the olive trees outside. A pure wind shakes the mauve thistles. The hillside slivers into infinite detail. Sky without end.

Something, Sara feels, is inexplicably starting to blossom, something impermanent and bruisable in which a kind of happiness is nonetheless to be found. The city seems to be filling up more than growing out, the way a child's mouth fills with teeth: a hill on which there had been one house, three, suddenly grows a whole street. Buildings rise on the empty lots of her childhood that had once been strewn with junk. Even Nissim Mizrachi, that is, Miracolo Orientale, has changed his burial cart for a fine black automobile, which it took him a long while to learn how to drive. On its side, in fancy white letters, he painted the verse, "And justice proceedeth before Him." "It's almost worth dying for the ride, Nissim," people in the neighborhood joke. But Nissim himself wishes to live: he is secretly in love with his hefty neighbor Victoria, though he doesn't dare approach her.

Subhi Bey and his wife Faiza come and visit on Jewish holidays, bearing gifts. Subhi is a well-to-do merchant, the scion of a large banking family with whom the Amarillos have business connections. Faiza had spent a good part of her youth in Europe and Constantinople, where her father, a Lebanese intellectual, served in the Ottoman diplomatic corps; she was betrothed to little Subhi, who is a head shorter, while he was on a banking mission for his father in Turkey, and never saw his face until their wedding. They have three grown sons and a daughter. Faiza wears a black veil, as is the urban Moslem's custom, but removes it in the houses of friends, and sometimes, near her home, even in the street: the fact of the matter is that she would gladly have thrown it away entirely. She has never traveled since her wedding, except once with Subhi to visit their eldest son, Taleb, who was studying agronomy in Berlin. She is on close terms with Gracia and fond of both her daughters.

Sometimes Hulda comes too, with Dr. Barzel, now Professor Barzel, who has fallen in love with the Amarillos' large house: *echt* Jerusalem, he calls it. Grandfather Amarillo joins the guests on the terrace in his black caftan, and instructs Professor Barzel (the red one, he calls him, as red as the porridge that Jacob served Esau), on the olive tree:

"Your olive, Professor, is the tree of light. Not your fig, or your carob, or your acacia: only the olive. Consider for yourself. The underside of its leaf is silver, of no other tree is this so. Each time the wind blows, the whole tree lights up. That's its silver. And from its oil, lamps are made that give a fine, soft flame. That's its gold. So there's a tree of light and there's also a tree of sweet scents. I'll explain that to you too."

"Olives have always looked grayish-green to me," Professor Barzel confesses.

"If you'll excuse me, Professor, that's because you have European eyes."

"Faiza's mother, God rest her," Subhi Bey comments, "used to hang olive-oil lamps from the ceiling. She'd fill little bowls with colored water, arrange them in a big glass dish, and put olive oil and wicks inside them. We'd hang the whole dish and watch the colored lights from below."

There is always some fragrance, some special smell, at Grandfather Amarillo's: frankincense or myrtle, a whole branch of it sticky with sap, and during the High Holy Days, branches of *rihan,* brown, green, and violet. On the fast of Yom Kippur he takes a bundle of them to the synagogue to use like smelling salts, so as not to pass out from the heat.

People in the neighborhood think it isn't so simple to go walking with Captain Crowther. But it really is.

Gracia sings. In a virginal, surprisingly strong voice, pleasant in its unwavering persistence. It rises, piercing the casements. Tony Crowther, coming to visit that Saturday morning, stands still in the street for a moment to listen.

In Seville there is a castle
Thousand wonders all around—

As she isn't done dressing yet, she sends the two girls out to stroll for a while with Tony in the field. It always takes her a long time to dress, mostly in purple, all shades of it. Her huge, nebulous hats look like the rings of Saturn. An unfathomable, enchanting, unapproachable widow. A galaxy of romantic suffering.

Neither water nor perfume
Can make his deep swoon disappear.
Only these three magic words
That she whispers in his ear.

"What a lovely voice your mother has," says Tony to the girls. They walk almost as far as Sha'arei Hesed. "It's as bold as a flower of the field."

Ofra giggles behind her hand.

"What kind of flower?" asks Sara, playing dumb.

Tony falls for it: "A white one. Lily of the valley."

Sara and Ofra frown contemplatively.

"It doesn't grow here."

"It doesn't?" Tony is taken aback.

"No. Name a flower that does."

He thinks and thinks and cannot think of one.

"Name any plant at all," they say to make it easier. "You've been here so many years, Tony. Where are your eyes?"

"All I can think of is carrots," Tony admits. "Let's see you name five plants."

He is deluged with them:

"In this field alone? Anemone. Cyclamen. Groundsel. Veronica. Narcissus. And now five more that begin with the same letter: Chrysanthemum. Clover. Campion. Chicory. Carob."

Tony throws up his hands:

"I surrender! I surrender!"

But Sara wants to teach him. She plucks a flower bud and gives it to him:

"Here, you can eat this. It's a mallow."

Ofra plucks a chicory leaf:

"Taste this too."

Tony takes a bite of the chicory and spits it out. Ofra laughs.

"You young scamp," he says to her. "All right, perhaps I need to brush up on my Middle Eastern botany. I'm a well-meaning ignoramus if you like, but there are other things here that I know something about."

"Like what?"

"Like the wars in the Bible, for example."

"That sounds interesting. Tell us about them."

Tony ignores their sarcasm and declaims:

The Assyrian came down like a wolf on the fold,
And his cohorts were gleaming in purple and gold.

Sara thinks it over and says:

"I doubt that the Assyrians wore purple and gold. More likely they wore ordinary linen or sackcloth. Who said that?"

"Byron."

"Well, he's not exactly an expert."

"Sara," Tony says, a bit hurt, "you're literal-minded to the point of pedantry. Where's your imagination?"

They are close to the house again.

They tell me the way that I'm going
Doesn't have any way back,
But if it costs me my life to keep on it,
I'll follow the same old track.

Gracia sings on and on in her room. Soon she'll come down, a purple, suffering queen.

There was a mysterious old man in the hospital: no matter how carefully his diet was watched during the day to lower his blood sugar, the sugar count when taken the next morning would be high again. Finally Sara looked in the drawer of his night table and found a hidden storehouse of chocolate, cookies, whatever was on sale at the stand below. Every day he stole furtively downstairs, restocked his treasure, hid it away, and nibbled it up at night like a rodent. He was a self-centered, cunning, half-senile old man who giggled with embarrassment when caught. The next day he would do it again. He pretended to be sorry and wasn't.

"He just doesn't want to be discharged," Sara told the doctors. "He lives in an old-age home where nobody ever looks at him, while here he gets lots of attention. Why should he want to leave?"

A noisy argument broke out on the ward between Professor Kapulski from Odessa and Professor Barzel. Kapulski was for throwing the old man out at once. Barzel wanted to reason with him, to give him another chance.

"Guess how it ended," Nahum tells Sara. "Kapulski pulls himself up to his full height and says to Bimbi: 'I'd like you to remember, Herr Kollege, that I'm a professor here too, and your senior.' So Bimbi pulls himself up too, nostril to nostril, except he's a little taller, and says: 'And I'd like you to remember, Herr Kollege, that I'm from Heidelberg!' "

Nahum and Sara walk far from the city, among the old olive trees in the Valley of the Cross. In the silently humming, soft evening air a partridge warns its chicks to take cover. He pulls the pins from her hair, which is done up so tightly, unsparingly, smelling its scent of day-warmed rose. He embraces her, short and hard, in the wild, shooty tangle of an olive tree. Sara traces his puppyish nose with her finger: a warm, shaggy, thick-coated little dog. His embraces, she thinks, are like himself: to the point and unimaginative.

"You rationalist," she says. She is feeling sad.

"Can I take you out again tomorrow?"

"You're too ambitious, Dr. Nahum."

They go out with each other two or three more times, but Sara knows well that she would find no new truth here. She rises, brushing the dirt from her uniform.

"That's enough, Nahum."

He is mad. In the hospital he doesn't talk to her for several days. Eventually things work themselves out. They are part of a team racing to save the life of a boy who has fallen off a scaffold. When Nahum can finally change his blood-soaked clothes, he says, in lieu of an apology, in a boy-man's voice:

"When you feel you can go to a movie with me, let me know."

"As far as I'm concerned, it can be right now."

They sit and watch an Egyptian film, cracking sunflower seeds, good friends.

"I feel so good I can't stand it," says Sara to Hulda.

"I feel so good I can't stand it," says Hulda to Bimbi. There is much good feeling all around. The days lead simply into the nights. Waking is easy.

Grandfather Amarillo rises early to walk with the dawn breeze. A cypress touches Venus, still shining in the sunrise. The feel of the hill is familiar. He picks up a God-fearing stone and breathes in the dry, khaki-colored shadows, thankful for the sinless sternness of the olive trees. He waits for the full weight of the light on the hill, his feet exploring the ground, the ground exploring his feet. Elder Amarillo's mornings are a daily re-encounter of his long black robe, his hands, and the light.

CHAPTER FOUR

"LEAD ON, TONY!"

Among ancient fig trees, in the streaming, flickery light, three
horses canter along the Roman road near Motsa. Captain Tony
Crowther rides in the lead, followed by his friend Major Jim Saywell,
expert equestrian, expert ornithologist, while the rear is languidly
brought up by Saleh, the Arab groom and father of six. Saleh knows
all about horses. Times are good. He gives vent to his sense of well-
being by singing long, flat desert songs that rise now and then like a
wave of sand to descend the other side of the dune, low, wind-swept
melodies with a tremolo at the end like the tips of a tamarisk branch in
the forgotten distance. The sky is too blue to be blue, pure cobalt: if he
were to paint it, Tony thinks, it would be with a blazing black iris at
the center. The stone is incandescent in the white light, as is the terra
rossa beneath it: barbed, sunbaked, hard-visaged stone. Shapes of it
like marbles, like loaves, spurt from under the hoofs of the horses,
large, gravelly pebbles like eyeless skulls. The terraced hillside is covered with flowering yellow broom, sheaves and sheaves of it among
the rocks. Swifts spear the figs and dart off, spear the figs and dart off,
with vivacious, provocative flight. Three horsemen on a hill. What

more could happen to them now in this sudden gust of wind, this copious year, this ascetic, unremitting mountain land?

"Swifts," says Jim Saywell. "Bound for Europe." He takes his notebook and jots it down.

The city still squats on its haunches behind them, a ripple of red roofs draped with a shimmering halo of heat like a clear muslin net that softens its colors and lines. Jerusalem is a veiled lady on a still, torrid day, feminine, forlorn, softly dreaming, self-absorbed, sucking time sweetly like an old sugar candy, her sons gathered under the many folds of her robe, picking rockrose and herbs. Other days she is a man, fierce, dry, and ancient, smelling of thyme and wild goat, his head covered with a sack against the wind, bare feet viny-veined, brusque-voiced and ornery, sniffing the slippery scent of sin in abandoned alleys, the odor of prophecy in public squares. The city lives without mirrors, each of its dwellers the key to an ancient, ironlike place, lattice-faced, wall-chested, sandaled feet skipping lightly over crooked, anonymous cobblestones, through openings, endless doors. Always an unsolved remainder, footprints belonging to no one, improbable clues, a taste of permanent mystery. A veiny, living tension from street to street, house to house. Each solemn girl in a courtyard is more girl than anywhere else, each baby wrapped in a shawl the only baby on earth, each single person the leaven of life. The city tenses its muscles under your feet. Put your hand on a wall and you feel the stone pulse. The very light percolates through it with each breath of the desert heat. Every house is itself. Alive. Alive.

But now it is behind them, dove-colored, far away.

"Jim, look!"

"A falcon," Saleh the groom says indifferently, chewing on the end of a stalk.

A smallish falcon has burst the circle of swifts, which it feigns not to menace. The swifts try keeping above it, spinning dizzily overhead in tight upward spirals, while the falcon seeks to outclimb them: a long, circling, almost indolent dance, a weightless pursuit around a tall, invisible pole, until they are lost to sight.

Tony lowers his gun, rubbing the cobalt flood from his eyes.

"I meant to take a crack at it, but that dance was just too splendid."

A deceptive stillness. A mendacious peace. The whole country is like that.

Softhearted, Saleh thinks. No hunter's blood in his veins.

"Who is the pursuer and who the pursued?" asks Tony Crowther. "Who is the potter and who the pot?"

"By the way, Tony."

"Yes?"

"There's been some silly grumbling in the department. Exaggerated, no doubt."

"About?"

"Reggie is convinced that in that neighborhood you visit there's a whole army of pyromaniacs with an arsenal of dynamite that could blow the holy city to kingdom come. Anyway, that's how he talks."

"The Right Honorable Reginald Welsley-More is a congenital idiot."

"Agreed. But he's also short, and short people have a way of attaching themselves to you and hanging on. If I were you, Tony—"

"Well, you're not, damn it."

They are quiet for a while before Tony adds mollifyingly: "Look here, old man, Reggie doesn't know them half as well as I do, Jim. If there's anything there at all, it's pathetic, pitiful. They're frightfully weak, Jimmie. The Arabs will eat them alive one day. It's absurd to think of them as a threat to the British Empire. Or to the great Islamic Kingdom. Besides, Reggie knows perfectly well that I have an informer there."

"Our virtuous sister, Sa'ada? Your Sergeant Starkie practically lives there."

"Sa'ada doesn't know a thing. The Jews don't go to her."

"Not kosher?"

"Either that, or not to their taste. No, I've got someone else. From an old, respectable family, in fact. A very Levantine gentleman. I can't say he's a likable chap. Sometimes when he comes to see me I'd like to kick his arse down the stairs. Talks a proper cockney, if you like. 'Yes, Cap'n Crowfer, at yer service, Cap'n Crowfer.' A civilian, but he always salutes. Thinks he's an integral part of the British Empire. The King is his. He'll come to London and they'll pat him on his greasy head for all the good work he's done. He has the shiniest shoes you've ever seen in your life."

"They're all like that," Major Saywell assents. "Where is your romantic, your idealist, who'd inform on his own mother just for the principle of the thing? There isn't a one of them that can't be persuaded to have his palm crossed in the end."

"With thirty shekels of silver, before prices went up."

"Tony, what about lunching in Ramallah? I'm beginning to be famished. We've been out seven hours without eating."

Tony turns to the groom and asks in Arabic:

"Saleh, do you know of a good place to eat in Ramallah? I believe you come from there."

A burst of oaths and protestations.

"I suppose he's saying that he just happens to have a twin brother there who runs the best, cleanest, and most inexpensive restaurant in the world."

"You're close. It's his cousin. Shall we chance it?"

"Let's."

They urge on their horses, ascending from the valley toward Nebi Samwil among dusty, scattered pine trees, along a grayish, rocky, barely negotiable trail, until they rejoin the main road at Kalandia. Passing through the village, they are besieged by a host of runny-eyed tots in strip smocks who shout: "Good mo'ning, good mo'ning." They ride swiftly by.

"What a beautiful country this could be if it had no people in it," Jim Saywell remarks. "Really, they *are* superfluous. Don't you think that their biblical God might be planning to get rid of them all soon with one of his famous disasters?"

"In which case Reginald Welsley-bloody-More wouldn't have a blessed thing to do. What a splendid idea."

"Saleh, lead us to your cousin."

They reined in the horses and hitched them to the entrance of a restaurant with a veranda paned in blue glass. Saleh went to water the horses. It was pleasantly cool on the veranda. Large jars of purple pickled turnip rested in the muted light beside containers of sour cheese balls in golden green oil, pickled onions with parsley, violet eggplant, and slices of yellow lemon, each a sour, caged little sun.

"If you tried painting these colors, they'd look trite," said Jim Saywell. "But here they seem natural. I say, Tony, I believe there are some friends of yours here."

The veranda was deserted, but in the dim interior, beyond an open bead screen, several men with mustaches, wearing European suits and kaffias on their heads, sat huddled around a small table. Among them Tony made out Taleb and Husni, Subhi Bey's eldest and youngest sons. He waved across the room to them. After a moment's hesitation Taleb came over, heavy-skinned, large-pored, eyes lost in thought.

"Hello, Captain Crowther. A pleasure to see you on a hot day like this. Major, how are you? I see you've been out riding."

"We were out in the hills and fagged out. Saleh recommended this place. Now that I see you and your brother, I feel better about it. Do you come here often?"

"Not anymore we don't," whispered one of Taleb's friends who had been eavesdropping on the conversation.

Taleb rejoined his friends. Bent almost double beneath his load of trays, the owner of the restaurant decked the table with a score of different salads, platters of golden roast pigeon, plates of saffroned, mouth-watering rice. The two Englishmen relaxed and ate.

"Saleh brought them here," said Taleb to his friends. "Right here. Of all the restaurants in Ramallah, he had to pick this one."

They nodded.

"I stopped trusting him long ago," said a thin young man with handsome eyes.

"Tony, don't you think there's something funny going on?" asked Jim Saywell in a low voice. "All the commotion back there. The whispering. What do you make of it?"

"I don't. It just surprises me that Husni and Taleb are being so matey together. As far as I know, Husni is in disgrace. The family doesn't like his being a singer. But I don't see what's wrong with them eating like you and me."

"They're not eating."

"Maybe they're done. Or maybe they just came for coffee."

"One can't be too careful."

"For God's sake, Jimmie, let me eat."

They resumed their meal in silence. Jim Saywell said:

"What annoys me most about our Reggie is the names he calls people. He calls all the Jews 'Beards'—and the Arabs 'Towels.' Why towels, come to think of it?"

"Because of the kaffias. Don't let it bother you. I served under him in Turkey before Atatürk outlawed the fez. He called the Turks 'Flowerpots.' "

"The fact of the matter is," said Jim Saywell, "that I could like the Middle East well enough if only they'd leave the garlic out of the food. It's the curse of the region."

"Its blessing, Jimmie boy, its blessing."

"A pistol?" The handsome-eyed young man hunched over the table.

"No. Too much noise. A knife."

"I don't want any part of this," said Taleb crossly, unhappily.

"What's the matter, Taleb, no balls?"

"If we want to revolt, let's revolt. But let's not have the first blood that we spill be an Arab's. I don't like it."

"Anyone working for British Intelligence isn't an Arab anymore."

Taleb made up his mind:

"Count me out. Come on, Husni, let's go."

He and two others rose and left, bowing slightly, as they passed, to the two British officers, who bowed slightly back.

A quarter of an hour later, while the two Englishmen washed down their meal with coffee and a satisfied grunt, Saleh lay half-sprawled and half-seated on the toilet outside, a knife thrust through the crude planks of the outhouse deep into his lungs, his pants pulled down, his life departing. Through an aperture in the door, in a sky gone mad with cobalt, he saw, or thought he saw, the falcon and the swifts once again. But perhaps it was only his eyes, spinning with black dots, before the final darkness settled in.

The two officers assumed that the missing Saleh had gone off on his horse to visit his family in town. Full of sun, sky, and food, they galloped wordlessly off to Jerusalem without even thinking to wait.

Professor Barzel passed the cedar of Lebanon in his garden every day. It gave him no joy. It was the third such tree he had unsuccessfully transplanted: a perpetually wilting refugee from the snow line, its earthbound upper branches rising and sagging fitfully by turn, it seemed afflicted with every illness in the plant books.

"Will it live, Hassan?" Professor Barzel asked his gardener.

"Never. It's a waste of time and work."

Professor Barzel ordered botany texts from Europe in the hope of finding some clue to treating it. None of them mentioned cedars, but he sought to apply what they said about water, fertilizer, and the culture of conifers in general to his own thoroughbred plant. It was hard to say in the end which the cedar responded to more, the treatments prescribed for northern larches and firs or the sheer attention that it got, but day by day it looked better. It perked up so that even Hassan grudgingly conceded:

"It's taking."

"It's taking," Professor Barzel triumphantly asserted.

He decided to throw a party for the cedar. He sat down and composed a heartfelt letter of invitation to his friends.

It was without a doubt one of the finest parties any of them could remember. There are days in Jerusalem, Professor Barzel liked to say, that are especially Schubert days—and though not all his guests were quite sure what he meant, this was certainly such a day. Gracia came with Sara and Ofra, all three in long, light-colored gowns, carrying new parasols in their hands. Subhi Bey came with Faiza, who wore the traditional black dress, now brightened by a colorful scarf and a smile that took ten years off her age. Husni came later, straight from the hospital, hungry and thirsty, with a red rose for Mrs. Barzel. The unruly-haired pianist Walter Rudi was there too, dark as a wild raven, perched predatorily among the women; Tony Crowther was there in his summer uniform; so was Hulda's twin brother, Amatsia, lounging with cosmic laziness; so was Madame Arthemis Savvidopoulos, who dreamed of marrying off her daughters to rich Greek tycoons but couldn't find one in Palestine; so were the violin maker Alfred von Kluck, who tied his fierce bulldog by the door, and the newly retired Professor Marcus.

"My dear friends," Professor Barzel declaimed by the cedar, toast in hand, "I am most fond of you all, each by himself and all together. I consider this banquet of love to be one of the last manifestations of civilization in a world which is being unfortunately taken over by *Barbarismus*. I don't know whether the next generation will still know what it is to feel the friendship and intimacy that we all feel tonight. Here's to all of us, and to the cedar tree that refused to give in and struck roots and lived!"

Everyone applauded. Hulda poured Sara a drink and said under her breath:

"Concerning friendship and intimacy, there's more going on than meets Bimbi's eye."

"What are you getting at?"

"That Husni's been poking around. He dropped by the other day. I threw him out politely. What do you think of him? I rather like him. Long arms and sweet charms."

Subhi and Faiza wanted to ask their close friends' advice about their oldest daughter, Suhaila, but had trouble finding an opening. Finally Faiza confided:

"You know, my friends, it's no secret that our daughter Suhaila is already twenty-eight years old. She's a fine, educated girl, a teacher in the Old City, and we hear she'll soon be made a principal, but we still haven't found her a proper match."

"We've turned down many offers," said Subhi Bey.

"We've turned down many offers. And then just two or three weeks ago a couple we know from Ramallah comes to see us with a message from a certain young man that he's interested in Suhaila. What did they know about him? That he's a pharmacist, never married, an educated fellow who's just returned from his studies in France and wants to open a pharmacy. We asked Suhaila. 'Invite him over,' she says, 'and we'll see.' A few days ago our friends returned with the young man. We spent the whole evening together, the three of them, my brothers, and my eldest sons Taleb and Kamal. We must have sat there for three or four hours without him even opening his mouth, not even when I tried talking about Paris, which I haven't seen for ages."

"The boy has heavy blood," said Subhi Bey.

"The day before yesterday our friends came back to inquire if the young man might ask for Suhaila's hand. 'But I don't know a thing about him,' Suhaila says. 'I haven't even heard his voice yet. I want to see him in private before I decide.' Our friends told the young man— and would you believe it, he took offense! 'If they want to examine me,' he says, 'I had enough examinations in France'—and he calls the whole thing off. It's hard to be an educated girl today. We brought Suhaila up to think for herself, to make her own decisions, and now we don't know what to do. We can't start sending her off to dances, after all. It simply isn't done."

"They've brought her up neither here nor there," Amatsia whispered to Tony.

"Suhaila's simply spoiled," declared Subhi Bey gloomily, his neck flushed. "All the girls are nowadays. This one she doesn't like, that one has to be examined, that one isn't educated enough. The result of it all is that she's nearly thirty and we're still waiting to celebrate."

"Never you mind," said Madame Savvidopoulos, pulling out a handkerchief and daintily wiping bits of strawberry from her pursed lips. "She's sure to find her true love in the end. Some wait more, some less. Did you ever hear of a flower, Subhi Bey, that grew and grew without blossoming? Give her another year or two, you'll see."

Amatsia snickered, but Subhi Bey brightened a little.

"Thank you, madame. Truly, you've sweetened our hearts with your words today."

Professor Barzel was telling old Marcus:

"You know, not long ago we received a government order to inspect all the brothels in town. Sa'ada's was first on the list. It was no simple matter deciding whom to send. In the end we picked the youngest and shyest of the residents, that puppy, Dr. Nahum. Let him learn some professional poise, we thought, it won't do him any harm. So off he goes to Sa'ada's and we made sure that he went by himself. 'How was it, Nahum?' we ask when he gets back. 'Fine,' he says. 'They're all in good health and used to being examined. They even called my speculum *zubb al-hukuma,* the government's prick.' We saw it was no use kidding him, so we dropped it. Only what do you think happens yesterday? Nahum shows up with a nonchalant look on his face, I do mean nonchalant, and shows us a piece of paper. Believe it or not, he received a love letter from one of the whores. You must admit, my friend, that's a rare compliment for a young man his age. You can imagine how his reputation at the hospital has soared. When they call for the man now, they mean Nahum."

Old Marcus laughed and laughed.

"Music! Music!" implored the guests. Professor Barzel and Tony took their places.

"An afternoon like this requires Schubert. *Rosamunde* would be in order, but we won't tire you with long works. Just one allegro from a sonata. A-minor, Tony."

They played, Tony fluently, with few mistakes, Professor Barzel with many, breaking on and off into song, waving his bow with true amateur passion. Gracia and Faiza, who didn't care for such music, sat at a distance.

"Just look at Doctor Bimbi, *ya* Mother-of-Taleb," said Gracia. "He's done Jerusalem a world of good."

"The very air is playing with him tonight."

Husni arrived as the allegro was nearing its end. He was besieged immediately.

"Sing for us, Husni! Sing!"

"One minute, I haven't eaten or drunk anything yet. Such distinguished company deserves me at full strength."

Hulda served him with a plate and a glass, brushing against him more than she had to, while Bimbi looked on uncomplainingly at this further note of harmony in his banquet of love. Madame Arthemis Savvidopoulos approached him on her swollen ankles, busily waving a paper fan. Lately she had been reading Saint Augustine.

"Professor, what do *you* think about feelings of guilt? When do they begin to appear?"

There was a stir among the guests. Subhi Bey, a believer, belittled all guilt feelings that weren't directed toward God. One must distinguish, he said, between shame, a purely social emotion that was best avoided to save face, and guilt, which was God's. Amatsia denied that God had anything to do with it. Gracia, wine-mellowed, confided:

"When my husband disappeared, we all felt guilty without knowing why. It was as though we were to blame. And yet we weren't, we really were not."

"The fact that I'm here at all makes me feel guilty," said Tony Crowther, caught up in the confessional mood. "Here I am, a pagan from the north, whom fate has put in charge of you ancient monotheists. We Europeans are the parvenus of civilization, my friends. You were law-abiding people when we were still living in the treetops."

Subhi Bey nodded.

"We respect your feelings, Captain. Unfortunately, not everyone is like you. Just the other day my brother, whom you all know, Hajj Kamal ad-Din, a man of great culture and the world's leading expert on Sufi poetry, was asked by a young upstart in the military dental clinic whether he brushed his teeth every day."

Hulda made a face. "Tony, you look at us as though we were all animals in some biblical zoo. We're human, you know."

"And you, Walter?"

"Why deny it? After an unsuccessful recital, I'm chock-full of guilt feelings. The piano was guilty, the auditorium was guilty, the audience was guilty, the critics were guilty—there's guilt wherever I look."

Laughter. Alfred von Kluck, whose turn it was to say something, was silent. He kept his thoughts to himself, inside his shaven Prussian head, and drank a great deal.

"And you, my dear friend Doctor Bimbi," asked Madame Savvidopoulos, "have you nothing to tell us? Are your angelic hands free of guilt?"

"No, I feel no guilt. Sometimes, though, I feel something much worse and much simpler."

"What is that?"

"Sin."

"Theology," whispered Amatsia. "Bimbi's getting old. Men get religion with age."

"Women are just the opposite," Faiza whispered back. "I can't tell you how little all these ceremonies mean to me now that I'm older. If I get hungry on the Ramadan fast I actually grab a bite before sunset— but don't breathe a word of it to Subhi."

"And the problem is," Professor Barzel continued his tortuous line of thought, "the problem is, my friends, that I don't believe in repentance one bit."

"Husni," Amatsia said coldly, "if my sister's done feeding you, I think it's time that you sang."

"Soon," Hulda interceded, as the figure of a new guest appeared at the gate, "let him rest a minute first." The newcomer was a tall and somewhat bashful-looking man.

"Elias Amarillo!" she cried out. "I'm so glad you came."

She ran to him and led him straight back, like a retriever proudly bringing its catch, waiting to have its nose stroked in praise, to where Sara was sipping her drink at a table in the garden. Sara made a fine picture just then: a large, dark-haired woman in a flowing white dress, shaded by a red-striped parasol that veiled and enveloped her in its light rose penumbra; her red-tinted wineglass, frosty with ice cubes, pressed to her cheek the better to feel its cold breath against her skin. Curious. More tuned to the world than to herself. The essence of woman in summer, thought Elias Amarillo.

"Sara, I've brought you another Amarillo. See if you're related. I'm sure you must be. His name is Elias. He comes from Tiberias and he's a big lawyer who's returned from abroad just in time to get our hospital out of trouble. Soon he's going to discover a paragraph in international law for us that will prove the British High Commissioner illegal."

"Call me Eli," he grinned. His mouth was long, generous, dark; when it smiled it grew even longer, narrowing to a slit like an old wound that no longer hurt, pulled downward at each end by two sharp, ironic angles. He had the lanky good looks of a cypress tree, of a tall, spare rabbinical student. Modest and excellent.

"And by the way, Mrs. Barzel, I'm sorry to tell you that the High Commissioner is perfectly legal."

"You're from the Tiberias Amarillos?" asked Sara, alert, raising her head. "A son of Tío Sasson's?"

"My father is Tío Sasson's first cousin. Ezra Amarillo, the druggist."

"That makes us second cousins once removed, Eli. I'm Elder Moses Amarillo's granddaughter."

"Then you're distant enough to get married," ruled Hulda, still sniffing, making them slightly ill at ease.

"You're Zaki's daughter?" he asked. There was no need to say more. Word of the scandal had reached Tiberias long ago.

She nodded.

"My mother and sister Ofra are over there in the corner. Would you like to meet them?"

"No," said her second cousin once removed, matter-of-factly. How could anyone's mouth be so long? Perhaps it had been charcoaled in. She liked his subtle impudence.

"Well, I hope you manage to get to the roots of your family tree. I'm off to cheer up Madame Savvidopoulos, she's looking rather glum. Von Kluck isn't talking to her. He hasn't earned his refreshments. He just sits there staring silently at Ofra in German."

Husni ran his hand through his hair and struck the pose of a romantic tenor for his audience. He cleared his throat, bounced a trial note off the ceiling and caught it, half-covering his ear with his hand,

and announced that he would sing "The Indian Love Call." His voice floated smoothly down the Rehavia street as though a hidden, honeyed tap had been opened in his throat.

"Sweet," said Madame Savvidopoulos, looking dreamily upward. "Sweet." Tony tittered.

"My husband is furious," said Faiza to Gracia. "Look at him. Haven't I told you? Subhi, God bless him, can't stand Husni's singing. He says that his family has always produced scholars and farmers, farmers and scholars, but never singers or entertainers. When we get home he'll chew Husni out for agreeing to sing. He's been very hard on him lately. Too hard."

"It was the host's request," said Gracia. "Husni couldn't have refused."

"I'll make that my line of defense," Faiza said.

"And you yourself don't mind, Umm-Taleb?"

"They're big boys," said Faiza in her mellifluous voice. "Let them fly the coop if they want."

Sara suddenly felt that she could not cope with it all anymore: not with Husni's syrupy song, which for all its commonness had everyone enthralled; nor with the overpowering, unbelievable scent of jasmine, honeysuckle, and snapdragon in bloom; nor with the sight of the light scattered half over the sky in the sinking red sunset, breaking against the fragile wineglasses, against the folds of the women's dresses, through a too-wildly flowering shrub; nor with the soft, pure, inno-cent air; not even with the little cedar tree that overcame and grew. It was all too much for her. The guests drew near each other as darkness was saturating the stillness, with a contentment that would never return. Even Amatsia seemed at peace.

Sara rose and went farther into the garden. She took a deep breath. The little wine she had drunk was taking effect. Elias followed her.

"What is it that you feel, Sara?"

She tried making a sweeping gesture with her hand, but it fell limply to her side.

"That this is all for the last time."

"Do you really think so?"

"I think that completely new times are ahead. That we're celebrating the end of something tonight. This city is full of tensions, Eli—they're even right here in this garden. We've managed to ignore them today—because it's Bimbi's party, and all of us love him, we've swept them under the rug. But how long can you go on sweeping tensions under a rug?"

Elias nodded.

"This city gets us all in the end," he said quietly. "I've been away for so long I forgot."

From within the house came the notes of a duet on the Bluethner piano: Walter and Tony were thunderously improvising on the love theme from *Tristan und Isolde*. Professor Barzel, a little high, approached Elias and Sara in the darkness.

"Ah, it's you? You're in love? Love each other, I say. It's all there is in this world."

He vanished.

Elias bent over Sara. "May I?"

"Not tonight."

"You just said yourself that it's all for the last time."

Her voice dropped. "It is, Eli. I'm as sure of it as I am that the sun will rise tomorrow. This lit-up garden, all these lovely people . . ."

She trailed off.

"I'm a man of reason, Sara," he said uncertainly, if not unhappily, for he took her sudden openness as a tribute to his attentiveness. "I believe in prophecy, but with a grain of salt. Are you an artist?"

"No. I'm just a nurse. A sister of mercy—and not even an experienced one."

" 'We have a little sister,' " Eli declaimed from The Song of Songs. He smiled his brown, wounded smile, looking quizzically down to check the rest of the verse: we have a little sister, and she hath no breasts.

She laughed.

"Come, Eli, let's go back to the party."

They walked slowly back. The magic spell had begun to dissipate. Faiza donned her shawl at Subhi's command; their driver was waiting outside. Madame Savvidopoulos had mislaid her purse and was ransacking the house for it. Walter Rudi drove Tony away from the piano and banged out a noisy rendition of Liszt that no one enjoyed.

Hulda walked them to the gate.

"Do you know what used to happen on evenings like this when I was a girl in Bet Hakerem? The poet Bialik, who came for rest cures, used to go for long walks with the novelist Agnon, and we children would turn out the lights in our rooms so that we could eavesdrop on every word."

"What did they talk about?"

"I really don't know. But they were terribly formal. 'You said the other day, Mr. Bialik.' 'I noticed in your latest work, Mr. Agnon.' "

"I always wanted to talk to Bialik," said Amatsia, "but I never knew what to say. Finally, when I was in eighth grade, I got up the courage to go over to him. 'Excuse me, Mr. Bialik,' I said, 'could you tell me what time it is?' "

"What did he say?"

"Half-past ten."

"We're talking about two famous authors," Professor Barzel explained to the other guests.

"Let's go, Faiza," said Subhi Bey. "This is not a topic we understand."

He smiled as he spoke, but a wall had already gone up. As though to leave no room for doubt, Faiza put on her veil. They stepped into their huge automobile and drove off. Tony, who was taking Gracia and her daughters home in his army car, seemed suddenly drunk, slow-witted, and thoroughly the Englishman. Professor Marcus was driven home by Professor Barzel, though he lived only half a block away.

In the car Gracia complained that she'd drunk too much wine and listened to too much European music. She was sure to get a migraine from it all. Tipsily nostalgic, Tony clung silently to the wheel.

"It was a fabulous party," said Ofra, looking off into the darkness. "Absolutely fabulous."

"Have you been seeing much of Elias Amarillo?" Hulda asked Sara several days later.

"No. We've just had coffee together once or twice. There's been someone else."

"Who?"

"You won't be happy to hear this. Husni."

"Sara, no!" Hulda was so beside herself that she hopped up and down on one foot. "Steve Harold? What on earth do you see in him?"

"He's the most arrogant thing imaginable in bed," Sara grinned. "There's nothing to it. It's all very technical. By the number."

"Then why are you doing it?"

"Do you really want to know, Hulda? I haven't the vaguest idea."

When Taleb had returned from Germany, he told his father that he was bringing new methods of farming that he wanted to try on the family's lands. Subhi, who had his doubts about both Taleb and the methods, gave his son a small vineyard near Kolonia to experiment with. There was something driven, self-haunted, about Taleb when he came back, as though he were in search of the biggest, most sultanic identity he could find and wrap around himself so as never to be anonymous again. His two years in Germany had been spent totally incommunicado. Each day after classes he shut himself dreamily up in his room, never venturing even as far as the local red-light district. The whole world, it seemed to him, was smarter than he and more important. He grew desperately homesick. The European winter depressed him no end. He loathed German food, the beef, the beer, the cakes with whipped cream.

Early in the morning he rode off to the vineyard. The first thing he told his father's workmen was to clear the land of all its stones, because his German professors had taught him that the soil should be perfectly clean. Next he instructed them to plow the furrows deeply, instead of simply scratching away a bit at the surface as they had done until now. The workmen looked at him skeptically. It wasn't easy to plow deep with their dark, brambly hands and thin mules that kept straying off course, but they did as they were told.

Taleb rode out to the vineyard each morning, issued orders whether they were needed or not, and pored over his German text-books to find something new to do every day. When harvest time came his grapes were few, small, and juiceless; their stems came apart in one's hands. All they were good for was raisins. It was then that one of his father's old hands came up to him and said: "*Ya Taleb effendi,* you told us to take out the stones and we took them out; you told us to plow deep and we plowed deep. But you might as well know that the stones trap the dew at night and keep the soil moist throughout the dry summer. And you might as well know that plowing deeply turns the subsoil up in the sun, so that the earth dries out right away."

Though Subhi was careful not to shame him and simply looked at him with fine irony above his cigar smoke, Taleb never got over the humiliation. When he finally emerged from his room again, he was raging with a fully ripened hatred for all things foreign, with their superior, condescending airs, their finely concealed loss of face, and their ultimate disgrace for whoever adopted them. He even tried destroying his diploma, which Faiza snatched from him at the last moment and hid in her French *secrétaire* that resembled a pregnant woman on beagle legs.

Taleb gave up farming after this. His brother Kamal, who was two years younger than he, took over the family's lands, while he himself moved into his father's office on Saladin Street in Jerusalem to learn the real estate trade. It was only now that he began to realize just how much land the rich Arab landlords were selling to the Jews. He began having nightmarish visions of the whole country being parceled away. Even wasteland shouldn't be sold to them, he insisted to Subhi, who replied with a wave of his hand, let them have it. He talked to Kamal, who simply laughed; he talked to Husni, who said that something impressive, spectacular should be done. Yet when Taleb started to organize the meetings in Ramallah, Husni stayed away nine times out of ten. There was always the same excuse of the hospital. Yes, Taleb whispered venomously, the Jews need you to empty out their chamberpots. But Husni didn't react. His connections with certain people at and after work were far more important to him than Taleb's young toughs, a band of inelegant adolescents, as he disdainfully thought of them. It simply wasn't his style. How could you compare it to the British Empire, whose royal crooner he was in his daydreams, starring sensationally in London and Nairobi, Sydney and Bombay? If only Taleb would leave him alone.

Sara hurries to her rendezvous with Husni, which has been arranged for that day on the narrow, oilcloth-upholstered couch in the room of the head nurse, away on vacation; yanking the bonnet from her head while still on the staircase, shaking out her hair, her insides contracting sweetly, as sharply as a jackknife, even before she opens the door. Just let him not talk, she prays pessimistically, just let him not talk. She is so deathly tired of all bed-patterers. If only he'd just hold her tight and shut up. But she knows that he won't, that she'll have to listen to him, halvah and rosewater in English, Hebrew, and Arabic. Always the same words in the same tone of voice. You could switch partners in the middle and he'd never notice. Sara laughs suddenly. The truth is, she marvels, that she doesn't want to love at all. She feels only one urge: to live fast, to move fast, because no one knows what tomorrow will bring. Elder Amarillo had once said that as the world neared its end, according to Spanish Kabbala, time would start to accelerate, to behave in strange ways. A day might take only an hour, but it might also take a week. Time would go out of its mind. Maybe it is happening now.

Professor Barzel also senses that something is in the wind. He unexpectedly cancels his vacation, much to Hulda's dismay. Their trip to Frankfurt is off. She'll have to wait to meet her mother-in-law another time.

One morning the vegetable man from Bet Suhur failed to appear in the neighborhood. That afternoon two Arabs from Malha hurriedly evacuated the boy from their village who sold newspapers on the corner. As Dr. Tidhar was sitting in his automobile in Wadi Joz, it was whispered to him that he'd better not drive out of town. People looked up, sniffing the air in silence.

The first fatalities were Lidochka Auerbuch, her Kurdish husband, and their one-year-old daughter. They were riding in a cart south of

Jerusalem, on the road from Nebi Daniel to Halhul, when local peasants attacked them with clubs and axes. The cart was stripped bare. Fresh casualties followed. Travelers, Jews out walking by themselves. Dwellers in lonely houses, on the outskirts of town.

Husni stopped coming to work at the hospital, whose lights now burned bright in each room through the night. "I'm very sorry," he told Professor Barzel. "I'm a Moslem."

"You're an idiot," Doctor Bimbi shouted after him.

The hospital staff all agreed that he was simply scared of the Jews.

The Arab and Jewish neighborhoods pulled apart in a senseless, unavoidable separation. Armed militia patrolled the streets. When the Jews asked Sir Reginald Welsley-More for the means to defend themselves, the local police being ineffectual, he agreed to send an arms crate to each neighborhood—with the proviso, however, that it be unsealed and opened only by an authorized British staff sergeant. Anyone else touching it would be punished severely.

"That's assuming," said Miracolo Orientale sadly, "that the sergeant ever arrives. We knew the Turks were like that, but the English? To think how we idolized them when they first came!"

A fiercely mustachioed Circassian sergeant continued to drill the militia in the three official languages of the country:

"Thees Engleesh rrrifle. Your father, he die. Your mother, she die. Only Engleesh rrrifle, it never die."

The tension kept building. Arab mobs armed with clubs rampaged through one Jewish quarter after another. When the Moslem fast of Ramadan came around, an Arab policeman went about among the Jews with a loudspeaker and announced:

"This evening will be two cannon shots. Please do you not be afraid. They are only for Arab Ramadan."

Women from Jewish settlements all over the country came to the hospital for a first-aid course. Sara met with them every day and taught them to give injections and emergency care. They were an anxious, serious, studious group: each knew that upon her return to her village, surrounded by a hostile Arab countryside, she could well be the most important person there. Sara thought she knew one of them, a middle-aged woman with glasses.

"Isn't your name Hanna?"

"Yes, it is," was the answer. "Where do you know me from?"

She was really barely recognizable. She had grown rounder, motherly, unlike before.

"I think I must have met you years ago," Sara said evasively. Hanna's expression reminded her somewhat of Tanhum: the same sense of injustice, of a blind, hot, disconsolate grief.

Hanna waited until the end of the course to approach her.

"Sara, several days ago I heard your last name, Amarillo. Well, it's good to see what a fine, productive person you've grown up to be. I want you to know that I appreciate very much all that you've done for us here, and especially the fact that you've treated me just like the others. If it wouldn't be psychologically hard for you, I'd like to invite you to our kibbutz. Do you still remember Tanhum? Do you remember the time he wouldn't let anyone feed him but you?"

How could she bring herself to mention it, Sara wondered. It was as though Hanna had stood before the smooth marble of her memory and scratched away to pick out a few fossils, marring the whole facade.

She didn't tell Gracia.

Professor Barzel was knifed in the lungs. He had gone to pay a call on an Arab woman having a difficult childbirth in Sheikh Jarrah. He saw the baby and mother through safe and sound and was on his way home, near the Bisharas' house, when he was set upon by a band of young men. There were about ten of them, careening wildly down the street, and they stabbed him almost casually as they passed. One of the Bisharas picked him up and brought him to the hospital.

His condition wasn't good. Old women, Jews and Arabs, gathered from all over the city to keen day and night in the hospital yard: "Doctor Bimbi, Doctor Bimbi, God punish us and not you, may you live to a hundred-and-twenty! God think no evil of you, Doctor

Bimbi!" The militia chased them away. They drifted back again each time.

Faiza came to the hospital in Subhi Bey's car, nervous and heavily veiled. She went straight to Professor Barzel's room.

"My dear friend. We're all praying for your health."

"Thank you," he answered weakly. "And where is my friend Subhi?"

"Subhi refuses to come to the Jewish neighborhoods now, Doctor. He says the Mufti has declared a holy war. What can I do about it? He sends you his warmest greetings and regrets that he can't come himself. But let's talk about you, Doctor Bimbi, you know that the whole city is praying for your health?"

He lifted a hand with great difficulty.

"These are hard times, Madame Faiza. Perhaps you should return home now and not stay here much longer. Subhi will be worried. It was very gracious of you to come. Please tell my friend Subhi Bey that I understand him perfectly, since he's a religious man."

Faiza made an angry gesture of contempt. She pressed her forehead to Professor Barzel's limp hand, put on her heavy veil again, and made a beeline for the car. The driver was angry.

"You were inside a long time, *ya sitt*. In another minute the Jews would have been all over me."

"You're all a bunch of idiots," said Faiza.

Dr. Tidhar packed and fled to Rumania. "This isn't for me," he declared.

"Yesterday morning," said Victoria, "I'm on my way to Barclays Bank when I suddenly see a gang of Arabs picking on this poor *pisgada* of a yeshiva boy. They are grabbing his earlocks, pulling the hairs out of what beard he has, and making him spin round like a top and clap hands. As little as there is of him, there's going to be even less in a minute. I look again and can't believe who I see: Husni, Mister Steve Harold the crooner, Subhi Bey's dumb little bastard of a son, may the earth swallow him up with all his friends! Well, you know me, I'm big and fat and it's hard for fear to get into me. 'Hey, Husni,' I shout, 'so you're a big man now, are you? You have a big mustache, have you?'"

"What did he do?"

"Cleared out in a hurry, that little fart, *hijo de puta,* except that Faiza's no puta. He and his gang were good and ashamed. Each damned one of them is worse than ten Hamans. I was so furious that I forgot to cash my check at the bank. Now it's not safe to go back."

Ofra made a scene with her mother.

"Maybe you'll finally stop having Captain Crowther over to our house now. You know the English are against us. You know he's a spy. It's time you showed him the door."

Gracia stood up for herself.

"My relationship with Captain Crowther is pure! Do you understand that? Pure! And he's a pure man. Purer than your own filthy mouth!"

To which Victoria's comment was:

"You bet it's pure. She's half a woman and he's a quarter of a man. It doesn't even come to one whole urge."

Tony Crowther, now swamped with work, did his best to make sure that no more armed Arabs entered the city. Jim Saywell personally confiscated a few clubs on the Jericho Road. Major Saywell was for letting the Jews defend themselves, but Sir Reginald put his foot down: the British alone would keep order. The mystery of Saleh's disappearance was never solved.

When watermelon time came around—in the midsummer month of Av, the time of figs and drought—and piles of ripe fruit lined the Hebron Road on the way down from Jaffa Gate so that the small, dusty Arab buses could hardly get by, whole families of Jews were slaughtered in Hebron and Motsa because they believed their Arab neighbors' promises that they would not be harmed. Miracolo Orientale spent a whole week carting the dead off to burial. Back and forth he went, from street to mourning street. Each block had its griefs.

Lying incapacitated and unable to help in the overflowing hospital, Professor Barzel lamented to each new visitor in his room: "We're so weak, my friend, we're so terribly weak!"

CHAPTER FIVE

LATE AUGUST. The city is shaky. Squills shoot straight up beneath straight cypresses, gathering close as though they were offspring. Miracolo Orientale no longer works overtime, but casualties from the riots still fill the hospital. Sara is terribly busy.

"Dead tired, like everyone," Elias Amarillo said to Sara, who had asked him how he was. She had arrived late for their date in a cafe on Ben-Yehuda Street, unrefreshed, after an exhaustingly long shift in the hospital. But she couldn't even think about it now; her memory had caved in on itself. She downed her coffee in hurried sips, thankful for Elias's nonmedical presence. A few days ago, she told him, when she'd felt the need to freshen up on leaving the hospital and had stood rouging her lips before a mirror, an old nurse had shouted at her for being shamelessly concerned with her looks at a time like this. Elias's questions about her work were dismissed with a despairing wave of the hand. "It's bad. We simply had no idea how weak we were, Eli."

Even the olive trees seemed nervously disheveled to her, stricken with vertigo, malevolent whirlpools on the evil hills. Each hill was up to no good. Each stone hut among trees lay in ambush.

"Eli, why don't you join one of the self-defense organizations?"

"I can't. I'm an employee of the British Government, and I owe it my allegiance. The day I join up I'll resign from the Attorney General's office."

She sighed.

"That's rather extreme integrity."

"That's integrity."

She looked at him: tall, thin, sad-mouthed, his voice quiet when he spoke. The strength of a reed that could bend without breaking.

"Look here, Sara, it's not as though I haven't thought of it. But the truth is that something in me recoils from all this bravado. I hate the fanaticism of it, the blind passion, this business of an eye for an eye. It's all devil worship. The politics of nationalism mean nothing to me. My way of doing things may be less romantic, but I think it sheds much more light."

"And what would you say that light is?"

"Let's say, reason. Order. We mustn't lose our heads, Sara. Nothing would be easier than to start another hundred years' war in this country. I know that what I'm saying doesn't mean much to you now, because you're still keyed up from all that you've seen, but in a day or two it will make more sense. Or do you think I'm just being foolish?"

"Foolish? Of course not. Look, I hate what's happened to this city too. If I'm a nurse, after all, it's because I hate sickness, not because I love it. And I'm more conscious of that than ever right now. I hate the Fridays with their talk of holy war in the mosques, this fever that everyone's come down with. You can't even walk safely anymore from one neighborhood to another. And all the ambulances. It's a disgrace, Eli, so much mutilated human flesh is a disgrace, a waste of people."

"That's just what I mean." A pale fire burned in his face. "Someone has to step outside of the charmed circle." He rested his hand on hers. "Sara, this may not be the best time for it, but then again, there may never be any better one. And I think that now of all times one has to try to go on living normally. To have children. To start a home with all that that means."

"I rather agree," she said cautiously. "But it's all still a little remote for me. A little theoretical."

"Fine, I know that you can't be expected to make any crucial decisions right now. But keep the possibility in mind the next time we meet."

"Anyhow, you've put it very nicely."

One hot afternoon, when the dusty branches of the fig tree seemed to hunker limply on the rooftop, a young man from the Haganah appeared at Sa'ada's. Sa'ada was reclining at the time on a plush couch in the anteroom, which was the coolest part of the house, groaning and fanning herself with a paper fan. "Not now," she said when she saw the young man. "The girls are all asleep. Come back tonight."

"I didn't come for a girl," he said in an English that didn't sit well in his mouth. "I came to have a talk with you."

"What kind of a talk?" she bristled, then began to pull papers from her dress. "Look. Everybody's been checked. Everybody's in good health. I swear to God, this place has nothing to hide. I run a clean house."

"I'm not from the health department. I'm from the Haganah."

"*A'uz billah!*" she whispered in alarm, glancing around her. "Where's your head, man? This is no place to talk. The High Commissioner has ears up the fluepipes."

She pulled him outside into an untidily swept courtyard of sorts. Under the fig tree was a wooden bench.

"Talk here, if you have to, not inside."

He explained what he wanted. Since her girls were likely to hear about such things as impending curfews and arms searches from the British soldiers who were their customers, the Haganah wished to pay them for the information. Naturally, he was quick to add, all the money would pass through Sa'ada's hands.

She looked at him sharply.

"Who do I tell when I know something?"

"You'll tell someone in the neighborhood. We'll think of somebody. Maybe Cordoso."

"No," she reflected. "I'll tell the grocer. Him I see every day. Since when do I have Jewish friends around here?"

He accepted her terms. The grocer was amenable. People dropped in on him at odd hours, so that not even a stranger was likely to arouse suspicion. Shrewd businessman that he was, though, he quickly realized that the more people in the neighborhood knew that a curfew was coming, the better it was, since everyone ran to stock up on groceries in time. And so he took to informing the neighbors of what was happening with Sephardic synagogue tunes. If he heard from Sa'ada that a curfew was due, he would sing in the words of the Psalmist:

Blessed are the home-dwellers,
They shall praise Thee for ever and e-v-er!

While if an arms search was in the offing, he chanted the verse about baby Moses:

And when she could no longer hi-i-de him, she took for him a basket of
bulru-sh-es, and laid it in the reeds by the shores of the Ni-i-le!

Once, toward the end of a month, when all were hard-pressed for cash, the grocery store owner sang his curfew song all morning. Everyone hurried to buy food on credit—and nothing happened. They all turned on him.

"Why blame me?" he countered. "Sa'ada passed me the word. Go ask her yourselves if you don't believe me."

He knew that no one in the neighborhood was going to demean himself by talking to Sa'ada.

"It somehow seems a little premature for you, Sara, don't you think?" Hulda asked.

"I'm not a little girl anymore," Sara reminded her. "I'm twenty-five years old."

"And you're sure you won't mind forsaking all others? You have to be quite sure."

"I'm tired, Hulda. And I don't think that anything will be much different in the future. It's all rather senseless to me, and I think it's perhaps time there was a little sense in Sara Amarillo's life. I know what you're thinking: Sara, is this what you've gone out into the big world for, just to bring home another Amarillo? But that's all that's in view right now, Hulda, and I don't mean to argue with it. Maybe I just want to be promoted a grade."

"Look, Sara, I'm a different type from you. If I can say to hell with everyone else now, it's not because Bimbi is God's gift to the world, or because I suddenly went blind on my wedding night, but because whenever I get sinful thoughts—and you know that I have them—I start feeling terribly sorry for him. But you're not like that. You aren't all heart."

"Sure," Sara grinned. "I'm also one part intuition, one part curiosity, and two parts mischief. But practically speaking, I feel I'm doing the right thing. I feel that I have to, you can even say should."

"Well, congratulations!"

"Not so fast. I haven't decided yet, and the ward is still full up. I hear that Bimbi is getting discharged by the weekend."

"Yes, I'm bringing him home from the hospital on Friday. I'm already cooking and baking. He's changed very much since the knifing. He just isn't his old self anymore."

"I've noticed that. Maybe he'll get over it as he gets back his strength."

"Maybe he will."

When Hulda came for Dr. Barzel that Friday and bent to tie his shoelaces, he began to cry.

"It's wrong to be so weak, Hulda."

"Come on home, you old Bimbi, you."

He didn't get his strength back that quickly. He passed the time reading, marking passages in the margins with a pencil. Perhaps that, thought Amatsia, watching him as he read, is the difference between our two generations: one makes notes when it reads and one doesn't.

Sara and Elias came to visit evenings. To everyone's surprise it turned out that Elias had once played the violin too.

"Wait, it's a long story. It happened back in Tiberias. I was about seven years old, and we had a Lebanese barber who played the violin. I used to hear him practicing in the next room whenever I went for a haircut. It made me so jealous that I decided to learn to play too. The Lebanese said fine, he would teach me, but I had to have an instrument first. Of course, not only didn't I have the money for one, but where in Tiberias could I have bought one even if I did? And so I swapped with him: I brought him an old Turkish rifle that I pinched from my grandfather, and he gave me a violin. A big one, he told me. And it really was, almost as big as a cello. My shoulder became sunken from holding it. And it was a little broken too. One of the strings was torn, the bridge kept falling off, someone had burned a hole in the frame."

"He gypped you?"

"Not exactly, because my grandfather's carbine was missing the trigger and its barrel was bent out of shape. It was a fair swap. He began giving me lessons. After I'd kept it up for a year or two, my parents decided it was serious. Just then a Jew from Italy, who was a real violin teacher, not just a playing barber, happened to arrive in Tiberias. I was transferred to him, at which point he discovered that the barber had been teaching me the other way round: to hold the instrument with my right hand and draw the bow with my left. My fingers had already got used to it. My new teacher had never seen anyone play the violin the other way round in his life, but as shocked as he was, I still wasn't good enough for him if I didn't play like Paganini by my second lesson. I saw it was no use, so I chucked it."

Bimbi laughed, perhaps for the first time since his accident.

The Barzels stroll slowly through the twilight. Slowly, because Bimbi still has pains and a cough in his chest, and Hulda is pregnant. The child is large; Hulda smiles whenever it kicks her moonlike body, now taut as a drum. She calls it Goliath. They are out for their evening walk, like good Jerusalemites. It is almost autumn and the nights are getting cold. The young trees of Rehavia are growing up. New buildings are going up all around.

"Every true native of Jerusalem," says Professor Barzel, "is always hungry for the absolute. Even if he reaches it, he goes on pining for it. That's what Jerusalem is about."

"The problem is," says Hulda sadly, "that everyone has his own absolute. Look at the sky, Bimbi, how the blue behind those scaffolds is so much deeper than the blue in front of them."

He stops to rest for a minute: "They're building too much. It's changing the whole character of the city. Jerusalem shouldn't be so crowded, or so square-angled. And those water tanks are an error."

"When I was a girl in Bet Hakerem, there was once an old stone-mason working down the street. One day Amatsia asked to be shown how to lay stones. There's nothing to it, the old man said. Just lay the stone however it wants to be laid."

A spasm of pain comes and goes as he smiles.

"Hulda, what will become of us? You'll have an old wreck for a husband."

"I'll have a Bimbi for a husband and a Goliath for a child."

In order to help pass the time, Professor Barzel conducts a study of the names of Jerusalem's neighborhoods, about which he writes to a friend in Germany:

> The question of nomenclature is most interesting. Some neighborhoods here have names like prayers for succor and strength that never seem to come. As the present is always bad, the Jews have learned to live in a future that is always sure to be better. Romema, 'Uplifted.' Ruhama, 'The Pitied One.' Ez-rat Yisra'el, 'The Aid of Israel.' Ge'ula, 'Redemption.' Talpiot, 'Great Heights.' Yemin Moshe, 'The Right Hand of Moses'— perhaps this last refers to Sir Moses Montefiore who built it, and perhaps to Moses the Prophet, who held both hands aloft while the Israelites prevailed. Some live in Mekor Hayyim, 'Life's Source,' while others dream of Sha'arei Hesed, 'Mercy's Gates'; still others who never planted a seed in their lives named their quarter Me'ah She'arim, 'The Hundredfold Crop.' And there are more modest, more secular names too: Nahalat Ahim, 'The Brothers' Estate,' Nahalat Shiv'a, 'The Place of the Seven,' Yegia

Kappayim, 'The Laborer's Lot,' Kerem Avraham, 'Abraham's Vineyard,' Bayit ve-Gan, 'House-and-Garden.'

The Arabs, on the other hand, are more concerned with illustrious figures from their past. They have a quarter named after Sheikh Jarrah, a healer in Saladin's camp; they have an Omariyyah after Omar the Great, and Talbiyyah after Taleb. Ahmed Abu-Tor, a warrior of Saladin's who used to ride on an ox, gave his name to the neighborhood of Abu-Tor, 'The Master of the Ox.' The name Abu-Dis derives from a forgotten Greek monk, Betabudission. The houses by the Saint-Simon Monastery were once called in Greek *kata monis,* 'by the monastery,' and the name Katamon has stuck to this day. A section of the city that was covered with sharp pebbles, *sarar* in Arabic, became known as Musrara, Pebbletown. And imagine, among the filth and caved-in ruins of an Arab slum, coming across the glorious street name of Gottfried de Bouillion! Thus we live, my friend, caught between a forgotten Crusader past and a yearned-for biblical future, with nothing to hold onto but the present, this damnably difficult here and now.

When the Arab vendor from Bet Suhur returned with his break-of-dawn cry of *yallah, burdegan, yallah, tomat,* there was no more disputing that the wave of disturbances was over for good. And when Goliath was born, he turned out to be a pretty, redheaded girl. They named her Nili. Amatsia called her Copper.

"I'm late," says Sara to Elias from the door of his rented room at the drop of Rabbi Akiva Street. The room has its own entrance, which is reached by descending a staircase flanked by tall dry hollyhocks. Wild marjoram grows in the cracks of the walls. The metal railing is askew. Elias stands below with his hands in his pockets, a long smile on his lips. There is a smell of scorched thistles in the air: someone is burning them, burning away the last of the summer, as though to quicken the coming of the winter rains by sending a cloudy reminder to the cloud-

less sky. A strangely nostalgic, moving smell. An ending and a beginning.

"It's all right. I waited."

A black cat that has been squatting like a sentry on the doormat
rises with obvious displeasure and looks balefully at Sara.

"You have a cat."

"Oh yes, I belong to him. Did he curse you out just now?"

"I think so."

"Then curse him back. Never give in to cats."

Sara stands facing it, glaring full-force with a make-believe primitive fury. The cat stares unblinkingly back. Sara bares her teeth like a
lioness:

"Grrrrrr!"

The cat slinks away, pretending to have noticed something among
the hollyhocks, and disappears with a face-saving, supremely indiffer-
ent wave of its tail.

"Bravo," says Elias. "Not everyone wins. He's a brave cat."

You mean not every woman wins, says Sara silently to herself. She
is suddenly curious to know what lies behind his fine, spare, impecca-
bly Sephardic good looks.

The room itself is wonderful, with a deep barred window full of
pigeons, narrow and high-ceilinged like a cell in a cloister. The afternoon light breaks through the window at an angle formed by a massive stone wall that cuts diagonally across the view. Sparrows are
nesting at the top of the shutter. A tall bed stands under the broad windowsill, covered by a geranium-red quilt, which seems to draw all
the light in the room to itself. Shelves crammed with books stand in
niches cut into the thick walls. A single rickety chair is piled high with
books too, and there are more books on the table. Spiders on the ceiling. Spots of mildew on the walls.

"Are the books on the chair for any reason?"

"Of course. To make us sit on the bed."

Sara lays the books on the floor and sits down in the chair.

"Does one get a cup of coffee around here?"

"Since you'll be making me my coffee for the next seventy years, I'll
be a gentleman this one time."

He prepares it expertly. The way it's made in Tiberias, he explains.
"Frankly," says Sara as she sips it, "the coffee's better in Safed."
"Sara. You've come to say yes. Otherwise you wouldn't be banter-
ing with me like this."
"Don't be so sure."
He looks at her and grins.
"But I am."
She is amazed by the swiftness of her response. Several days later
she discovers that Elias has thirty or more pairs of underpants and not
a single undershirt.
"Why so many?" she wonders out loud.
"Because they're good for all kinds of things. For wiping the floor.
Or for after shaving. Or for cleaning the soot from the kerosene stove."

She is getting to know the angled light, the red of the quilt, and Elias
himself, whose time spent with her always seems to be a fleeting vacation from the complicated world of indictments and legal briefs.
Sometimes she curls up naked on the bed, milk on geranium, while he
works in a circle of light. He has the power not to look at her for long
periods of time. It is clear that she will never be able to share the world
that most matters to him, nor does he bother explaining it to her. She
too doesn't try to explain herself very much. We'll live parallel to each
other, she thinks to herself in a sudden flash of insight. Why shouldn't
it be possible?
There is much humor between them. Much of what the Bible calls
"sporting."

Gracia decides that it is time to put the fear of God into Sara.
"If you're going to come home at one in the morning on a night
when you aren't on duty, you needn't bother to come home at all."
"Mother, I don't know of anything that people do at one in the
morning that can't be done just as well at one in the afternoon."
"You should wash your mouth out with soap. Foo! You're just like
your father."
To listen to Gracia, sin sleeps in its den all day long until half-past

ten in the evening, when it sallies forth lantern-eyed like a lion for its nocturnal fling.

The truth of the matter was that she never really consciously decided, but simply let herself float on a current whose direction was clear. There was no need to make up her mind. The first person she told was Grandfather Amarillo, who was very moved and gave her his blessing.

"*You,*" he stressed, "deserve the very best."

For the first time since their childhood she realized that her grandfather had never really cared for Ofra.

Victoria, on the other hand, raised Sara's chin with her hand and asked searchingly:

"Have you leveled with each other, Sara?"

Sara blushed a little. Victoria persisted.

"Have you?"

"Yes," she whispered.

"You've got yourself a fine young man," said Victoria.

"Ofra complains that he's too thin."

"Don't let it worry you," declared Victoria. "A man and a woman should be like a knife and a spoon."

"Victoria, why didn't you ever get married?"

"It wasn't marriage that scared me, it was a family. I was afraid that if I had children I couldn't be Victoria anymore. This way I have my peace and my habits, I come when I want and I go when I want. If I want to climb up on the roof and go cock-a-doodle-doo, there's no one to stop me. Besides which, look here, your grandmother drove us crazy with her *cama matrimonial.* It once occurred to me that those of us who were born before she moved out of your grandfather's room— that's Avraham, Rafael, and Shlomo—turned out all right. And then there were the three others who died when they were small. But your father Zaki and I had to grow up with all her crazy tricks: she delivered us flat on her back and never got up again. She never took us anywhere. She was always in bed. And so when Zaki went off and left you two little *chicas,* I said thank God I have no children and never will have, amen. That way there's no one to mess up."

They sat saying nothing until Victoria roused herself again:

"But you'll be all right, Sarika. You're not tied down to the family. Look at me, everyone thinks I'm so brave because I do whatever I want, and yet the fact is that I've never even had the guts to move out of this neighborhood. I've lived ten feet from my parents all my life. You'll do better in the end than any of us."

As Victoria had predicted, the wedding turned out to be a grand reunion of *todos los* Amarillos. Elias's parents came from Tiberias: Ezra Amarillo the pharmacist with a red fringed fez on his head, one of the last of its kind to be seen on a Jew in the country, his little wife, Allegra, and their sons Sasson and Zion. The latter did and didn't resemble Elias; they laughed all the time and had none of his fine laconism. Druggist Amarillo was a punctilious man. He sported pince-nez and a well-groomed exact little mustache, and explained to Sara and Gracia:

"There is much violence in the materials that I store in my pharmacy. What I keep on a single shelf is enough to wipe out not just one or two people, but a whole city. And yet I help people to live, not to die."

Gracia bowed her head in acknowledgment. Despite his laughable Galilean accent, with its *r* that spluttered in the throat, Druggist Amarillo impressed her as being truly the master of all the dreadful perils that he spoke of. He was a man of proportion and limits who weighed things out wisely in hundredths of the gram and measured them to a hair—precisely what she herself was not. He seemed to her an admirable embodiment of masculine good sense.

Druggist Amarillo conversed seriously with Sara, in a Galilean French mixed with Arabic, about Jean-Jacques Rousseau and natural education. Nowadays, he said, *l'éducation* was more *scientifique.* Sara wasn't impressed. She had already heard from Elias that Ezra Amarillo had been the most draconian of fathers; Rousseau had been one thing and sparing the rod another. Just like the French themselves, said Elias; all reason on the outside, and a cold, egoistical core.

Allegra, in a sky-blue brocade dress with golden trimming, cried under the wedding canopy. Gracia cried in violet. Victoria nearly cried. All felt anew the gnawing absence of Don Zaki Amarillo, whom all had managed to forget until now. Sara's eyes sparkled behind her veil, which softened her pointed features a bit. Her lush, strong hair had already thrown off all the pins and wires driven into it by Lisa, the Russian hairdresser, in accordance with the latest fashions taken from an old Odessa magazine. She and Elias, who looked tall, calm, and distinguished, were in the first-weeks' bloom of mutual discovery and seemed contented and at ease as they swam effortlessly through a tearful, frenzied sea of family. *Los* Amarillos turned the wedding ceremony into a three-day convention. They came from Safed, Hebron, and Tiberias, filled hotels and the houses of their relatives to overflowing, chased away flies with illuminated fans, misplaced shawls and ornamental combs, and ate meat with pine nuts, stuffed burekas, and honeyed sesame cakes. And ate some more. And reminisced. In Spanish, Hebrew, Arabic, and French, all spoken in a single breath. If all the Amarillos are here celebrating in Jerusalem, they told one another, it's a sure sign that the times are looking up. Even Miracolo Orientale came, excitedly bearing as a wedding gift a marbly pink statue of Diana resting one hand on the horns of a deer while she hid her private parts with the other.

Sara and Elias rented a house at the narrow end of Melissanda Street, where it dipped toward the Old City wall. The house belonged to a rich Arab from Sur-Baher and stood by itself in a long-neglected garden. If you happened to glance to your right as you left the front gate, you suddenly saw the Mosque of Omar like a blue, dreamlike surprise, much bigger and nearer than you had somehow expected to find it. The tumult of the Damascus Gate was not far away, but Melissanda Street itself was always perfectly quiet. The house was whitewashed inside, and each morning the vaulted rooms became a blinding display of arched surfaces in varying degrees of white, light, and shadow. It was furnished with a few solidly comfortable pieces and many ferns in copper pots. The curtains were white, the bed was huge, and enormous chests-of-drawers filled the rooms. Gracia, who had never ceased considering herself a princess in captivity, couldn't get over the absence of tapestries and gold picture frames, of pink lampshades and gilded Parisian chairs with thin, beagley legs. Your house has no refinement, Sara, she would say, absolutely no refinement. But the refined vulgarity of things was something that neither Sara nor Elias could stand. In a drawer of a chest Sara kept a packet of dried lavender picked from Victoria's balcony that gave the room a rustic fragrance all day long. Elias uprooted the thorn bushes in the garden. Sara planted fruit trees.

About a month after all the excitement, when the city in its sleep at night still clutched the mountain at any sharp noise, Grandmother Amarillo died of a stroke. Sara, who happened to be in the ancestral house at the time, unsuccessfully tried to revive her. The sumptuous white body that met her eyes when she stripped her grandmother's frock off looked as though it had been preserved in milk. Sara stared with emotion at the blue veins of the breasts, the strong nipples, the youngish-hued flesh. Why, to what purpose, had this woman spent her whole life hysterically in bed? How could eight births have left no mark on her?

Sara shut her grandmother's eyes more sorrowfully than she'd have thought, pulled the blanket over her, and stood up.

"Grandmother's dead," she told the agitated onlookers in the room.

She might at least have said passed away, Gracia was afterward heard to remark.

Grandfather Amarillo performed the ritual tearing of his clothes. He sat mourning in his office, both for his wife and for all the death and desolation that had been caused by the disturbances. His brother Yosef, "The-Messiah-Is-Coming," sat in mourning with him.

"The Peace of Heaven forgive me what I say," said Tío Yosef, "but she certainly made your life miserable. I pray they don't take it out on her in the world to come."

"She had a meanness, it's true," said Elder Amarillo. "But she held the house together."

"It's enough to be thankful for that they bear us our children and keep us out of sin's way," agreed Tío Yosef.

"What can you possibly know about it, Yosef? You were never even married."

"I keep my eyes and ears open."

"Well, then, I tell you, a woman in the house even if she's no saint is better than no woman at all. Sometimes when she was sleeping, even after she'd left *la cama matrimonial,* I used to go into her room and see her lying there as quietly as a baby, with her white hair blowing a little, this way and that, like a dandelion tuft in the wind. Blessed be God the true judge."

And he wept.

When the seven days of mourning were over, Elder Amarillo said to his daughter-in-law:

"Look, Gracia, it's impossible for me to go on living with you here in this house. It isn't proper. You stay here and look after Ofra until she finds a husband—who knows, perhaps Zaki will even come back to you one day. I don't have to worry about finding a place, because when Avraham and Malka were married I gave them the house I owned in Ezrat Yisra'el. They can get rid of that communist who lives in the attic and let me have it for myself."

"Now, at the age of seventy, you're going to move? Are you sure you know what you're doing?"

"If we don't shed our old skins when we're seventy, when will we ever get the chance?"

"I still think you should stay. Not one person in Jerusalem will think the worse of you for it."

"Why risk even one? You stay, Gracia, you'll have a big house for *pasatiempo.* For entertainment."

"There'll be no one left here but us women."

He shrugged:

"What can I do? *No puedo nada.*"

Bukas quit and went to live in an almshouse in the Old City. Grandfather Amarillo sent her a pension. "Thank God we're rid of her," said Gracia, "she was filthy." She hired a young girl in her place, who worked days without sleeping in.

Elder Amarillo packed his things and moved out. There really was
no one left in the house but women now. It was too clean, too polished
and starched; the furniture was always waxed and no one dared lay a
finger on it; the shutters were never opened because of the dust and no
one moved a footstool from its place. The large main room turned into
a kind of showplace in which no one lived and nothing was done.
Gracia scrubbed and cleaned it of every trace of dirt, sweat, loud
voices, human presence, life. She put pink knit shades on the lamps,
sewed lace on the curtains, covered the chairs and couches with anti-
macassars, and scattered about potted plants of which it was difficult
to say whether they were still furtively alive or discreetly dead like
strawflowers. She didn't rest content until she had put mothballs in
every corner, tied the bedclothes in the closet with violet ribbons, and
closed off the rooms upstairs so that no one would enter them.
Eventually she even had all the rugs covered with felt.

"She's embalming the house," said Ofra to Sara. "You're lucky
you've left."

"Why don't you leave too?"

"That's easy to say."

Elder Amarillo now lives with his many-sonned son Avraham and his
daughter-in-law Malka. Half of their patio is covered with cans of
flowers. Whenever they finish a tin of olives they fill it with earth and
plant something new in it.

"*Los halutsim,*" says Avraham to his father, "our pioneers, they
don't want to have anything more to do with the occupations Jews
worked at in the exile, like *cambio de* money, brokers, and the like.
They want to return to the soil, to teach their children all the things
that their forefathers forgot. In a word, agriculture. But that's not all.
They want to make a revolution in the world too. This communist
who lived here upstairs, Mr. Monya, he also wanted to make a revolution. Only he didn't want any agriculture."

"Once when he was living here," adds Malka, "I asked him to pick
up three kilos of oranges for us on his way home. He turned up at the
house with four oranges. What happened? I asked. That's what the
Arab gave him for the money, he said. Excuse me, Mr. Monya, I said,

I understand that you want to make a revolution in the world, but how are you going to make a revolution in the world if you can't buy three kilos of oranges in the street without being cheated?"

"After he moved out of here," relates Elder Amarillo, "I ran into him one day in the street. Hello, Mr. Monya, I said, where are you living these days? In the Montefiore Quarter, he says. Listen, I say, I have no intention, God forbid, of interfering with your affairs, but isn't it a little strange that you, Comrade Monya, should be living in a neighborhood named after an English baron? Yes, rabbi, he mumbles, you're really right, but it's too late to move again now. He went away crestfallen."

The grandchildren laugh. Grandfather Amarillo passes his hand slowly over his face.

"How it's grown on us, this city."

The patient city gathers in people with the strangest ideas, philosophers, freaks, madmen, all of whom add to her a measure of themselves and disappear. Sometimes she seems to be built as much out of obsessions as of stone.

The streets of the city teem with inventors, mad geniuses, incorrigible buttonholers, writers of petitions to the League of Nations. Here today, gone tomorrow. One day Sara is traveling on the bus to the hospital next to a chain-smoking, butch-haired woman of about sixty.

"These cigarettes will be the end of me," says the woman to Sara. "But enjoy it, I tell myself, you only live once."

"How do you know?" Sara asks.

The woman looks at her with surprise.

"Aha, I can see you're an intelligent girl. In that case I'll tell you a story. Listen carefully. I've been shot with the same bullet three times in the last five years. Not three different bullets, the same one. And once I was already up there. I knocked on the gate, and suddenly I heard a voice call out from inside: Don't open it. It was my late husband. Guess what? He was living up there with a woman younger than myself and wouldn't let me in. So I came back down. That's just one story. If you travel on this bus often, I'll tell you a new one every day."

She leans over and whispers in Sara's ear: "I know when the High Commissioner is going to die."

She is never seen again.

A light-and-shade-struck city of light-and-shade-struck people. A narrow, arched passageway, gravid-shaped, wide enough for a small donkey; the soft light behind it incandescing not on the man but on the red flaps of his clothes, his dark patch of a head barely brushing the moss growing out of the wall. A burro slowly climbs the narrow steps. Around the corner the aquamarine mosaic of the Dome of the Rock, a sudden treasure to look at, a prismatic jewel in a setting of stone.

"I wonder," says Professor Barzel, "whether the Hebrew verb *l'hat-sil,* to save, mightn't come from the noun *tsel,* shade? In a hot country like this, where the sun is a medical problem, shade is truly salvation."

"It never occurred to me," says Hulda, shading her infant's face. "You have to have not been born here to think of such a thing."

A city you long for the more you are in it; in which you are most yourself and most miss yourself; in which whatever you find, you will want again from afar. A dichotomous city in which everything is its own looking glass, forever mirroring, always the same sky reflecting domed rock cut from sky, always the same broad evening light casting back in reverse the red roofs of the houses. People draw near and recede as in mirrors. A few last gilded roofs. Still the spires of the minarets. Evening comes with an avalanche of longing, and you walk slowly through Zion Square as the first lights go on and buy a coal-hot order of stemmed *hamleh m'lan* from the scarfaced Sudanese vendor, eating it as though there will never be food in the world and no you, only this one perfect hunger that must be shared with a friend because everything is in it, this entire evening, and that is more than one person can bear.

"When I was a girl," Sara tells Elias and the Barzels while they are out walking one evening, "I used to think that Egypt was a country under the ground. It wasn't a place you could get to by ordinary travel; it was a secret, hidden land that could only be reached by going straight down, right into the ground beneath your feet. It had a Pharaoh and a great blockhouse for slaves. There were whole subterranean cities lit by lanterns, tunnels with hurricane lamps, warehouses full of grain, gold, and seeds. Sometimes I used to touch the sharp point of a rock sticking up in a field and tell myself that it was the tip of an underground Egyptian pyramid of which nobody knew but myself. And each spring came the exodus from Egypt, everything budding, sprouting, shooting up. Right here in this field near our house."

"And I used to think," says Hulda, "that time was a river. If only you wouldn't swim in it, you would never grow old."

"Sara, is it true that Subhi Bey and his family came to visit you every Passover?" asks Professor Barzel.

"Not just every Passover. And when they came it was always with a basket of presents, and dressed in their best. And we used to call on them for Id-el-Fitr, to bring holiday greetings. The things in those straw baskets! Date syrup from palm groves they owned near Gaza. We were crazy about that syrup. What Faiza and we didn't cook for each other! I remember how one Passover they came to visit Grandfather together with Taleb, their eldest son. He had just returned from studying in Germany, where he had apparently spent two years in total isolation. He must have been a pathetic sight there. He's not terribly bright and it's an effort to get him to talk, but there's something serious about him."

Dr. Bimbi shakes his head. "He must have gone on living there by his own inner clock. And among all those Lutherans! Good Lord, who sent him there?"

"Subhi, who else? So Taleb very apologetically said that he had a question to ask. *Is'al ya ibni,* said my grandfather, ask, my son. Taleb wanted to know if it was true that the Jews baked their Passover *matsas* with blood, because that was what he had heard from Christians in Europe. Faiza jumped on him of course, and said he should be ashamed of such talk, while Subhi got all red and huffy; I thought he was going to murder him then and there. But Grandfather didn't lose his temper. He told Bukas to bring some cheese, took a piece of matsa from the table, and said: "*Ya* Taleb, you and your father are familiar with our customs, and you know that no observant Jew would ever eat milk and meat products together. Look!" And he put the cheese on the matsa and ate it. There was nothing showy about it, it was just a simple act, but we all had gooseflesh. For a second I thought I saw that Grandfather was wearing shrouds beneath his clothes."

"Was Taleb convinced?"

"I'm not sure. He's much more pious than his father, by the way. As soon as he came back from Germany he married a very religious girl, the daughter of a *ḳadi,* who's always veiled and never leaves the house. She's already had three children and no one's even caught a glimpse of her. Very orthodox. God only knows what Faiza thinks about it all."

Ofra is bored. She asks Gracia's permission to invite a few young people to the house.

Gracia says certainly not. During the year of mourning for Grandmother Amarillo not even an evening of Mr. Bialik's poetry will be allowed—and she doesn't care what Mr. Bialik writes, though whatever Sara snidely says about her, she knows perfectly well that it isn't Spanish *romanzas.* In general, Sara is getting a little too smart for her own good lately. She, Gracia, hasn't the slightest intention of taking the felt off the rugs and the slipcovers off the couch for a few young fools or doctors' assistants who aren't even dry behind the ears yet.

One evening Sara takes Ofra along to a staff party at the medical club. In the middle of a dance Ofra swings by her, beaming.

"Don't wait for me, I've got someone to take me home."

"Who?"

"Dr. Nahum."

Though they try hard to leave inconspicuously, Nahum and Ofra don't succeed. Nahum cannot get Ofra's coat sleeve on right. Ofra knocks over a hat-and-umbrella stand while searching for it with her arm and everything falls to the ground. The two of them slip away in the confusion.

"A handsome couple," says Elias, watching them as they leave. "How did they ever avoid meeting until now?"

Ofra keeps Nahum in check, jailing his passion with her polished red fingernails, always squirming loose at the last moment, driving both him and herself to exhaustion. Her little knees that rouse the compassion of men stick violently together. One day Nahum breaks the good news to Sara in a corridor of the hospital.

"I'm terribly happy for you, Nahum, really."

"I'm happy too. I really hadn't planned on getting married this year, but that's how it is. Just looking at Ofra's face makes me feel peaceful. Does anyone else in your family have blue eyes? Where did she get them from?"

Sara almost physically has to stifle her doubts.

"There's one more thing, Sara. I don't know how to put it. I'd like to ask something of you: if Ofra still doesn't know anything about what happened between us, I'd appreciate it if she never found out. I don't know whether you two talk about such things, but that's a favor I'd like to ask."

"She doesn't know and never will," Sara promises. She feels a hundred years old, a cosmic, all-knowing ancientness.

The wedding was a modest one because the year's mourning was still not up, but Ofra sailed through it triumphantly, waving the corner of her white dress like a flag.

"I wish I had a better feeling about them," said Sara to Hulda.

Gracia, who had never loved her daughters, now flounces flirtatiously around her sons-in-law without stop. She cooks them whatever she knows how to make without Bukas—elderly, watery dishes that she has to urge them to eat. With Sara and Ofra she hardly exchanges a word anymore, as though they had outlived their usefulness the moment they acquired husbands. Everything about her seems to proclaim that women don't matter. It is for Elias and Nahum that she now dresses up in earrings and shawls with a large Spanish comb in her hair. Once they even found her sitting on the veranda with a hat on. The two men barely conceal their aversion to her annoying flattery; it may have been a product of her loneliness, but Gracia's loneliness is itself somehow repellent. It makes one long for a breath of fresh air.

"My daughters are *brujas,* witches," she whispers to Victoria. "They don't let their husbands come near me. They've turned them against me."

It isn't true. The two men simply prefer to come as little as possible. Gracia keeps pawing them, keeps resting her more and more talonlike hands on their jackets and sleeves, as if to attach herself to them by force. Her red lipstick, which keeps getting all over her teeth, is too bright; so is the red polish on her nails. It is excruciating to be with her, a Circe whose manacles are her puddings and dry cakes, whose prison bars are her incessant demands.

Taleb saw dark visions of Jerusalem. The quarrel with his father started afresh every morning: Father, don't sell any more land to the Jews! Subhi Bey would lose his temper and slam the door.

Now Taleb walks in the old walled city from the Muristan to Sheikh Lulu, along the unchanged Jebusite donkey trail that is now called El-Wad Street. The marketplace teems with people whom he passes by unseeing. He watches as the street splits for him, lengthwise along its axis: the houses on its righthand side vanish, and a great naked mountain, the color of goat hide, rises in their stead. The earth is reclaiming its own. Why, *they* were built of it. The stone of the houses has been hewn from the mountain itself. From the bowels of the mountain it cometh, to the bowels of the mountain it shall return. The noise. The dice and backgammon games. The babble of tongues. Superfluous exhalations, all. The rock will rear up and take back what belongs to it, all this hewn stone chipped into rattling dice. Silence will return with a thunderous clap of the hills.

He hungers for that silence with an actual physical hunger. He craves the moment when the tumult will cease and the wilderness swallow up the swarming, insectlike horde. No more modern life. Just a lone flock of goats in the twilight, a single barefoot shepherd boy. No more. No more. The earth belongs to God, Taleb thinks with all his heart's passion, not to this race of loud peddlers.

A city on the desert's edge, its populace holding on with bare nails, high-strung, quarrelsome, haggling, wrangling, cupidinous. The weaver weaves and hawks his wares; he sells his wares; the buyer buys. None turn to look at the desert from which their forefathers had come, scaling the heights from below to conquer this place.

And yet on certain warm nights, when a dry sirocco wind that has assembled its forces on the Plain of the Jordan, that has marshaled them again on the Mount of Qarantal, that has gathered reinforcements in the ascent of the Edomites, bursts through the streets of the city like the footfalls of an invisible invader, the desert overruns Jerusalem again. There is a groan, a stillness, a wound. And then silence once more. The broken tablets of the Law. Until morning.

"Father, don't sell any more land to the Jews," Taleb weeps inwardly. "Don't sell any more to them, Father."

Dreams are stronger than people, Taleb tells himself, stopping at a stand for a suck of nargileh smoke. Entire mornings now pass in such reveries. He is ashamed of his father: a compromising, sanctimonious trader of a man, forever fingering his prayer beads, every bead a sin. He should not let Faiza and Suhaila go about unveiled. He should not take Faiza visiting with him. He is destroying the purity of manly society, the noble fellowship of brothers to whom honor matters more than lucre or women. Father, weeps Taleb, can't you see what you're doing?

Dream-driven, he has gone many times to Friday prayers in the great Square of Omar, has been pierced to the quick by the majestic power of the simple choir of men's voices, of the great throng of believers, snow-white kaffias on their heads, diapasons from the Holy Qur'an in their mouths. Tremendous. Tremendous. But it has left him unpurified in the end. The markets of Bab-el-Silseleh, with their fawning merchants and their wares, lie in wait for him each time beyond the square.

The city has been the ruin of the Arabs, Taleb muses. It has made Jews out of them, Europeans, an effeminate world of women, thieves, avarice, and sorcery. Taleb knows what he will say to his friends the next time they meet in Ramallah: "Brothers, does the Arab still know how to keep the desert in his heart?"

Ofra burst into tears.

"Sara, I've never told you about it, I know, but believe me, I don't want to go on living anymore. You don't know how many times I've gone to bed with the sleeping pills by my side and had to convince myself not to do it. It isn't a life that I'm living, it just isn't a life. I'm a prisoner like at mother's, only now it's even worse. There at least Bukas did all the work, I never had to worry about washing and ironing and all that. Nahum's never home during the day, he's never home at night, if he's not on duty at the hospital, it's some patient waking him up from his sleep. And before I can say to him, Nahum, maybe this one time you won't go, he's already dressed and out the door without even looking at me. Listen, Sara, I'm not just anybody. I'm a woman who needs a little attention, a little special consideration. If only he would look at me sometimes or bring me a flower; if only I could cuddle up to him and know that we'll have a couple of hours together without some old witch ringing the doorbell to tell him that someone is dying. Do you know what I do all day long? I wait for Nahum. Six hours. Seven hours. I sit there and wait."

"Didn't you know when you married him that that's what being a doctor's wife is like?"

"I thought I would be a lady. A free person. That at night I'd go out with my husband to all kinds of nice places. Do you want to hear what happened last week? Nahum had helped take care of some minor illness for the High Commissioner's wife, who'd been referred to him by Bimbi, and so last week we were invited to a garden party at their residence. Well, an invitation from the High Commissioner doesn't turn up every day. I had a new dress made, I had my hair done, and then it's time to sit and wait for Nahum. I waited, and I waited, and I waited. The Messiah could have come in the meantime. The invitation was for six, and at a quarter to eight Nahum walks in. Where on earth were you? I ask. What could I do, he says, there were complications in the operating room. And he goes off to shower, and when he sees that there's no supper on the table, he goes straight to bed. And would you believe that after all that he still wants to play around with me in bed? The nerve of him! Thanks a lot, Dr. Nahum, I told him, but tonight you're sleeping in the other room. You might as well come and see the dress at least. What a waste."

Sara sighed. She spoke slowly.

"I don't know what it is about the women in our family. First Grandmother, then mother, and now you. Believe me, there are days when I know just how Grandmother felt. One just doesn't want to get out of bed."

"You're not like that, Sara. You'll always get out of bed."

"Well, the fact is that I do. Listen here, Ofra: Nahum isn't your nurse, and he isn't your father. After spending all day in the operating room he deserves a bowl of hot soup from his wife when he comes home."

"You're talking about another woman, Sara, not about me. I'm the woman who gets the bowl of soup brought to her. By a waiter with gloves on."

One day several weeks later Sara ran into Hulda.

"Sara, do you know that Ofra had an abortion?"

"Hulda, no!"

"Bimbi happened to be in the maternity hospital in the Old City and just saw her there. She had gone to a midwife who botched things up and sent her there for repairs. Bimbi tried talking to her, but she wouldn't answer. He says there's a wall around her."

"Where's Nahum?"

"I have no idea."

Ofra lay there very pale, her dry lips tight against her jaw, hinting at the skull bones beneath them. She lay as though she had made an ominous decision from which there was no being budged.

"How do you feel, Ofra?"

"I'm fine. With luck I'll be out of here in a few days."

Her voice was strong yet hollow, as though it came out of a metal pipe. It occurred to Sara that she had changed drastically, even the sound of her.

"You have no regrets?" Sara wondered softly. She thought she might be pregnant herself but still wasn't sure.

"For getting rid of some frog in my belly? Of course not. I am a young woman and I intend to live like one. No one's going to make a mother and a grandmother out of me."

"Or of Hulda, or of me, or of thousands of other women?"

"Fine, so you're all saints."

Sara took her hand:

"Ofra, I want you to promise me one thing: that you won't make any decisions in your condition. You're weak, you've lost a lot of blood, you can't be expected to decide anything now."

Ofra shrugged. "It makes no difference. Today, a month from now—it's all the same."

"Do you have pain now?"

"Not anymore. I'm not afraid of it either. I'm not such a weakling as you think."

"I can see for myself."

"Sara, before you leave look under the blanket and see if they sewed me up properly. I don't want to walk out of here like a barnyard door."

Sara felt taken aback, disgusted, without knowing why.

"I'm not the one to examine you. I don't know enough about it."

"Fine, I'll go ask that butcher of a doctor."

She must have felt pain again, for her face grew suddenly livid. Sara put a hand on her forehead.

"Would you like a shot?"

"No," she snapped between clenched teeth.

"Don't punish yourself. I'll go get you a shot."

"Just go."

Ofra pulled the blanket over her head and groaned underneath it. Sara didn't move. Her hand was still on Ofra's forehead, under the blanket. She could feel her sister's pain in every concentrated nerve of her own body, could sense each spasm, each smothered cry that fought to break loose, yet could do nothing to help. She could sense, too, the exact moment when the spasm passed, and Ofra went limp and began to breathe regularly again. But she still wouldn't talk or come out from under the blanket. It was as if, slowly, she were leaving the corridor of pain to enter a fresh, white, slightly misty room in which the assaulted body could finally sleep. Sara imperceptibly removed her hand and left the room.

"I can understand everything," said Nahum, "except where she got all that hate from. A young girl like her, with such a sparkle in her eyes, such love of life, such exuberance—and all of a sudden, a snarl of hatred."

"I'm terribly sorry, Nahum," Sara whispered. "The Amarillos haven't brought you much luck."

"*You* are all right, Sara." He flushed and turned quickly away.

Gracia threw a fit in front of Sara. "It's all because of you. It's you, you who taught her to run around with men and put ideas in her head. Once a girl starts up with a man . . ."

"She can never stop, mother, isn't that so?"

Within three months Ofra officially moved in with von Kluck. Some time later she told her family that she was going with him to Paris. In Paris there was real culture and really cultured people who knew how to live. And just so Gracia should set her mind at ease, they were planning to get married as soon as they solved the problem of religion.

"You'll never guess what, Professor Barzel," said Sara in the staff room one morning. "Von Kluck refused to become Jewish and Ofra refused to become Christian, so the two of them went to the *ḳadi* and became Moslems, and he married them. They're Muhammad and Hadija von Kluck now. Ofra Hadija Amarillo von Kluck."

"Everything happens in this city of ours," sighed the doctor. "I'm sure it was Alfred's idea. But it wasn't nice of him not to invite me."

"I wasn't invited either. Ofra informed us by mail. After the fact. My one hope is that we don't find out that von Kluck's father is a fez cleaner too."

"You won't. I know the family. Prussians. His mother runs a dog kennel."

"Ofra never could stand dogs. I wish her luck."
"Amen. I just hope Elder Amarillo doesn't take it too badly."

But Grandfather Amarillo had no time to take it badly, because that Saturday he was run over by a furniture truck near his home. He never knew what hit him. He hadn't even bothered to look, because in all his life no truck had ever gone down the alleyway before, certainly not on a Sabbath.

Elder Amarillo's black horse has come, wailed the old women in the neighborhood as they followed the bier. Miracolo Orientale transported the coffin in his hearse in grand style. He who dwells in the shelter of the Most High, he sang out loud, wiping the tears from his eyes, who abides in the shadow of the Almighty. Even the Cordosos followed the coffin all the way to the Mount of Olives, where a new tombstone was added to the rows of gray monuments scattered over the hill like silent sheep. Sara, heavy with child, felt as though the last bridge connecting her with herself had been cut. A swollen river raged through her streets.

Gracia had no intention of becoming a grandmother so suddenly. She took the inheritance money—"You'll manage by yourself, Sara, you always do"—and went off with Madame Savvidopoulos and her unmarriageable daughters to Cyprus.
All the contours of Sara's childhood had vanished within one year.

When her firstborn son, Hillel, arrived and was given her to hold for a while in his swaddling clothes, Sara uttered a fervent, addressless prayer for mercy. The lack of her father and grandfather had seemed most acute of all during the birth. The small gift in her arms made the lack worse. Bless him, Grandfather, she prayed, holding the no-longer-bawling infant protectively near her, wherever you are, Grandfather, and I don't begin to know where that is, bless him from there. Ask whoever needs to be asked, because you know and I don't, to look after my son Hillel. Try to hear me, Grandfather, because I've never felt so defenseless before. Help me.

"That's enough," said the nurse. "Let's have him back. Both you and he need to rest."

"Just one more second."

She looked at him and counted his fingers one by one. The eyes were closed. An engraved, shut, absorbed slit of a mouth. Still remembering what other earth dwellers had long forgotten. Still half-living there, the latest messenger from a fogbound world, an undecoded message brought by a stern-faced old man who refuses to converse with mortals. Only in a few weeks' time would he begin to get used to them, to open, to shine, to get to know, to forge a new life. A hostage.

At night she soared over the rooftops with him, took nonstop express trains to the stars and beyond, searched for wizards and fortune-tellers to consult, beseeched the pity of all creatures, all who were wiser than she. She nursed him apprehensively. Yet from the start Hillel proved to be a most manly baby who could manage quite well without all her motherly fears. He sucked lustily and cried in a deep bass voice, giving fierce vent to his protests. His hair was black already, strong, like Sara's own.

Later on, when Noam and Nadav were born, Sara no longer felt quite so primitively defenseless. Elias agreed with her.

"The first child forces you to define yourself," he said. "When the second comes, you're already defined. Not just as a parent. Whatever you are and aren't, you can be sure that's what your child will learn to demand from you. I was very critical of my own father from an early age."

Elias liked to spend time with the children, to walk and to talk with them. Unknown to Sara he kept a diary in which he recorded all the stages of their development. For some reason he refused to show it to her, or even to tell her about it. He was afraid she might think it intrinsically opposed to the process of growth, a vain attempt to translate the untranslatable into mere words. Yet once he began to know his own mind, Hillel preferred his father's to his mother's company. He was less earthy than she and more forgiving.

Sara stopped working at the hospital. She and Hulda wheeled their carriages together.

"Tell me, Sara, does it make any difference that you and Elias are cousins?"

"Yes. A lot. It creates a kind of tribal confidence, which really has no justification. I'm from the bad Amarillos, the ones who are always quarreling with life. Elias is from the good Amarillos. Still, it's nice to have a common ancestor."

"My mother once had a cleaning woman who was born in Nebi Samwil and married a man from Lifta. They were married for nearly forty years, and had lots of children, but when anyone asked her about her husband, she would say: 'How can I possibly know him, he's not from my family.' "

"There's something to that."

There is a moment right after sunset when the stones of the city grow terribly pale, like a man at the end of his strength, waiting in spent silence to be transported as he is to whatever lies beyond. Night then falls with softly stunning kindness, a blessing certain and swift. One adjusts one's breathing to its breath; each street and its houses, each house and its breathers, attending their nocturnal fate. On such nights Sara lay curled by Elias's side, *en mi cama matrimonial,* as she liked to say to herself, and imagined that the steps of her house led infallibly down to the sea. Suppose the whole street should suddenly lift up and be washed ashore in Brindisi? She was certain she had once been in Brindisi, in another incarnation perhaps, had sat there in the twilight behind bolted shutters in an embroidered, wine-colored dress, a yellow citron lustrous on a table, her head shaven beneath its wig, listening to the sound of seawater as it lapped against the steps of her house.

On the subject of reincarnation, Elias was sure that he had lived in Jerusalem in Herod's time and had been trampled to death there by a horse-drawn chariot in a narrow alley. In his nightmares he saw the horse bearing wildly down on him and the frightened eyes of the charioteer; he felt the wall against him, sudden and hard, and knew he could back off no farther. The dream kept recurring.

He felt at home, so he said, in the Herodian remnants of Jerusalem, in the ruined towers of Phasael and Antonia with their margined, finely dressed stones. A toga would have befit his tall frame. His sad, knowledgeable mouth could have spoken all the tongues of that complicated city without tripping. Greek sounded well on Elias. Not the Greek of Madame Savvidopoulos, but the blunt, wise, stinging Greek of those times.

No city lives closer to the almost visible ghosts of past lives than Jerusalem; no city is better at blind, secret love. Hermetic, ironic, a sink of cold tempests, the city stands upright on the mountain against the cold night, most strong and most vulnerable, something in it never falling asleep. All places outside of it are like a somehow undeserved vacation. Or is there any place at all outside of Jerusalem?

And once, on a nearly violet-skied autumn night, when sleepers lay most unprotected, an abyss surrounding each bed, Sara managed to see Elias's horse in her dream and to feel the hard wall at her back. The two of them awoke and lay with hearts pounding till morning, while the waves of the city washed over them again and again with a harsh, moonlike obstinacy.

Toward evening the setting sun takes possession of Elias Amarillo's white room, illuminating his head as it bends over documents. Sara brings his coffee up to him, with a glass of arak and a glass of cold water by its side. It is forbidden to sit in the living room below; Noam has five winkies, invisible creatures that no one can see but himself, and whenever anyone sits on a chair, or the couch, he wails:

"A-y-y! Get up quick! You're sitting on a winky!"

Which means that the sitter has to get to his feet and escort the winky outside, a task that is by no means simple, inasmuch as it cannot be seen. Lately Hillel refuses to see the winkies to the door. He has simply outgrown them.

Sometimes Noam makes a fuss:

"They don't want to leave the house."

It then takes a considerable amount of entreaty and formal persuasion to get rid of them.

"There'll be loads of fruit this year," says Elias Amarillo, sipping cold water as he looks down at the garden from his second-floor room.

"Grandfather would have loved to see it."

The crenellated Old City wall near the Damascus Gate can be seen well from Elias's room, though not the young rowdies who have taken to congregating beneath it and accosting non-Arab women: "Madam, come with me to Ramallah, I will show you Nablus, Madam." Nor can you see Subhi Bey's slim-shouldered, bitter-souled brother, old Hajj Kamal ad-Din, as he walks with heavy heart and courtly steps to prayer at the Sheikh Lulu mosque. "*Hajj Kamal, ya dayus, ba' al-balad bil filuss,*" the children chant after him, the traitor Kamal is selling Jerusalem for money. But it is not money that he wants, it is peace. Over and over he tries to persuade the Jewish leaders to stop the flow of immigration from Europe, which they insist on calling rescue work. What are they so afraid will happen to all those Jews in Europe? Hajj Kamal knows Europe well; it is a civilized place. And without immigration there will be quiet in Palestine. Truly there will be. Only nobody wants to listen to him. Even Mr. Shertok of the Jewish Agency, who had grown up among Arabs in Ein-Sinya, refuses to lend an ear.

The western light grazes the wall and the roof of the Church of the Dormition, then fades like a last reverberation of brass cymbals.

CHAPTER SIX

SHOTS AT NIGHT AGAIN. Not a night without them. The victims are found stripped of their identities, cast bloodily like empty sacks in some shot-up car on the road, or in their own homes far from town. A young couple in the street. A family in an isolated house on a slope leading out of the city. More shots. Who is it this time? Where? People stiffen silently in their houses, listening out into the night. Police. An ambulance. Quiet.

The city lies wounded, heavy, hurting. The innocence of a budding branch in the morning brings tears to one's eyes. So frail. Anyone could step on it, break it, uproot it, and run away. The streets are filled with malice. The children cover their heads with blankets, afraid to fall asleep, until a dreamless slumber comes and takes them, though it gives them no rest.

Walking through Mahaneh Yehuda, Elias Amarillo sees armored plates being riveted to the front of a bus.

"Lie-ber-man! God speed, Lie-ber-man!" shouts the sooty-faced Yemenite welder to the driver.

Lieberman, fat and balding, raises his hand in a brief salute, a captain whose passengers' lives are in his hands. He wedges his broad bottom into the driver's seat and switches on the motor.

"Three Arab roadblocks have been cleared near Lydda," a young dispatcher with a cap on his head tells him quietly, resting an elbow on the open window of the bus. "I don't know what you'll run into beyond that. Did you have any trouble on your way here?"

"Just some stone throwing. One broken windowpane."

"Well, have a good trip."

The passengers huddle behind the bulletproof shades of the bus. They sit their children away from the sides, on baskets and suitcases in the aisle. They don't say much.

Elias is at war with his own inner demons. All his instincts tell him to back the forces of existing order, to stay aboveboard and avoid clandestine bodies, to keep faith. He knows that he wasn't cut out to be a Lieberman, that it simply isn't like him to go zigzagging at crazy speeds with a bus full of passengers through some Arab roadblock before too many shots can be fired. His fortes are his patience and stubborn trust. Thin, anxious, long-legged, he often goes to meetings of the Brith Shalom, where he chats with Professor Buber and Hajj Kamal ad-Din amid pleasantly intellectual surroundings. The suited, robed, and briefcased Arabs and Englishmen in the Attorney General's office are his friends. Standing before a wigged British judge, they all feel like brothers. My learned colleague Elias. My distinguished friend Tewfik.

Still, there are fissures. He feels as if some part of him has been altered, and one morning, as though under duress, he asks Sara what she thinks of changing their last name to Amir. It sounds more Hebrew, he says to her, embarrassed.

She agrees right away. Since her grandfather's death, the name Amarillo no longer means much to her. She sees little of Gracia, who has meanwhile returned to Jerusalem, or of her pudgy mother-in-law, Allegra, who occasionally sends them jars of olives and olive oil from Tiberias, to say nothing of all her tías and tíos scattered throughout

Jerusalem. Hillel is enthusiastic about the change. By the standards of the Ashkenazi school he now attends, Amir is certainly a nicer name than Amarillo. His teacher Tsippora thinks so too. Botanically derived names are in fashion this year, and Amir, which means treetop, is right in keeping with the style.

One evening, after a hard day's work treating casualties at the hospital, a day of amputations and unavoidable deaths, Dr. Barzel, smelling of disinfectant and wearing a white surgeon's hat that made him look like a butcher, passed down a corridor where a group of men stood praying, one of whom asked him to don a prayer shawl and join in reciting blessings and psalms. His anger, which had been building up all day and had only barely been restrained from giving vent to blows or to tears, suddenly burst forth.

"I have no time to waste on prayers," he snapped at the old man who approached him. The latter was not offended.

"Doctor, if you should one day die at the ripe old age of one hundred and twenty yourself, and reach the gates of heaven . . ."

"If I ever get to heaven, which I very much doubt, I'll tell whoever is responsible for this revolting mess just what I think of him. Any five-year-old would have planned things more mercifully. There's a sadist up there, that's what there is, and there's no point asking him for favors. You make me laugh. I have nothing but contempt for you and your carryings-on. Why don't you all go help the nurses mop the floor in the emergency room instead?"

"We can't know what all His calculations are," the old man said placatingly.

"If he has calculations that he isn't telling anyone about, then he's simply a rotten commander."

"The doctor has been working hard to save lives," a young yeshiva student said. "The Law states that a mourner isn't responsible for what he says while his dead are still before him. May his sins be forgiven."

Dr. Barzel almost physically tore into him. "What's sin? It's just a word. You might as well say it backward. Nis! Nis! Where does it get you?"

"Don't you know what a sin is, Doctor?" the old man asked in amazement.

"I know, I know." He waved his speckled hands like a large red heron. His wits were not about him and he needed to get away. He walked into the darkened garden of the hospital and lit a cigarette. His shoes were still caked with blood.

We must learn to go from the abstract to the practical, he told himself, feeling chaos—all of us. In a sense he had already made the transition in medical school; yet he had left himself his redemptive outs there—they all had. Medicine had never before seemed in contradiction to soul making, which Professor Barzel had always considered a wholly abstract occupation.

And now?

Secretively, stubbornly, suicidally, Professor Barzel went from crisis to crisis without anyone knowing about it—not even Hulda, who was too busy with her daughter to guess. He felt all of a sudden that he had given too freely to the life all around him, that in his unreserved and uncalculated openness he had kept nothing for himself. He had been too soft and lubricious; he had failed to sharpen himself, to learn to concentrate on a single end. Somewhere he'd left a flank unprotected. Heretofore, even though he had never thought of returning there, he had felt covered by the presence of a strong, enlightened Europe at his back. Now his Europe too—the opera house of Memphis—had crumbled into nothing. It made him wonder what it could have amounted to in the first place. And being the quintessential European, it made him wonder what he amounted to himself.

"I don't have to tell you what it means," he said to Amatsia, wringing his hands. "There's no Europe anymore."

"For me there never was," said Amatsia, bemused. He noticed that his brother-in-law's hair had begun to turn very white.

The world was no longer the same for Professor Barzel: he met it suspiciously now, warily. The eternal duel with death in the hospital seemed to him pointless, absurd, like a poker game played by a condemned man with his jailers on the eve of his execution. His love of life was an emptied bag of tricks. Hulda with her emotionalism, her dishes that kept dropping and breaking, seemed insignificant to him, small, and ultimately, tiresome. At times her peals of laughter reminded him of the bleatings of a hysterical goat. Only Nili was still somehow miraculous, but even she, he told himself, cracking his knuckles in the deep black armchair in his room where he sat without turning on the lights, was a gratuitous miracle, without substance. Nothing human seemed substantial anymore—while of a God who transcended questions and challenges, he wasn't able, or willing, or going, to hear. At least three times a day he planned his own death with marvelous precision—and no one had any idea. Were he to shut the door of his office in the hospital and bite off the tip of the cyanide capsule that he kept in his drawer, it would be considered a tragic accident, for why should the popular Doctor Bimbi want to kill himself? His *accidie* was indefinable, intangible.

I'm suffering from a miracle deficiency, howled Professor Barzel to himself, diagnosing his pain as he felt it—and from an unbreakable addiction to hope. Maybe the postman will pull a lightning bolt out of his satchel tomorrow. Maybe I'll find a shred of prophecy at the bottom of Hulda's shopping basket, underneath the tomatoes. Maybe an epoch is about to end and another to begin.

Professor Barzel wrote, this time in Hebrew:

Will we wake again this morning with dry mouths?
The coming wave will wash away the pain.
Look: the body opens like an eye,
and silently, a sea anemone,
awaits the kingly hour and the distant gust.
Now let the signal be.
The word will become flesh.
Through this dryness there will flow a living sea.
Epiphany. Epiphany. Epiphany.

The days passed without revelation. His mother wrote bad news from Frankfurt. Their property had been confiscated. Most of their Jewish friends had been marched off to concentration camps on trumped-up charges, while his Aryan colleague Professor Reichenbach was too scared for his own skin to be of any help. Dr. Barzel pulled what strings he could and procured an immigration visa to Palestine, but it still wasn't easy to get his mother out. The Germans, Frau Barzel wrote with anger and hurt, kept demanding the most absurd documents from her, such as a certificate that she was free of lice, or a notarized statement that she had received a nonexistent vaccination at the age of three. It was a farce, a scandal, a bad joke, all simply to extort from her what money she had left, for the greater power and glory of the Third Reich. He bit his nails in the dead of night while Hulda was asleep, certain that his mother would never be allowed to leave. He developed insomnia. He sensed strange presences in the house, for which he could find no better description than such banal words as old age, sickness, malaise, imprisonment, death. And yet he knew it wasn't that, not at all. I'm not a believer, Professor Heinz Barzel fought with himself, so why do I have such feelings of sin? such expectations of a miracle?

I've been hexed, he would say to himself every morning: off to work with you, Bimbi. But it wasn't any use. Despairing of sleep, at three o'clock in the morning, despairing of all intimacy with Hulda, he shut the windows, turned on his heavy table lamp whose globe was the color of egg white, and read Hölderlin, or wrote:

Who else skims on the air of the room,
cutting its dark planes
with a motionless motion?

A face in the mirror. The mirror opens up.
Old age rises slowly
out of the four corners.

Who are you? A passerby in your house,
surrounded by presence.
All your alonenesses are at fault,
you echo of no sound.

At fault, at fault!
There's nothing in your bulging fist.
Before you can know before Whom you stood,
even the traces of your hand shall vanish.

It dawned on him that in order to go on living he would have to sacrifice most of himself. He wasn't sure whether life at the price of such self-abandonment was really a sacred commandment, but he wasn't convinced of the opposite either. I'm not authentic, Professor Barzel said to himself, I cast a solid image of myself in Frankfurt and in Heidelberg, and now I'm trying to force my way into it in a different time and a different place. I am not the medical savior of mankind, nor the all-round Renaissance man, nor the universal mind. In the Persian Gulf I could get away with it, but not here in Jerusalem. This city abides no one's decision about who they are. It decides for them, it makes them, with the pressure of stones and infinite time. It teaches humility. But after humility, what?

"Bimbi, you mustn't work so hard, you look terrible, look at yourself in the mirror, I beg of you, what kind of father are you to Nili?"

Starved for greatness, crying for a miracle, Doctor Barzel was a shadow of his former self. He threw himself into his work as though nothing else existed; for the first time in his adult life he found himself living within the narrow sphere of his profession alone. The bloodshed hardened him. The fear that gripped the city, the screaming headlines in the newspapers, gave him a gray, quotidien, unbreakable strength. Jerusalem seemed no longer a perpetual holiday to him and had become a tough secular reality instead. At times when trouble broke out he rarely bothered to return home from the hospital. Hölderlin and the violin were forgotten. He talked only about his work. He even abandoned his famous philosophical lectures at the hospital, as though he had lost the key to them.

"You're committing workicide," said Hulda sadly. But he wasn't really. He had just stopped thinking of himself, had skipped right over himself. The only dawn to break at the end of his long, dark nights of the soul was that of the long, ugly war at the hospital, a war without outcome, without choice. He felt like someone emerging from a period of mourning without ever having known what it was that he had mourned for. Imperceptibly, his relations with the younger doctors had improved. They were partners.

An early afternoon sky: at the zenith a Prussian blue, breaking off into laundry blue, the color that houses are plastered throughout the Levant. Along the ridgelines, touched with haze, the pale, opaque blue of plumbago blossoms. The squatting city is the color of flesh.

Sara sits on Victoria's balcony with Hillel and Noam at her knees. The two women watch Elder Cordoso coming home below, huffing and puffing with importance like his politician son Leon.

"Just look at him hop," says Victoria. "Like chickpeas in a frying pan."

"They say he's been meeting lately with Hajj Kamal ad-Din. They're trying to form some sort of public committee to bring peace to the city. Elias has gone a few times too."

"What can come of it? These days every Jew has his Arab, and every Arab has his Jew. They sit around adoring each other."

"Does anyone ever see Faiza?"

"Nobody. They say that she's shut herself up in their house in Jericho and never goes out. Imagine, Jericho in midsummer! And Subhi's in Alexandria. One really ought to write Faiza a letter."

"Another one of those things one ought to do and never does."

"You're tired, Sarika."

"Dead tired. Everything is so . . . small. Everyone lives in his own little box. There are more dangerous boxes and less dangerous boxes, but they're all still so small, Victoria. We keep thwarting each other, everything keeps getting in everything's way."

"If I were your mother," says Victoria irrelevantly, or perhaps not so, "I'd come to help you a little around the house."

"Let my mother be."

In fact, Gracia had become quite impossible. Even in her sunglasses, even in her huge hats, she could no longer keep up the image of the

romantic widow, the abandoned Señora Amarillo who was once
Tony Crowther's great love. Her legs swelled. A second chin grew
under the first. Her body gave off a scent of lavender, candies, and
medicine, a smell of aging female hate. Her hands clawed the clothes
of whoever sat next to her. She was sure that others were better off
than herself, that everyone but she had all the money, the possessions,
the *pasatiempos,* that their hearts desired. She kept a hungry ear to the
world, certain that she alone was being had, that she was missing out
because she was such a soft touch. I let myself be pushed around, she
would say, that's always been my problem, that I let myself be pushed
around. Only her voice remained as marvelously clear as always:

Like a white lily
In a rare season of the year,
You are my soul, you are my very eyes.

Tony Crowther no longer had the time to drop in very much.

Elizabeth Barzel arrived.

Hulda told Sara about it over the telephone:

"We'd been waiting so many years for this hapless refugee, and she
really had a hard time over there, she was even beaten up in the street
before she left—and here, there turns up this tight-mouthed little old
lady with kid gloves who throws a scene the very first time she hears
me call Bimbi Bimbi. What kind of name is that, she says, my son's
name is Heinz, Heinz Barzel. You can call him Heinzchen, but
Bim-bi? . . . The next thing she did was tell Nili to call her 'Omi'
instead of 'Savta.' And, oh, I forgot to tell you, she also started calling
Nili Ursula. It had completely slipped our minds that after she was
born we'd received a letter from Elizabeth ordering us to call the child
Ursula. Bimbi simply forgot about it, and me, you know what a coward I am, I wrote her that we'd given the child a middle name, Ursula
Nili. I took Nili aside and said to her, 'Look, Nili, Omi's an old
woman and she'd like to call you Ursula, it's a name that she likes, do
you mind?' Well, you know Nili's an angel, she said right away that
she didn't. So we had an Omi and an Ursula, and everything was just
fine for three days, until the old lady began to catch on that Ursula was

not exactly Nili's real name. She thought and thought until she said over supper one night with tears in her eyes, '*Na, ja,* I can see that her real name is Nili—that's how it is when you're a stranger in a new country and have to get used to all kinds of things.' You won't believe it, Sara, but we actually felt so guilty and ashamed of ourselves that dope that I am, I said to her right there at the table: 'No, no, we really call her Ursula too, don't we, Ursula?' But she just kept shaking her head and saying no, it wasn't Ursula anymore, it was Nili. And she pronounced the word *Nili* like it was a bullet she was shooting us with. She sat there with tears in her righteous eyes, and so help me, we all felt like heels. But wait, there's more to come. A few days later Nili came to me and said, 'Imma, when will we shut Omi up in the bathroom?' I asked her what had happened. It turns out that Nili had said something to her that she didn't like, and so she spanked her and locked her up in the bathroom. Bimbi and I nearly went out of our minds. Bimbi let her have it. In the choicest German. He told her that she'd better not behave like a dirty old goose, or some expression like that. They're always calling each other names, you know. Elizabeth once hit Bimbi with a broomstick because he walked into her room. And do you think Nili cares about it all? She said to me, 'What is abba getting so mad about? Omi likes shutting people up in the bathroom, so what?' What can I tell you, Sara, I love Bimbi, and I love Nili, and Elizabeth can't get out of here a minute too soon for me, so that the three of us can be alone again. Why the hell do people have mothers? And now we'll be stuck with her until . . . until she dies."

But they weren't stuck with Elizabeth Barzel, because she got married instead. Within four months of her arrival she became the bride of old Professor Marcus. The two of them had a joint age of nearly one hundred and fifty. Hulda got emotional at the wedding and couldn't stop kissing them both. She bought them a huge present. Elizabeth, who looked very elegant in a short veil and tailored cocktail dress, scolded the cantor because his shirt was stained, criticized the flower arrangement, which she thought Asiatic, and carried on royally. For a woman her age, marveled Hulda, she's really sensational, isn't she? Bimbi said that was all well and fine, but he was damned if he was going to start calling Professor Marcus "Pappi." Marcus agreed that this would be absurd, and suggested that he be called "Onkel" instead. In the end the two men stood in a corner and talked shop during most of the wedding party, calling each other Herr Kollege and Herr Professor as usual. At exactly ten o'clock Frau Professor Marcus collected her gloves and her husband and said, "Ladies and gentlemen, thank you very much, and now we'd better all be going home, hadn't we?"

"She looks marvelous," said the guests, watching her climb into the waiting automobile in her elegant blue cocktail dress, lifting up her little veil to show a face as strong as life itself. Just five months before she had been slapped in the streets of Frankfurt am Main and had lost all her property there. Hulda wailed into Bimbi's handkerchief. Weddings always made her cry.

Two weeks after the wedding, when Professor Marcus went for a ride in their car without informing her first, Frau Professor Marcus called the police to tell them he had stolen it. Fortunately, the Arab desk sergeant who picked up the telephone understood none of the languages that she spoke to him. By the time someone was found to take down the complaint, Professor Marcus was back with the car, at a loss to understand what the fuss was all about.

"The car is joint property," said the Frau Professor. "If you take it anywhere, you have to ask my permission first."

The world-famous Professor Marcus, holder of numerous international prizes, admired her more than anyone he had ever admired before. She became an almost legendary figure in the family. They all had their Elizabeth stories, one more incredible than the other, each of them ending with the same flabbergasted sigh of a smile: she's incredible.

One hot, dry day that summer, when the headlines of the newspapers seemed to tire of shouting their letters as big as black windows, several young Jews from the neighborhood jumped the Arab newsboy from Malha who sold *La Bourse Égyptienne* on the corner and beat him up savagely.

"That little kid who sits on the corner and chirps *La Bourse, La Bourse?*" asked Sara, repelled.

"That's the one," said Victoria. "Ten years old and looks like eight. And the leader of our gang of heroes was none other than Hayyim Cordoso. Kicked him right in the stomach with his well-shod feet. Smashed one of his kidneys or something. We're as disgraced as they now. This whole city is crazy."

When Elias heard about it, he started as though bit by a snake.

"Victoria, are you a hundred percent certain that you could identify Hayyim Cordoso? Are you willing to swear to it in court? Because I'll have to call on you to testify."

"*Como no.* Leon's son, I've known him since he was a baby. He was always a little stinker. I'll swear on a stack of Bibles. Miracolo saw him too, go ask him."

A few days later Elias returned home tired and depressed.

"It's impossible to file a complaint against Cordoso junior."

"Why?"

"I don't know. The British decided to close the case. For lack of public interest."

"Maybe he works for them?"

"Maybe. I haven't felt so sick to my stomach for a long time."

Sir Reginald Welsley-More, pipe in hand, sticks his finger into the cage and pokes a nail into the plumage of the frightened, cornered bird.

"Coochey-coochey," he says, blowing smoke at it.

"What is it, sir?" It is a species unfamiliar to Tony Crowther.

"They call it a bandook. It's part canary, part finch. Or vice versa. The Towels breed them. I just bought it an hour ago, for Angela. It has a fine voice, but it won't do us the honor of letting us hear it. Coochey-coochey," he pokes it again. Through the bars one can see the bird panting in shallow, frightened waves.

"I believe the cage is a bit small for her, sir."

"You do, do you, now? We'll tell Starkie to bring a bigger one." Sir Reginald sits down in his chair. "Have a seat, Tony. I have some news for you. In light of your brilliant success in Jerusalem"—his voice takes on a sarcastic note that reminds Tony more than anything of the teachers in public school—"and inasmuch as you have proven yourself lately so indispensable for the advancement of His Majesty's Intelligence Service, there is a proposal on my desk to transfer you to India."

"India, sir?"

"India, y'know, that unimportant little country in the lousy belly of Asia. Endemic cholera and all that. Fresh chutney, not Fortnum and Mason's. A new world for you, Captain Crowther. An excellent opportunity."

"Is that final, sir, or am I permitted to appeal?"

"Ah, Tony, Tony, how can you ask that? You know that His Majesty's Army wouldn't do a thing to hurt your feelings. You do know that we want our officers to be as happy as can be, don't you?"

"Then I can think it over?"

"Think it over all you want, man, as long as you're on the plane to India on the thirtieth of this month. Via Bahrein." He bangs a fist on the table and shifts tone. "You can't say you haven't been warned, Captain Crowther. I have here before me four warnings of the most explicit sort. You haven't been doing a bloody thing, Captain Crowther. On the fourteenth of this month you received a tip from your informant that there was an arms cache hidden in his neighborhood. You knew all about it, Captain Crowther, yet you didn't make a move until the twenty-second, when you found absolutely nothing. You haven't been a very successful intelligence officer, have you, Captain Crowther?"

"I've done my best, sir. You're quite right, sir."

"Between the two of us, Tony, I don't pretend to understand you. *De gustibus* and all that, you know, but what pleasure you find in this country of sun and flies, between the Towels, and the Beards, is beyond me. I've seen native-lovers in my years in the service, but you're quite the most incorrigible case I've come across yet. Starkie at least enjoys buggering the little Towels in the halls of the YMCA, but to the best of my knowledge that's not how your tastes incline."

"No, sir."

Sir Reginald Welsley-More crossed his legs.

"Two delegations came to see me yesterday. First the Towels came to inform me with holy wrath that the Beards had brought a bench and folding chairs to sit on by their Wailing Wall, thus constituting an infringement of the status quo in the holy places. Then the Beards came to tell me that the Towels have been knocking over their bench and violating the sanctity of their holy site. Each side requested a decision in its favor."

"What did you decide, sir?"

"Strictly by the book, Tony, strictly by the book. The status quo in such cases is clear enough. The introduction of any bloody bench or bloody chair to a disputed site is categorically forbidden. Just last week the Copts and the Armenians, or some such blokes, were here to see me regarding the status quo of three floor tiles—three whole floor tiles, mind you—in the Holy Sepulchre. I was asked to decide which of the two sects had the right to stand incense burners there. To get back to the matter of the bench, though, the Beards say that they need it for old people who are fasting, pregnant women, and so forth. I simply can't be involved with all that. As far as I'm concerned, they needn't fast or get pregnant at all."

"A very Roman decision, sir."

Reginald Welsley-More squinted sharply over his pipe at Tony.

"You're a clever bastard, Tony, but I'm no Pontius Pilate, for the simple reason that there will never be another Jesus here. That's precisely what you fail to see. All grandeur is gone from here forever. Nothing will ever happen here again, Tony, nothing of any importance. The flies have eaten it all. This is an obnoxious, petty little land, consumed by religious and irreligious rivalries that will never be resolved. Hundreds of years from now they'll still be fighting here over benches at walls and floor tiles in churches. It's a decrepit, dead-end place, Tony; their mission in life is played out and they don't even realize it. In the best of cases this city will survive as a museum, an antiquarium for lovers of the past. If it weren't for our forcing them to build in stone here, they'd already have turned this place into a concrete marketplace, a second Tel Aviv. Or into a second filthy Amman. Go to India, old chap, there you'll see things in perspective, you'll realize their proper magnitude. Amid all these little quarrels and fanaticism, with one sect maddening another and the sun maddening them all, one tends to forget."

"I believe, sir, that I'll put in a request for a discharge."

Sir Reginald is taken aback.

"Good Lord, Tony, what will you do in mufti? Go to work behind a desk in some miserable little town?"

"I really don't know yet myself, sir."

Tony Crowther applies for his discharge, goes off to England for a few weeks, and returns in a civilian suit which he cannot seem to get comfortable in. Though his shoulders are less impressive than before, there remains something military about his bearing. His friends, Jews and Arabs, gape, congratulate him, love him as before, and procure him the job he desires in the music department of the Palestine Broadcasting Service, where Husni works as an announcer. Tony likes nothing better than to go every day to the old building in its luxurious garden on Queen Melissanda Street. He loves the ponderous feel of the soundproof studio doors, the special, cavelike smell of the recording chamber, the businesslike atmosphere of the control room, the cacophony of the record library in which everyone sits in his own corner listening to the music of his choice, the clocks that rule, inexorable, from the walls. What an enormous lever, he once remarks, it takes to lift a flower on the air. His own specialty at the station is classical ballet, a subject that had always been a favorite. As the studio is near Sara and Elias's house, he sometimes drops in on them after a broadcast. Once he relates:

"Last night I was in the middle of playing Tchaikovsky's *Swan Lake* during my ballet show, when a technician rings me up from the control room. 'What's wrong, Captain Crowther, I can hardly hear you!' It was right during the pianissimo, when the viola could break your heart. 'I'm terribly sorry, old man,' I said, 'it isn't my fault, it's Tchaikovsky's.' 'Who?' he says, all in a rage. 'Jukovsky? Put him on the inside line and I'll give him a piece of my mind! What the devil is he doing in the studio during a broadcast anyway?' "

At last Tony feels that things are beginning to move. He and Elizabeth Marcus become active in Jerusalem's musical life. Tony organizes a choir, which within a few months of his discharge he is already putting through its paces, with more enthusiasm than know-how, in the *Exultate, jubilate.* Later he takes to organizing record concerts at the YMCA, sometimes in the auditorium and sometimes in the twilight garden outside. Elizabeth doesn't miss a single concert. She brings all the scores and follows with her finger.

"He's finally found himself," says Hulda.

"But first he had to lose himself," says Bimbi. "Like all of us. A true Jerusalem metamorphosis."

"And yet he's also getting to be more and more like a fussy old bachelor. One never noticed it when he was in uniform."

Busily, benevolently, smilingly brimming with small, unpretentious love, Tony Crowther, intelligence officer *manqué,* Jerusalem's very own, galumphs through the streets of the city with a briefcase full of records, notes, and musical announcements. An ocean of music foams through him in great waves and keeps on going. In his pleasant little room that looks out on the Old City his loneliness never reaches cosmic proportions. Occasionally he tipples a bit, by himself. A modest fellow.

"Aren't you a Cordoso?" Sara asks a boy whom she has helped to his feet on Hassolel Street. He had fallen and scraped his knee while running.

He grins.

"You bet."

"Which one?"

"Ya'akov."

"Hayyim's son?"

"Uziel's. Hayyim's uncle."

"What do you do all day, Ya'akov Cordoso?"

"I go to my Grandpa's Talmud Torah."

"Do you like it?"

"Hate it. He wants me to be the best student, just because I'm his grandson. He hits a lot too."

She finishes cleaning off his knee and slaps him on the behind.

"On your way now!"

"Who was that?" asks Hulda.

"The scion of The Family We Hated," Sara explains with a smile. "My grandfather and his grandfather didn't talk to each other for fifty years. Did you see what a darling?"

"Did you ever have a romance with one of the Hated Family's children?"

"Never. The only one who was the right age for me, Hayyim, didn't appeal to me. And besides, there was someone else then."

She suddenly thinks of Matti Zakkai: young, raw, nutty, that strong mouth. She sighs. What a chaos everything had been then. And what tenderness. There'd never be anything like it again.

"No Romeo and Juliet?" Hulda is disappointed.

"Romeo was someone else. So was Juliet."

There is an announcement in the paper that Subhi Bey's daughter Suhaila, now principal of a school, appears on the Royal Honours List for her extraordinary contribution to the education of Moslem girls. Her Jewish friends send flowers and congratulations. None of them come to the ceremony.

One evening Miracolo Orientale plucks up his nerve, puts on his best clothes, knocks on Victoria's door, and proposes to her. She is wearing her flowery wrap knotted low over her knees and holds a bucket and a rag in her hands. She was about to mop the floor.

"We're neighbors anyway," he explains to her.

She throws him out.

"Do you want the whole world to laugh at us? A big girl like me and a pipsqueak like you? You'll come to me, I'll mistake you for a mosquito who's bitten me in a place where it isn't nice to scratch."

"I'll be back, Victoria," he says with dignified mien, and departs.

"The nerve of that pipsqueak," she says out loud for him to hear as she runs water into the bucket. "Him and me, what a laugh! The poor little bird. A one-man holy burial society."

Miracolo doesn't give up. Not long after, he brings Victoria a fancily wrapped present. She opens it to find a pink nightgown covered with ribbons and pink muslin butterflies.

"I'll bet you stripped it off a corpse," says Victoria.

"Victoria, why are you so cruel to me?" he asks. "I never thought you could be so mean. I come to you respectfully, with honorable intentions, and you treat me, God forbid, like dirt."

Victoria folds up the nightgown and hands it back to him.

"Don't you go buying me any more nightgowns, Nissim. And don't you go imagining me in them either, because it won't get you anywhere. Besides, you might as well know that pink is a color for whores. Take it to Sa'ada, she'll know how to thank you."

Nissim Mizrachi is mortified. The truth of the matter is that Sa'ada herself had picked the gown out for him. He'd met her by the door of a lingerie shop, where he was standing too embarrassed to enter, and had shyly asked her to buy it for him. She had even bought it at a discount. Had he told Victoria, she would have no doubt roared with laughter and accepted the gift. But fear cost him this round as well.

"That graveyard gosling," she says when he's gone. "That corpse on a wagon. He needs a wife to fatten him up, he does."

In Mawlawiyya, in Bab Khan ez-Zeit, in Derwish Street, they sing:

We will go forth to the Jihad with devotion,
We will go forth to the Jihad in a storm,
We will go forth to the Jihad with a sword of vengeance,
We will go forth to the Jihad with the flag of the Prophet,
We will slaughter, slaughter, slaughter, slaughter, slaughter.

"It h'always starts on a Friday, sir, in the square by the Mosque of Omar," says Starkie. Since his promotion to second lieutenant he has taken to using Sir Reginald's expressions. "You never know in advance if the Towels are going to go h'out and take a whack at the

Beards. They're always screaming all day long anyway. Per'aps, sir, we should 'ave a bloke h'up there by the mosque."

"There's no need for a bloke by the Mosque of Omar, Lieutenant Stark," says Sir Reginald. "And I'll thank you very much not to call the several Palestinian nationalities by such pejorative names as Beards and Towels. *Quod licet Iovi* and all that, Lieutenant Stark."

Starkie glances up resentfully. Him and his damn Latin from Oxford. He oughtn't to remind me all the time that I've come up from the ranks and never had a proper education.

"The crucial spot is by the Mosque of Omar," say the men gathered at the staff meeting in a wing of the Jewish Agency Building. A fan whirling overhead dispels the heat a little. "Especially when the Mufti comes to preach and stir them up. There's absolutely no way of knowing when they're going to break up quietly, and when all hell will break loose."

"There is a way," says one of the men. "Someone has to start hanging out in that square until they get used to him."

They look at him.

"Do you have anyone particular in mind?"

"I think I do. Zion. A Yemenite boy. He knows his Qur'an like any of them, if not better. Let's ask him."

Zion agrees, but on one condition: that his superior keep him in view all the time and never take the binoculars off him for a second. "They're my good-luck charm," he explains. "Put down the binoculars and they'll grab me. They'll make shoe leather out of my skin."

Each time he returns, shaking from tension, his teeth aching because he unconsciously grinds them all night, slipping into a house in the Jewish Quarter of the Old City in order to change clothes, he stubbornly quizzes his superior to make sure he had really been looking. He never quite believes him.

"All right, so tell me, tell me who I talked with. And with how many people. And when I sat by the left-hand wall. And when I was by the ablution fountain. Or was I? Go on, tell me."

"Zion, sometimes my arms get tired."

"I get more tired. Just stand there and look and don't ever, ever stop."

Until Chamberlain came back with his umbrella from Munich to tell the world he was bringing it Peace In Our Time.

CHAPTER SEVEN

HULDA IS ENTERTAINING AGAIN. Most of her guests are in uniform now, and the refreshments are modest, in keeping with the war effort. She circulates among them, keyed up, swirled around by her red, almost ankle-length dress like a big bell of which she is the tongue. Her hair is shot through with white strands. Tony Crowther stands in the doorway of Nili's room, a drink in one hand, arguing with her over the correct way to perform the *Appassionata*. Nili accuses him disdainfully of slobbering romanticism. Tony counters that she has no tenderness. They are dreadfully fond of each other.

Amatsia is high on his own imaginings, though not at all drunk. Hulda, you spinning top, he thinks, watching his twin sister, who seems to be everywhere at once. She looks older than he now: long, nervous lines run from the corners of her eyes and from her flared, filly nostrils. What would you say if you knew that I wanted out? Out and away. I could make my shoes ships, my sign the high seas, I could shut all these jabbering parrots up in their cages and never look back, no, not even to look at a single photograph all the time I was gone. To be on some salt flat by the sea, with a little knapsack, wearing khaki. To find final words and to say them. To fill myself with fog, and the smell of salt, and lots of water. To breathe.

I'm nearly forty years old, he reminds himself, and I've never been myself yet. Anyway you look at it, it's my right. I've simply been dreaming all these years, a lazy, comfortable dream.

Hulda comes up to rub against him as usual but he pushes her aside.

"Leave me be, Hulda. I'm a little tipsy."

He no longer cares for her caresses, for the little nips that she takes at his ear from behind. She senses this and tries to hold back. Suddenly Amatsia has begun to worry her, badly—and it isn't just this evening, either. His catlike Philistine eyes are veiled.

"Amatsia?" Her voice is barely audible. "Is something bothering you?"

"No. I drank too much."

Something is ending and something is about to begin: a dim understanding of this flickers through Hulda's mind, but it isn't enough to cast any light. She claps her hands against her red skirt and goes off to look for Bimbi.

"Imma, can Hitler get through to us?" Nadav asks while at play, without looking up from his blocks.

"No," Sara says, "we won't let him in."

He nods, satisfied.

"Lookit that yellow block, it's the biggest. Look, I'm putting it way up here. Wait, don't fall, I tell you—oof! Imma, who won't let him in?"

"We all won't. Your father and I and Tía Victoria."

"Tía Victoria won't for sure," Nadav declares.

The Germans are near El-Alamein now. Sir Reginald Welsley-More personally telephones the world-renowned Professor Marcus and offers to evacuate him and his wife to India. He knows, Sir Reginald says, that Mrs. Marcus had barely escaped from the Germans once; why risk it happening again? A number of well-known boffins in England and America had contacted him and requested his assistance.

But Elizabeth, who answers the telephone, says no thank you right away. They are two old persons and have no place else to go to. Besides which, she says, a people is composed of all its ages, children, adults, and old folk too. Once you start evacuating the elderly, or the women, or the children, or the leading scientists, it isn't the same anymore. Everyone has to stick together. And thanks to Lady Angela too.

Nahum approached the Amirs' front gate to find Sara watering in the garden and Elias sitting on a bench beneath a grape vine.

"Come on in, Dr. Nahum."

"Drop the Doctor. It's Nahum, and I've come to say good-bye."

"You're joining up?"

"Tomorrow morning."

Sara pressed both his hands. Elias laid a hand on his shoulder.

"Well, I'll be seeing you both. I'll write you a line from time to time."

"When did all this happen to us?" Sara asked softly. "In a month? In a year?"

"I don't know, but it did. Sometimes it seems to me that all the years until now belonged to a different world. A not entirely real one."

"One you feel you're still in?"

"Not anymore. What a kindergarten it all was."

There was a pause.

"Good luck, Nahum. We'll answer your cards."

"Good luck to you too. Say good-bye for me to all the bigwigs. I don't want them to make a fuss, so I'm slipping away while I can."

They hadn't yet got over their emotion when Hulda phoned:

"Sara, come hold my hand. Amatsia just came to say good-bye. He's joining up."

"He'll be together with Nahum then. Nahum was just here to tell us the same thing."

"They won't be together. Nahum's sure to be commissioned as an army doctor; if I'm not mistaken, that means lieutenant, or even captain, right away. Amatsia wants to be a flier, but the British will never let him. They say Jews can't make good pilots. He'll end up a sergeant getting fat on his behind in some miserable hole in Africa. Let's hope so, anyway. Sara, my brother complex is getting out of hand—believe it or not, I want to go to Africa too. They're perfectly dreadful, these good-byes. Just imagine not seeing Amatsia for the next two or three years. Imagine if something should happen to him without my being nearby. And Bimbi says that it's only right that Jews should be fighting too. He sits in Rehavia, too old to be drafted, and carries on."

"Be quiet, Hulda."

"I *am* quiet, so help me. We're even going today to a student concert at Nili's conservatory, together with Elizabeth and Marcus, and we'll all sit quietly listening to the *Appassionata*. Would you like to come listen to the *Appassionata* too? With Elias? I'm sure you can hear Nili practicing in her room right now. Be quiet for a second and listen. Doesn't she play like an angel? Sara? Tell me, isn't she just an angel?"

"If you'd stop crying for a minute, I might be able to hear something."

La Voix de Jerusalem. This next hour of French-language broadcasts is dedicated to the soldiers of the Free French Army.

> *La Madelon pour nous servir à boire,*
> *Quand on lui prend la taille et le menton*
> *Elle rit, c'est tout ce qu'elle sait le faire*
> *Madelon, Madelon, Madelon.*

A truckload of drunken Australians in ten-gallon hats pulled up outside the Edison Theater, by a corset-and-brassiere shop.

They barged inside and bought out the store, showering the counter with pound notes before the eyes of the half-shocked, half-delirious lady shopkeeper. Back in their truck they slipped over their uniforms pink brassieres, stiff fishbone girdles covered with roses, lewdly glittering black silk garters, all the comic and vulgar private underworld of women. The whole street applauded them, saluting when they broke into a hoarse, tipsy rendition of "God Save the King."

"And I want you to know, Sara," Elias told her, "it was really like running up the flag. I know that sounds crazy, but it was."

"How did it end?"

"Four jeeploads of MPs came along and made them take it all off after a pitched battle. Then they arrested them all. Contempt of His Majesty's uniform, you understand. They surrounded the truck with their jeeps and escorted it off in a convoy. The shopkeeper ran into the street and collected everything in baskets. Baskets and baskets of pink and black silk. It was terribly sad when it ended. That was the solemnest military ceremony I've ever seen. And the truest."

Miracolo Orientale was a worried man. For some time now he had suspected that someone was signaling to the enemy with a flashlight from the roofs of the city, yet each time he ran outside to have a look, the mysterious lights would mockingly disappear. He had already informed the police several times, but the latter, in typical foot-dragging fashion, had done nothing. They're nincompoops, Miracolo groused, until one of those fat slobs gets himself up on a roof, twenty spies could come and go twenty times. Everyone knew the police were slow-footed and that a spy must be spry. There was no choice left but for Miracolo himself to take to the rooftops and catch the criminals single-handedly before they spelled the doom of the entire city.

Night after night, skinny and sad-faced, Miracolo prepared himself a cup of strong coffee, washed it down with a jigger of arak, clapped a dark beret on his head, wrapped himself up in a dark, cloaklike coat, and sallied forth from roof to roof like a pessimistic alley cat.

He became an expert on roofs. He knew who was drying raisins and who clumps of figs, who was putting up hay for his animals and who needed to have his water tank retarred. He knew whose roof was piled high with torn old mattresses, their insides long spilled out, and who had lovingly assembled a junk collection on top of his house: straw hassocks and chairs that could no longer be repaired, broken table legs and stoves, closet doors and dustpans, chamberpots and old upholstery and discarded wooden crates. He knew which couples spent their nights beneath the open canopy of a sky strewn with ripe stars that could almost be touched. More than once in the course of his perambulations he had stopped to look silently, inquiringly, upon such trysters as they lay baring themselves to the heavens. More than once, too, he had had to restrain himself from whistling with surprise, because some of the couples he saw were most unexpected.

Such investigations, however, were strictly a side pursuit. The object remained to catch the signaling spies. Often it seemed to him that he could make out the flicker of their flashlight on a far-off roof; there it was, unmistakable, dash–dot–dash–dot; yet no matter how quickly he covered the distance, he never found more than an empty roof beneath a glorious sky whose inky blue tint was dribbled blackly on the horizons by the thin brushes of the cypress trees.

The whole city was at his feet. He began to love Jerusalem from above, sprawling in the darkness. Most roofs could be reached easily by jumping from house to house, if not by means of an exterior staircase, then by leaping from a terrace, a high stretch of wall, the hefty trunk of a fig tree, or the reddish clustered branches of a pepper tree. Each time he came home, tired and disappointed, he would have to brush from his coat, after a brief, restless sleep that lasted till morning light, the rooftop debris that had clung to it: bits of sparrows' or bulbuls' nests, the crushed, staining leaves of stinking acacia, rusty metal tacks, little red peppercorns. And yet it all seemed worthwhile to him in those hours when he felt like the city's aerial lord. They're all asleep, the poor, tired darlings, he would say to himself with prodigal royal compassion; let them sleep, let them sleep, as long as I'm here to watch over them. It occurred to him that he was now two whole levels above the dead whom he helped bury during the day, for they were, so to speak, below the ground floor, in a land of ultimate silence, underneath the apartments, the markets, the automobiles, the school buildings, while he was on the top floor, closer to heavenly things and high secrets of which few men knew, to the uppermost kabbalistic spheres in which the Shekinah merged with Tifereth and the divine black light was conceived.

Months went sleeplessly by without his once laying hands on the accursed signalers. Finally one night he decided to outwit them. He took a flashlight himself and began to flick it on and off to get them to reveal themselves: dash–dot–dot–dash; dash–dot–dot–dash. He was on the high roof of a house near Hassolel Street at the time, overlooking an alleyway known as Assis Lane, which he had reached by means of a stairway and a precarious iron ladder that led to a catwalk for water tanks. He had chosen a high house deliberately, the better to trip the spies. Cunningly he stood there signaling, on, off, on, off, his eyes like an owl's, straining to hear every sound, his hands shaking slightly from the chill of the late, high-mooned hour, of the city beneath its dark pall.

"Blimey," said Lieutenant Stark, who was on his way to the broadcasting station in a jeep, " 'oo's that h'up there?"

"Bless my soul," said the driver. "If it ain't a bloody spy!"

They jumped from the jeep and dashed up the stairs as one man. Miracolo Orientale was apprehended and marched off in handcuffs to jail.

His neighbor Victoria appeared at the Amirs' house the next morning with her usual wrap and cigarette to request Elias's help.

"That *pustema,*" she said. "An old bachelor like him must have gone to peep at the lovers, poor man, and got himself caught. *Claro.* If he's a spy, I'm Elizabeth Marcus."

Elias first went to sound out the underground organizations. None of them, it turned out, had the slightest interest in aiding Nissim Mizrachi, alias Miracolo Orientale. The Haganah claimed not to know him, the Irgun snickered at his name, even the ultraorthodox Neturei Karta refused to acknowledge him as their own. At the burial society they panicked and anxiously asked Elias if their driver was in trouble with the law.

"If he really *were* a criminal, or a member of the underground," Elias told Sara, "it would be much easier, you'd simply have to press the right buttons and the machinery would start. But a wacky case like this, Sara—it doesn't pay to be an unknown nut in Jerusalem these days. To say nothing of a nut who happens to be perfectly sane. Even the psychiatrist wants nothing to do with him."

Elias talked and talked, arguing and cajoling with his long, thin smile, until the British were convinced that Miracolo Orientale was no danger to the war effort. That same morning Lieutenant Starkie entered Miracolo's cell, and spat from under his mustache:

"You there!"

"Yes, officer."

"You're not a spy."

"No, officer, I swear to God I'm . . ."

"You're an idiot!"

He threw him out of the cell. "You disgusting Peeping Tom," he said to him in the corridor, "if it was h'up to me I'd give you ten years I would. Go on, get h'out of 'ere, you dirty old scum, let's not see yer fice around 'ere again."

Miracolo went skinnily home and suddenly felt how sleepy he was. He slept for thirty hours and rose purged of spies, rooftops, and the kingdom of the night.

Elias and Sara went to see how the redeemed man was doing and brought him some arak as a present. He had finished his long, resuscitating sleep and looked his old self again. He dusted off a seat for them, removing his night robes that still lay there stinking from an acacia branch, come in, come in, welcome, what guests, what an honor. He ran to the pantry to bring them sucking candies and sunflower seeds. "When I was a young boy," he related, "there was a *bruja* in the neighborhood, you should pardon me telling you, who read my fortune in coffee grounds and told me to watch out for the night demon Lilith. She even made me an amulet against her. And just look how I forgot. Lilith, you should know, can disguise herself as she likes. Even as a German spy signaling in the night, she can, if that's what she wants to be. Anything."

Little Ya'akov Cordoso finally got even with his grandfather. He came across a group of Australians who were looking for Sa'ada's place.

"You want girls?"

"We sure do. You know where it is?"

"You come with me."

He led them down the lane to his grandfather's Talmud Torah and stopped them at the gate.

"You each one pay me shilling."

They threw shillings, pounds, whatever they had in their pockets, into his hand. Money meant nothing to them.

"Now you go up. Three floors, on the right, behind iron door."

The Australians went upstairs. There was a tremendous commotion. Benches toppled to the ground. Then down they came again on the run with Elder Cordoso pursuing them in full fury, waving his stick at their heads. After him whooped the Talmud Torah boys, peppering with their rolled-up notebooks the running soldiers, who defended themselves with mock blows.

"Where's the little chap who took our money?"

"Ya'-a-kov! We know it was you. You better come home quick, Grandpa's going to give you a hi-i-ding!"

Then why come home at all? Ya'akov logically asked himself. He carefully counted his shillings and put them away in a hiding place.

"Grandpa'll murder you black-'n'-blue!"

"Abba, aren't you joining up too?" asked Hillel one evening. Many fathers were already gone. Sara tensed for his answer.

Elias replied carefully:

"Not everyone can join the army, Hillel."

"Why not?" Noam asked.

"If some men didn't stay behind to perform vital jobs, the whole country would fall apart. If I went, and a few more men like me, the courts wouldn't be able to function."

"And then the criminals could do what they wanted?" asked Noam.

"Well, it would make things easier for them, that's for sure."

"That's for sure," Nadav agreed from his highchair. "There'd be so many of them, even, there'd be no room for them in jail, even."

Sara, who was in the middle of serving dinner, stopped for a minute to sort herself out, and found a combination of disappointment and relief.

With your hand come and wave me good-bye,
Cheerio, here I go on my way . . .

In a kibbutz cabin, far away from home,
Sits a young Palmach boy, guarding all alone,
Counting up the days since he's been gone . . .

Sara, attuned to the vibrating city, went back to work. Not to the hospital: the thought of that great dungeon of suffering oppressed her. She looked for, and found, a job as a field worker, visiting needy homes on welfare all over the city. The work came to several hours a day. She was usually paired with another nurse, a Christian Arab named Thérèse. Neither of them had known before what depths of misery there were in the city, what poverty holed up in burrows, buried in mildew, stirring amid the huge stones covered with slobber and moss. An age-old underworld of poverty. Holes in the walls. Stinking puddles on the ground.

Thérèse had been raised by French nuns. She still talks in a whisper, keeps her eyes on the ground, and walks with her legs close together. She writes in a tiny, calligraphic hand and can do the delicate embroidery of the convent, whose handiwork is famous throughout the world. In her gray nun's robe she looks like a nestling dove with its wings tucked in. At the height of the day, when the afternoon sun beats down on the dusty exhalations of the alleyways, her eyes see sudden glimmerings in the open gutters that pass for sidewalks, mysterious pinpoints of light, as though the puddles were gilt-bottomed; in the rock-strewn, debris-covered urinals through which she passes, there are portents of the many numinous powers at work beneath her feet, in correspondence with the visible world. Since she and no one else sees them, she keeps it to herself. There is a mystery about her and a light. Her eyes never quite focus and she is infinitely kind.

An old nun stood in the doorway of the convent school each morning with a tape measure in her hand to check on the prescribed length of

the girls' hemlines and sleeves. Penmanship was the main subject: if
you couldn't learn to write exactly like the nuns, your days in school
were numbered. The priest, whose soft, buttery hands smelled of perfume when you kissed them, never listened very hard to their confes-
sions. And yet what horrible sins they had sinned: the sin of envying a
friend whose collar was starched crisper, whose hair was prettier, than
one's own; the sin of gossip; the sin of not listening to the paternoster
on a fine spring day when the sky was crisscrossed with swallows. The
soft hands, the enveloping clouds of incense, the all-forgiving, all-
absorbing soft chaos of it all, wiped the girls clean of the broad avenues
of their childhoods, of the histories, traits, legacies, legends, of their
families and homes. In what was left of them after this thorough
French erasure, a new, prosthetic consciousness of *nos ancêtres les
Gaulois* was instilled. No more olive, vine, and fig. Henceforth, they
were implanted mind-and-soul with great spruce and fir trees such as
they had never seen in their lives, though everyone in the convent
knew that these had cast their shade on young Jesus of Nazareth; with
unknown cherry groves; with winter tales as brilliantly white as the
frost balls on a Christmas tree; with thatched roofs; with broad rivers
frozen over with ice on which simple midnight angels skimmed while
a barb-tailed, cloven-footed devil hopped and jigged. The girls took to
all this as to a strange, all-effacing dream. Be good, honor your superi-
ors, speak properly, keep your ankles together—and one festive day a
taste of the promised paradise will be yours: a glittering, gold-laden
procession of crosses through the narrow streets, artificial flowers of
lucent, frozen wax, the ruby-red stones on the bishop's robe and mitre
tipped by the last rays of the sun, the choirs of candle-bearing votaries
washed free of sin, the sonorous tones of the organ that resounded
right through you as they spread and spread all around.

Expandi manus meas ad te,
anima mea,

sings Thérèse, before stopping with embarrassment. Sara urges her to
continue. "Sing, Thérèse. It's lovely. Much nicer than that heavy
German music of Bimbi's."

Sicut terra sine aqua, tibi . . .

Thérèse sings. Sara loves the old Gregorian chants, which call to mind those simple, gray, massive, pre-Gothic castles from the days when men built without windows because who needed windows anyway, in a setting of scraggly flocks, thickets of wild berries, and filthy chickens scratching in the straw that covered the lowered bridge of a moat. In Thérèse's singing one can clearly make out the quarter tones of the Orient. Perhaps the Crusaders had brought them back across the sea with them to France. Now the melodic circle has been closed: down it has curved, through the innocent, cruel, heartbreaking Middle Ages, to return to its source, here, at the foot of the Temple Mount.

Sometimes Sara makes fun of *nos ancêtres les Gaulois.* She tells Thérèse about Monsieur Gaston in the rain, but Thérèse just thinks it is lovely. One has to love, Sara, she says softly, one has to love, human beings are so pitiful, we can't prevent a single death, all we can do is stave it off a little. Give comfort.

"That's what Dr. Bimbi says too, but he sees that staving off as a sign of human strength."

"Oh, no," Thérèse recoils. "Human beings have no strength. We live like flowers, by the grace of God."

That Christmas she bashfully brings Sara's children a present: a small tree made of colored celluloid, its trunk set at the center of two intersecting pieces of wood. She has decorated it herself with gold and silver stars cut from tinsel, shiny, bubblelike beads, absorbent-cotton snow, and a fat paper angel on top staring down from a star. Little Jesus and his cross have been tactfully left out.

The city sings, it swings like a pendulum on the radio airwaves, it grows excited, it writes letters, it weeps, it waxes sentimental, it hates, it listens. Olive picking follows grape picking, orange picking follows olive picking. Jeeps drive down the street, topless in summer, covered in winter. Sara and Thérèse walk and walk like two tall doves, sometimes together, sometimes alone. There isn't a corner of the city to which they haven't dragged their weary feet.

Serene, transparent, her mane of coppery red hair falling over her face, Nili plays Czerny études and Beethoven sonatas with power and finesse. One day she accompanies a young singer from the conservatory in the role of Leporello boasting to little Madamina of the exploits of his master Don Juan. So many and so many women in Italy, so many and so many young maidens in Germany, but in Spain . . . ah, in Spain . . .

in Espagna . . .
mille e tre, mille e tre!

"One thousand and three," Bimbi sings quietly along in his own room, careful not to disturb what he considers a sublime message from eternity itself. What an unusual sublimation of the escapades of that scoundrel Don Juan Tenorio these two young people are giving, though they themselves have no idea of what the aria is really about, of the shame, the sweat, the sadness, the vanity, the loveless gymnastics of naked bodies. Loveless, Bimbi thinks, totally loveless,

Let her be pretty, let her be ugly,
Let her be rich, let her be poor,
As long as she wears a woman's skirt . . .

Angels, thinks Dr. Bimbi, plain angels, the seriousness, the harmony, the way Nili stops just then and corrects her partner:
"There's no need for a ritardando here, you've already got all the emphasis that you need in that phrase. Don't overdo it."
And elegantly, exactly, she plays the coda on her piano. *Mille e tre.*

Madame Savvidopoulos took the last of her ugly unmarried daughters and set off with her to Bahrain.

CHAPTER EIGHT

ONE FRIDAY AFTERNOON, when Elias was about to go for a walk with the boys, four Arab peasants knocked on the door. They came from the Sur-Baher area, kaffias on their heads and long gray coats over their shirts, their brown arms protruding from too-short sleeves. Their faces were sullen, and a demanding insistency lurked in the politeness of their manner. They opened and shut their fists as they talked, huddling together in the doorway as though their physical closeness gave them strength.

Elias invited them inside. They were, it turned out, the nephews of the Arab who had rented the house on Melissanda Street to him and Sara over twelve years before. The four men's uncle had included them in his will, and now they had come to reclaim their property, on which, they said, the Amarillos' lease had run out.

"It's only right, *ya hawajjah,*" they repeated over and over, with a persistence that was half-entreaty, half-threat. "It's only right."

Elias took out some documents to show them. Several years ago the accumulated rent money had already reached the purchase price of the house, the title to which had then been legally transferred to him.

Their own father, the deceased man's brother, had signed the papers himself.

"Don't you recognize your own father's signature?" he asked. "I'm sorry, my brothers, but someone has misled you in this matter."

In other times they would perhaps have taken no for an answer and gone their way. But the Jews were buying land everywhere these days, and their general sense of injustice was too great for them to give in. Who's talking about money, they growled, we want our property back. They lowered their eyes before Elias's proofs, but the wave of defiance still crested within them.

"The effendis have sold all our lands, *ya-Ustaz,*" cried one of them. "Where shall we go, to the desert?"

"It's your right to take me to court. We're not living in Turkish times anymore. You can be sure you'll get a fair trial."

"What do we know about trials," said the tallest of them, a broken jaw upsetting the symmetry of his face. "It's our land, and that's that."

"The court rules for the Jews," spat a second, who was amazingly like, though shorter than, his brother. There was something violent about him.

"They've picked the meat off our bones."

A nervous, guttural, peasanty speech, a volley of words followed by silence, another burst and silence again. Hands used to the earth. They stole a glance at the fruit trees in the garden. Sara had planted them. Fine trees. They coveted them with their eyes.

Elias talked slowly, quietly. He tried to explain. The fact was that he sympathized with them. He knew their situation. So much land had been sold out from under them, from under their feet, that they themselves didn't know anymore what was theirs and what wasn't. As far back as 1929, peasants from Sur-Baher had razed the kibbutz of Ramat-Rachel, whose land had been bought from them with good money. The law, no law, could justify this—yet he, Elias, understood how they felt. There was something about land. If you owned one dunam of it, you wanted five; if you owned five, you dreamed of planting on twenty. It wasn't easy to look at the fruit on a neighbor's tree that had still been yours the minute before it was sold. What were documents or contracts next to peaches that you'd eaten from the day you were old enough to remember? Peaches as old as the world, *your* world, the world of your childhood.

In the end they rose to leave as if convinced, or at least as if persuaded that they had no tenable case. They finished the coffee that Sara had served, thanked Al-Ustaz Amarillo, and departed with their faces in frowns. An ancient taxi with two more companions was waiting for them outside. They crowded into it and drove off. Both sides were left with the uncertain feeling that the matter was not over.

"They'll be back, Elias," said Sara, worried.

"Like as not. We may have to call in the authorities yet."

But before Elias had time to call in the authorities, they returned. It was on a Sabbath morning, while Sara was in the kitchen and the boys were off in the old neighborhood visiting Gracia, who since her panicky flight had begun to accept her true age. The men barged suddenly through the front gate without knocking. There were five of them this time, and they spoke in near shouts. It seemed their purpose to put on a show of force, or at least to make a scene. Elias was alarmed.

"Sara, run out the back door to the neighbors. Quick. I'll lock up."

Sara, frightened, did as she was told, sweeping aside the vegetables she was peeling and hurrying outside with the paring knife still in her hand. The moment she turned her head to look back around the corner of the house, though, she saw the five of them treading deliberately, maliciously, on the row of phlox she had just planted that morning. Something peasanty reared up in her too, washing in a blind rage over her face and eyes. Without stopping to think what she was doing, she ran out on the front steps of the house.

"Get out of my garden," she said in a voice choked with rage.

They squinted and looked at her as though from a red cloud. It only now dawned on her that she was facing the five of them alone. She retreated, backing up the steps toward the house, before realizing that Elias must have locked the front door. She was in for it now. She clutched the little paring knife behind her back, squeezing the handle until it hurt. There wasn't a soul in the street.

They began to move toward her on the staircase as one man, slowly, staring at her as though mutually spellbound by the violence in the air. The first of them put a hand on the railing. Her mind blanked out. A whitish mist drifted momentarily before her and then vanished. She felt very cold now, as though she had gone outside on a snowy day without her coat on. She could hear Elias inside the house, frantically trying to dial the police from his room upstairs. Her face curled with contempt.

Before any of the five could tread on the steps themselves, two men appeared suddenly in the gateway. One of them, brawny, not young, seemed to drag one leg; the other was a shaggy, overgrown adolescent. Quickly they approached the five peasants, taking advantage of the second in which the five looked back with surprise to station themselves by Sara on the steps. Her head reeling, she made out the older of the two, who was wearing a khaki shirt, the one who dragged his leg, as Matti Zakkai. The other looked to be about twenty and was tall and bearlike; he wore a gray undershirt and a peaked cap on his head, from beneath which his hair shot out wildly in all directions.

"What's going on here?" asked Matti quietly, in Arabic.

The spell of incipient violence was snapped. They knew it and hung their heads.

"We've been robbed, *ya hawajjah,*" said the oldest of them, the fifth, unfamiliar one, who was missing a tooth in his mouth. "They've taken away our land, they've taken our house, God punish the robbers for their iniquity."

"Shut up!" said the tallest, dragging the man away. "*Yallah,* let's get out of here."

"And don't step on my flowers," Sara wanted to add, but her voice faltered and couldn't be heard. They left in a hurry.

"Sara Amarillo!" said Matti. "I'll be damned. I'd like you to meet a friend of mine, we call him Bear. From Zefaniah Street."

Sara reached out to shake hands but was still holding the paring knife. She felt utterly embarrassed.

"What's that in your hand? A knife? Are you serious?" His warm eyes, a pile of walnuts in a wooden bowl, sparkled as he regarded her fondly in her pale dishevelment. She was still quaking with what had happened and couldn't keep her hands still.

She put down the knife on a windowsill and shook Bear's hand. He bowed to her, ironic. She must have seemed a bit crazy to him, a woman of her age. She pulled herself together.

"Matti Zakkai, you couldn't have picked a better time to come."

"You just whistle and the whole old neighborhood comes running. Who were those men?"

She explained.

"Come on in, you've earned yourselves a cup of coffee."

"We can't," said Matti. "We're in the middle of work. We just happened to be taking a break. We'll take you up on the coffee some other time." He stood there for a minute looking at her. Only now did she notice the long, ugly scar that ran down his neck from his ear and disappeared into his coarse khaki shirt. Who stitched you up so terribly, she angrily wanted to ask. That strong, sane mouth. He had the sweat-smell of a laborer. And something else that smelled like grease. His skin was white, as though it hadn't seen much of the sun.

"What are you doing these days, Sari?"

"A bit of nursing, on and off." She smiled at him. Sari, he'd called her. It was suddenly easy. Too easy. Like twenty years ago, or more, she wanted only to submerge herself in those half-sunlit, half-shaded eyes. Her twin in anxiety, in resolution. "And you?"

"A bit of lathe work, on and off." He grinned. "If you ever have a free moment, ask for me at Cohen's lathe shop over on Yosef ben-Matityahu Street. They'll call me." He took her hand. "And next time don't take on five Arabs with a paring knife, because I don't often happen to come by this way." He pressed her hand to his cheek. "*Yallah,* Bear, let's go. I doubt that they'll be back today."

"If they try, the police are bound to get here sometime too."

"Either they'll get here or they won't," drawled Bear.

"My husband works in the Attorney General's office."

"In that case, maybe they will."

They waved good-bye. Sara followed them to the gate and locked it carefully. She took shears and some string from the toolshed and went to work on the damaged plants, pruning the broken shoots, splinting what was left of them, firming up the ground around them. She needed time, lots of it, before she'd want to see Elias again.

Elias was angrier than she had ever seen him before.

"You took a terrible risk, Sara, and a totally unnecessary one. It was quite irresponsible of you. I really don't understand how you could have done such a thing, a mother of three children."

"Why didn't you come out on the stairs?" she asked, dry-mouthed.

"Because it would have been perfectly stupid of me to come out on the stairs. The best way to handle it was to keep them out of the house until the police came."

"Didn't you see that I was outside too?"

"It never occurred to me. What kind of a fool do you take me for? Do you think I'd have stayed in the house if I knew you were out there?"

He didn't speak to her the rest of the day, and she felt it was just as well. She herself couldn't decide if he was right or wrong. She could only feel the locked door of her house against her back.

As though trying to prove a point to her, and to himself, Elias set out that same evening for the agitated village near Sur-Baher. He didn't go by himself; a police officer came too, and Hajj Kamal ad-Din, Subhi Bey's brother, who made it his business to help as best he could in patching up differences between Arabs and Jews. They conferred till late at night in the village headman's house and then drove back in the police car. It was after midnight when Elias came home. The rooms were dark and he didn't turn on any lights. He washed and undressed by the light of the street lamps, which filtered through the branches of a large fern that Sara had placed in the window—a leafy light whose long shadows made a dark plant on the floor where none stood.

Sara held her breath.

"Sara?" he whispered. "Are you asleep?"

"No. Was anything settled?"

"Of course it was. The headman gave us his word, and so did their oldest son, and the head of the family, and all the uncles. They themselves admitted that they got carried away and lost their heads. And that's the correct way to do things." He lay down beside her, angry. "Are the boys home?"

"Yes. They're sleeping. Victoria brought them."

"Did you tell her what happened?"

"I told her there was almost a fight. She said that she wouldn't have gone to the village if she were you. That she doesn't trust them."

Elias sighed.

"I'm telling you, there weren't any problems. You're unreasonable, Sara. You get yourself into trouble and want others to get you out again. How primitive can you be?" he asked plaintively, summing up.

She didn't answer him. The man has so many words, she thought, and he's never seen a real corpse in his life. They lay next to each other very straight, without touching. It took them a long time to fall asleep.

A few days later, while making her nurse's rounds, Sara, dressed in her white uniform, stepped into Cohen's lathe shop on Ben-Matityahu Street. Three men were at work inside, one of whom was Bear. The two others were working in a corner, in gray undershirts and peaked caps too, their lean muscles sticking out on their thin arms like the white vesicles of a pupa. All were pale-skinned—as gray and prosaic-looking, it seemed to her, as could be. There was a smell of oil and metal filings in the air.

"Good morning, Sister Sara," drawled Bear in his slightly swaggering voice. "How are you? Are those men still bothering you?"

"No, we've seen the last of them for a while. My husband is taking care of them," she added, confused by her own need to be loyal. "Where's Matti?"

There was a moment's silence.

"He's out," said one of the other two workers.

Sara didn't believe him. She didn't know why, but she didn't. And yet she sensed no hostility on their part. It was simply as if they were waiting for some code word she didn't know. Each waited for the other's next move.

"Couldn't you call him?" she persisted.

They exchanged glances.

"Maybe. In a quarter of an hour. Go take a little walk and we'll get him."

"Listen, you two," said Bear, "let's not play games. If this whole thing blows sky-high on us tomorrow, who'll take care of us if not Sister Sara? . . . Come on, I'll take you to Matti."

One of the workers shrugged:

"It's your lookout. I don't know from nothing."

They turned pointedly back to their work.

She followed Bear. He opened a side door leading into a backyard that was filled with rusting junk and surrounded by a crooked stone wall layered with concrete. The yard was neglected, full of dry brown brambles, and smelled like an outhouse.

"I take it this is your restroom," said Sara.

Bear grinned.

"We like it to stink, that way no one comes poking around. If you feel like contributing to our security zone yourself, I'll be glad to look the other way. Excuse how I talk, I'm that way with everyone. It's my character."

He approached a manhole hidden beneath a sheet of rusty tin and pulled aside its cover, whose handle was smudged with whitewash and dirt.

"Step right this way, modom."

She fought back a moment's nausea, repelled by the foul stench, and started down the ladder. Soon her feet made contact with solid, level ground, while above her she made out more openings for light and air. These were covered with piles of dry brambles, which, from the darkness of the tunnel, glittered against the sky like gold set in indigo. Unlike the filthy yard, the tunnel was an orderly place whose proprietors seemed to know exactly what they were up to. She stepped easily down to the ground with Bear right behind her and heard him close the manhole cover from within, wondering for a second how it was done. After walking some twenty yards she came to an unlocked iron door painted against rust, beyond which several steps led to an underground chamber lit by naked bulbs. By a large worktable that took up

most of the space stood Matti, whitely naked from the waist up, peer-
ing at something through a face mask that he wore. He was busy
welding with a small torch. For a minute she stood there, taking in the
sight of his back as he worked. There wasn't a wasted or nervous
movement to him; it was as if he were tuned to some very regular and
precise inner rhythm of his own. Not until he switched off the torch
and removed his mask did he sense them behind him and spin around.

"You," he said quickly, letting his blackened hands drop. His eyes
sparked.

"Matti," said Bear, "you might at least wash your hands. Can't you
see she's wearing a white dress?"

"Mind your manners with Sister Sara," said Matti mildly without
taking his eyes off her.

"Well, then, the escort's heading back," said Bear. "You're responsible for the return convoy, Matti."

He waved good-bye and retraced his steps.

"You," said Matti again, pleased. They stood a long time, welded in
wonderment and desire, shooting sparks.

"So here's where you live."

"Here. You can sit on that crate. There are some old Mills hand
grenades in it that I've been fixing up to make less nervous."

"It won't make them more nervous if I sit down on them?"

"No, they don't get upset when they're not primed."

She sat down.

"Sometimes this place is full of dinosaurs and elephants," said
Matti. "We make all kinds of things out of junk. It's pretty empty here
today, just little odds and ends."

"And this all comes from your training at the Alliance school?"

"At the Alliance, with a few later installments. Those Frenchmen
didn't know themselves what they were teaching me."

"And you work here all the time?"

"We take shifts. Bear's a terrific worker. You mustn't mind his big
mouth, he has fine hands."

"Just a minute, Matti. If that's how it is, you never get any sunlight
at all. Do you drink milk?"

"The fact is that there's a standing order to bring us milk, all of us galley slaves, but with Jerusalem in the state it is, it doesn't often get done. About one time in five. You won't believe how disorganized everything is here. Out in the countryside it's easier, they keep a special cow for you. Straight from the barn to the bunker."

"Matti, you'll get sick. I'll bring you people milk myself."

"That would be most gracious of you."

They said nothing for a while.

"Did those men ever come back?"

"No, it's been all taken care of."

She couldn't bring herself to mention Elias this time.

"Sari?" He lowered his voice. "How are you?"

"All right. I guess."

"I'm dying to hug you, but my hands are black."

She rose and went over to him, passing two cautious fingers over his face, along his gross scar. They looked deeply at each other, silent, unarmed.

"It's been at least twenty years," she said under her breath.

"They never passed."

"True. They never did."

He stood facing her tensely, careful to keep his hands to himself, transmitting without words.

"Matti, I have to go now. People are waiting for me. I'll be back during the week, with that milk. That doesn't mean that I'll always be able to come down here."

"Don't worry about it," he said. "I'm not always down here either. The fact that you came at all today is a gift to me. I've hit the jackpot."

"Come, walk me back up to the yard."

He followed her, regarding her from behind as she climbed the ladder, as tall almost as he was, a woman with cradling fundaments of thighs, strong legs, bristling, electric hair, and a laugh. The way she had come back to him. Had fallen right into his life.

Bear had left the manhole open against regulations, covering it only with the rusty tin sheet, but Matti decided to let it pass. This time. This day that his eyes had made him a happy man.

"Bear didn't ask you to contribute to our security zone?" he asked, rubbing his eyes in the sunlight.

"Of course he did." The strong light called for a different language, one they didn't yet share. "I'll see you soon, Matti."

"See you soon, Sari. Watch your step by the door."

At sunset Sara and Matti left the lathe shop and walked slowly through Me'a She'arim and down Saint George Street, Matti dragging his foot a bit, and how comely is thy hair in the light, O my beloved.

"So when exactly did you lose your foot, Matti?"

"Just half of it. It was during the Switzerland course. You never heard of it? There was this small-arms course that everyone in it told their family they were going to Switzerland, because it was a bit long. I had a disagreement with my platoon commander about the reliability of a certain grenade. He was wrong and I was right. You needn't look at me that way, a commander's entitled to make a few mistakes. So this year I'm filling in here in Jerusalem, they needed an armorer, but it's only temporary. It's a bit of a rough time for me, actually. We're hard-pressed at home, it's not easy for my wife there. And my smallest boy has asthma, which isn't helped any by the hut that we live in. I've already been promised that a kibbutz will take them in, and that I'll be able to go back to full-time work with the Haganah. You and I just happened to meet again in a little crack in history, Sari. All my friends are off on operations or in some course. And here I am, with a bum leg in Jerusalem, greasing a few pitiful guns—you wouldn't believe how pitiful. But for a reward, you silly hero, I got to see you playing soldier yourself with your paring knife. You looked just like your Aunt Victoria then. By the way, do you remember old Hankes, whom you all hated so much after that business with Shabu? He was really one of the few decent people around then. Two little guns were brought to Jerusalem then, just imagine, two little guns that were the pride of the whole Haganah, and Hankes let us keep them in a barrel in his wine store. They were right there, in fact, that day you came to pester me in the cellar. Don't hit me now, I'm not complaining, not about that cellar or about anything else. I'm just mentioning it for the record."

"Right under Tony Crowther's nose."

"Under Tony Crowther's nose, and under Hayyim Cordoso's nose, who was working for the police."

"We guessed as much, only not until much later."

"Sari, what happened to Elder Amarillo? Is he still alive?"

"He died thirteen years ago."

He threw a quick glance at her, fathoming an entire dimension.

"And Ofra, what happened to her?"

She told him.

"We haven't heard a word from her since the fall of France. And they're shipping Jews off to the camps from there now."

"Maybe the 'von' will stand her in good stead, because I doubt that the conversion will help much."

"That's what we all say."

They stopped near Melissanda Street.

"Sari, this is too good to be true. It's a luxury. And I don't believe in luxuries."

"You call this a luxury?"

"Do I have to explain myself?"

"No."

They stood immobile. Without touching, he let her have all of him, planted himself in her body, which had opened to him wholly, between her unlifted arms.

Lead me among the clefts of thy voice, that we fall not among heartbeats, O my chief joy.

All villages are more villages at night, all the neighborhoods more themselves. Each place burrows down, lit from within, noisy with suppertime, as though the out-of-doors had been expropriated from human beings by a dark, odorous ocean in which every house is now an island, an impregnable asylum for the night. Between the villages, between the neighborhoods, the distances grow vast; one does not just step outside anymore, one takes a flashlight, one casts rings of weak light on the low branches of a huge cypress tree, on a crevice in the ter-raced earth, on a path hurriedly crossed, as though on a thousand legs, by some little night beast. The quick, cautious, snuffing nose of a jackal or fox between Theodosius and the tombstones on the Mount of

Olives. The hopping flight of a barn owl above the rooftops of Ezrat Yisra'el. Hoot owls keening over the valley beneath French Wood, that forms a melancholy triangle with the tomb of Sheikh Jarrah and the tomb of Shimon the Just. Every creature has its own sounds, every bird its own call, to warn away others from a territory whose borders it alone knows, an unmarked estate the slightest trespass on which leads to a flurry of bared fangs, beating wings, crooked claws, to treetop scuffles in the dead of night, the quick pounce, the final gasp, angry bluster and threat. Neither Sara nor Thérèse likes to go far at night, but with some households, where the man comes home from his work after dark, they have no choice. They walk quickly, until back on lit streets again, tall in their habits, temporary friends. Of their fears they never speak.

The naked bulb cast its light in the bunker. Matti and Sara sat on a blanket that had been spread upon a crate.

"I'd like to go down to the coast. There's talk of illegal immigration again, it's the most important thing now, and I've all but been promised a part in it. Meanwhile Hadassa had to take the little boy to Gedera for three weeks, he just can't shake that asthma of his here. For a whole lot of reasons, we have to get out of Jerusalem."

"Her name is Hadassa."

"It's Hadassa, but she really was named Esther. She hated it and changed it to Hadassa."

Esther-Hadassa began to be real. There once was a girl who felt ashamed of her name. She had her loves and her hates, and she had borne Matti four children. Hadassa Zakkai of Shimon the Just Quarter, not far away. A blinding mirror that mercilessly showed her herself. Sara felt utterly crushed.

"What's his name?" Matti asked roughly.

"Elias Amarillo. Now Amir."

"A relative of yours?"

"A distant one."

The word "distant" took on its other meaning. They felt unsure of themselves.

"You see, Sari, there's so much we don't know. I have the feeling of living in something that's not mine."

"What's not yours, Matti?" she asked gently. "Myself?"

"I don't know. Something's twisted here. Or maybe I am."

"Look, Matti, let's bring it down to earth. Come home with me, meet Elias and the boys. We'll straighten things out."

"It would never work out. And that's why I don't want to meet Elias and your boys. Just the thought of it kills me. Why drive each other crazy? You yourself just said, 'Come home with me.' I call it home too. That makes two homes."

They fell silent.

"It's like I say, Sari. A crack in time. I'll be gone before you know it."

She didn't answer. He only now noticed that she had a Band-Aid on her finger. It made him wince more than it should have. He still couldn't stand the thought of her suffering pain. That old compassion.

He took her hurt hand and pressed it to his mouth.

"What happened to my Sari?"

"Nothing. I burned myself on the iron."

He kissed her fingers one by one.

"Are you sure it's all right?"

"What's the matter with you, Matti? Of course it is. If you make such a fuss over a little burn, what kind of crazy father must you be?"

"You'd be surprised. I'm not really even a good one. I leave it all to Hadassa. She's a real—how should I put it?—mother hen. She doesn't miss a trick. I'm not so good at this fatherhood business, I haven't been home enough for it. Courses, other things. Sometimes it seems to me that they're only on my lap when I want them to be, never when they do."

A hard, melodic face, and for so many years she used to draw the map of it after he'd gone, always with the same empty, unexplored spaces.

"What was that story you once started to tell me about your father?"

"Well, it's like this. My parents were apparently never married. Or in any case, they never lived together. He was a typical Russian intellectual bore, something of a linguist and part anarchist too. And she was a working girl. On principle, so as not to have to work in some office during the day, he worked as a night watchman in a furniture warehouse—though I never really did understand the principle, since why should an anarchist be against thieves? His big thing was that he wanted everyone to write Hebrew in Latin characters. He even wrote me letters like that, in Latin characters. I couldn't stand them. During the day he wrote linguistic pamphlets and did research that nobody gave a damn about. It makes me sick to this day to think of those piles of pamphlets written in his beautiful calligraphic hand, mountains and mountains of worthless paper covered with cobwebs. All that effort. And all in the same shrill, pompous tones. A man as gray as a sack, but he wrote in screaming red. After the age of ten I hardly ever saw him. I think he bummed around along the coast for a while. He was probably organizing a secret group of terrorist linguists, or something like that."

"In Latin code."

"In Latin code. My mother worked hard. For a while she even worked in the building trade, laying floor tiles. She was a union member. Now she lives in an old-age home for invalids in Gedera. She never talked much, but it was she who brought me up, more or less. And when I was fifteen years old, he committed suicide. He hung himself here in Jerusalem, in the furniture warehouse where he once worked. I don't know what it was supposed to symbolize. And believe me, I thought even less of the way he died than of the way he lived. He must have seen himself as the totally involved man, but he was really the total dropout. My mother was the involved one. Involved by him. A man of words. Well, that's enough fairy tales for the day, Sari. Tell me, did you happen by any chance to be on Geula Street today? I heard they slapped a curfew on some houses there, that they were looking for some Stern Gang people, is that true? Bear didn't show up for work."

"I was there. Depressing. Barbed wire everywhere. Some people hadn't done their shopping yet, and the neighbors were throwing them loaves of bread over the wire. A police car kept driving up and down, trying to stop it. Armed soldiers. Whistles. Screaming children. Hysteria."

She could feel his body growing rigid next to her.

"Matti, don't make yourself completely into a tool of war, like Bear."

"Look, when there's a war on, someone has to be its tool."

"But you don't have to love it."

He looked at her reproachfully: an intentional, unevadable wrong.

"Sure. I'll keep it in mind."

Their mood was spoiled.

"Sari," he said pleadingly, "I have to stay sane. I have to. You should understand that better than anyone."

Sara rose to go.

"Sure. I'll keep it in mind."

She didn't return to the bunker, or bring him milk, again.

Nadav rode across the garden on his tricycle and cut her off.

"Tweet-tweet! Clear out, I'm making a curfew."

"I have a pass."

"Let's see it."

She fumbled in her purse and showed him. He relented momentarily, then pushed the tricycle in front of her again.

"So what if you do, even."

How could one leave them.

One day Elias Amir came home with a book that a British colleague had brought him from India, a practical treatise on lovemaking in the best Hindu manner: what to say and how, which sounds to make when, the best time to scratch the left shoulder with the fingernails.

"It's all such nonsense, Eli."

"But you've been bored lately in bed. At least it's good for a laugh."

She dreamt that she was standing with the two of them under a wedding canopy. Matti, who was on her right, slipped the wedding ring onto her hand with a single, characteristically purposeful movement.

Then she extended her left hand to Elias, who awkwardly maneuvered the ring halfway up her finger; she and Matti looked at him with fond patience, like an adult couple at a laggard child, while he applied himself and succeeded. Applause broke out and Sara linked arms with both men. The three of them grandly descended from the proscenium, while the guests gaily cried, Look how simple it is, there's really nothing to it. She awoke with a delicious sense of victory, as though she had just invented something of universal importance, so simple yet ingenious that no one had thought of it before.

Coughing, catarrhal, indignant, suspicious, Sa'ada came to Elias's office one day. She and some of her girls had been caught in the NAAFI, the British army store, with ration books that they had no right to have.

"The soldiers gave them to us," Sa'ada fumed. "How were we supposed to know?"

Elias thought for a moment.

"Look here, Madame Sa'ada. As long as your relations with a soldier are purely commercial, there's simply no way that you can be considered to be even his adoptive family."

"So what do you want me to do, give them my girls for their lousy butter?"

"I wouldn't suggest that, but every now and then you might invite a few of them, just like that, for a free cup of tea or some cake, and then we could claim—it's worth a try, anyway—that your house is the residence abroad of the soldiers in question, which would entitle you to make use of their rations for the purpose of entertaining them. Do you get what I'm saying? If you charge for everything, you can't be like a family; but if you entertain free of cost, we can tell the judge that you are."

She struggled at length with the thought, but in the end her instincts proved stronger.

"No. I don't give away anything for nothing."

"In that case, you'll have to give up the ration books and not use them again."

"That's all you can do for me?"

"I suggested a way out. If you don't want to take it, you can't use the books."

She mumbled angrily as she got to her feet, knotted her heavy kerchief, and started for the door. When she reached it, she turned around:

"How much?"

She drew from her bosom a sewn linen purse still warm from the giant breasts that had surrounded it like a fortress, wet her thumb, and grudgingly ticked off a few bills that had been in the pocket of a New Zealand soldier several hours before, and several hours before that, under lock and key in the chest of the regimental paymaster. The King's shilling. Just like olden times, when each soldier signed for his shilling in an English town square to the accompaniment of a crier and a trumpeted fanfare, except that now it was a barking, whiskered paymaster dressed in desert khaki, whose bugle had been exchanged for a field telephone.

"Don't mention it. I'm a civil servant."

He didn't doubt the point would be lost on her.

"Actually," Elias told Sara, "I'm sorry that was her decision, I would have been very curious to see how such an argument would have sat with the court—a cheap whorehouse as a soldier's residence abroad. *In loco parentis*. Now we'll never know. She ruined my chances to make legal history."

Though business was booming, Sa'ada decided that life in Jerusalem was becoming too difficult. Starkie kept pressing her for information in a way that Tony Crowther never had, and she really had none to give him. Starkie didn't believe her. Well, then, he would say, you'd better get some, or I'll 'ave you locked up, see? Sometimes one of the "hello-George" boys below would come to tell her about some terrorist he had seen in the alley, but these reports were undependable; the young men had vivid imaginations and enjoyed sending Sa'ada and the British off on wild-goose hunts. You couldn't trust a word they said, and in any case, by the time Starkie and his men would arrive, the neighborhood was always clean. Once they informed her that they had captured a dangerous saboteur armed with a pistol in his pocket and were holding him in custody. Starkie came on the double in a desert-colored jeep, pulled up with an arrogant screech of the brakes, and saw that they were hilariously holding little Miracolo Orientale and keeping him from entering his house.

Miracolo was in the midst of throwing a despairing glance at Victoria's balcony, from which he hoped his salvation might come. Victoria, Victoria, he wept inwardly, you're up there and I'm down here, and nothing but calamity in between. But Victoria wasn't home, and her balcony was deserted except for the usual garlics and peppers that were drying there in the sun. At that exact moment Starkie arrived with his jeep. "A jeep, Lord, the righteous shall be saved from travail," Miracolo whispered under his breath, "the righteous shall be saved from travail."

"You there!" growled Starkie menacingly. "You Peeping Tom, you! Get out of 'ere, quick march!"

"Yes, officer."

"And you, you bunch of bloody h'idiots, break it up! 'Op it!"

To be on the safe side, he swung his stick at a few of them. They ran, pretending to howl with pain.

"Those hoodlums are taking over the neighborhood," everybody said. "Something really has to be done."

"Never mind," said Mr. Cordoso, "it's just as well that they're concentrated in one place. Imagine if those ne'er-do-wells were to scatter, the police wouldn't begin to know where to look for them."

A night or two later, Sa'ada made up her mind. She slit open her mattress, took out the wads of bills that were hidden there, and dug up by moonlight a large jar buried beneath the fig tree that was full of bills too. The next day she was gone for good.

Time passed and the Food Control Bureau opened an office in Sa'ada's old house. Pregnant women requesting extra rations and toothless old men with medical papers sat on wooden benches beneath the shade of the fig tree and grumblingly fanned themselves with folded newspapers.

Sara had had a bad day. She had gone with Thérèse to visit the family of an unregenerate alcoholic and had found a bruised, beaten woman and sick children, including a two-year-old girl with a burn on her cheek where her father had hit her with a frying pan. It was too much for both of them. Sara had repeatedly consulted Elias about the case, yet she knew there was little he could do. The police preferred to keep out of family quarrels, while the woman was too scared of her husband to file a complaint.

She made supper and put the children to bed, but she couldn't seem to calm down. Her head felt as though it were bursting.

"Elias, I'm going out for a walk."

"By yourself?" He looked up from the folder of documents in which he was immersed.

"I won't be gone long. An hour or so. Perhaps a bit longer."

It was a dark, moonless night, a sticky darkness that made your heart beat faster. At first she didn't know where she was going. Her feet took her downhill, down the steps that led to the tomb of Shimon the Just. It was pitch dark. She felt frightened. She switched off her flashlight so as not to be seen herself. High brambles suddenly grew all around; the unkempt field, strewn with rubbish during the day, was now a whirlpool of night sounds and night shapes. She kept her eyes on the lights that flickered weakly from the huts across the way. She tripped, regained her footing, and then, in a single panicky moment, twisted her ankle and fell from the footbridge she was walking on into the shallow conduit below. When she managed to climb out again, her purse, with her identity card and all her notes and money in it, was gone. Her forehead broke out in a sweat. She cried but walked on. Just a little farther, she kept telling herself, it isn't far now, just a little farther.

A dog barked. The first fences of the neighborhood appeared. A jagged, rusty piece of tin caressed her foot. The shacks loomed large around her. She drew a beam with her flashlight on door after door, trying to see. Hadassa and Mattan Zakkai. Mattan? She had always supposed it was Matityahu. A can of geraniums stood outside. On the freshly painted door a child had drawn something with chalk. A home. Pallid light shone out from within.

She knocked.

Matti opened the door. He stood wonderingly in the narrow doorway, blocking it with his body and with his hands that rested on the jambs. A dusky kerosene lamp silhouetted him from behind. He was wearing an undershirt. Something quiet and unassuming about him. In his fingers he held a needle, with which he had been trying to mend, grimy-handed as usual and without notable success, his daughter's dress. The threadbarest of rooms could be made out over his shoulders.

"You!"

"Matti, I lost my papers, my shoes are soaking wet, and I haven't an ounce of strength left."

"Take them off, Sari."

He put the kettle up. He said nothing. He ran a loving finger over her face, down the inside of her arm, over her eyes that were shut with accumulated fatigue, perhaps of all the years since Zaki had run off. Be it the death of him, he knew he could do her no harm. The children were asleep; the smell of their breathing filled the room, the milky, animal vapors of three washed little bodies. One of them whimpered, snorted like a steam engine, and turned over in his sleep.

He came in her as though into his own among all the families of earth.

CHAPTER NINE

MATTI WAS FULL of undistilled doubts. The night Hadassa returned with their son to Jerusalem, the boy had another asthma attack.
The whole trip had been in vain. Matti went feverishly out into the
night to look for a doctor, took a wrong turn in the driving rain,
missed two more, and lost several valuable minutes. Had anyone
stopped him to ask where he was going, he wouldn't have known just
then. The rain flooded down his face. He didn't bother to wipe it.

It can't go on like this anymore, he told himself. He was full with Sara
as though he'd exchanged his bodily heat for her own, implanted in
her, in her and this city, which was one big bunker now, an impene-
trable warren, his own warm, private hole, the cave of Matti the Just.
So close to the lull of your breath I can touch it, all the time, even at
home, I pronounce you a secret line cut into the flesh of my hand that
I clench harder and harder. I ought to fence myself in with Hadassa,
he said to himself, but I can't even see her. How can you fence yourself
in with thin air?

When the doctor had left and her son felt better, Hadassa wept quietly. Matti listened with total abnegation to her choked, broken cries, on his way with a towel and a bowl of warm water to bathe the boy's sweaty body. I'm not a child, he kept telling himself, I'm forty-two years old already. When she finally fell asleep, he buried his face in his hands and sat without moving. Inside the shack the low flame of the lamp trembled above the sleeping heads of the children.

A letter from Amatsia arrived from the Egyptian desert, stamped with the censor's approval. Hulda sniffed the paper it was written on. It smelled of army.

Dear Hulda and Bimbi,

This desert is dull, pointless, inchoate, full of heavy khaki objects that bounce from place to place and light khaki objects that you carry on you—and it is absolutely crucial. Even if sitting in this flapping tent, bent over a map that keeps tearing loose in the dry wind, one can see no connection between what one is doing and this war against the Great Fiend, there's still something that so obviously unites the snows in Russia, thousands of kilometers from here, with the sand that I eat with my bully beef. It's hard work, but it's meaningful. And it's all so clear. Do you remember, Bimbi, how you once told me that you longed for a language that had no green lawns between its words? Here there aren't even sidewalks between the words, not even a winding Jerusalem path. Our talk here is monstrously laconic, the code of a practical tribe of men caught up in that most stirring, boring, dreadful, and marvelous of things, a just war. Sometimes I think that this is perhaps the last just war that will ever be fought. I don't know how well defined the forces of Good are in it—they're too dispersed and sometimes even hidden—but I know that the forces of Evil are unmistakable.

As for myself, personally, I've chucked here a lot of what was superfluous, perhaps even ostentatious, and it may be that on my return to Jerusalem (when?) I'll no longer be as broad-minded, as worldly as you who are my family. I've become frightfully unenlightened. You'd be shocked to see how crude my humor has become, how simple my needs. What's mine is mine, I'll bash whoever doesn't like it in the teeth, and that's that. Terribly simplistic, Hulda, isn't it? And by the way, I think that our friends Taleb and Husni and that whole gang of theirs, because they're doing nothing against Hitler, and even a few things for him, are losing out on the significance of this century.

I think a lot about Nili, and the cedar tree, and the two of you in our city that I hardly dare allow myself the luxury of longing for. Swimming in whisky from the sergeants' club, my taste buds ruined by too much tea and tinned meat, moronized by meteorology, tired tired tired, I ask that you make me when I come home, if I come home, a big bowl of salad with fresh mint and green olive oil, and a cup of real coffee. No concerts, no books, no art exhibitions, please. My friends, there are men here who haven't seen their wives and their children for nearly five years. Who am I compared to them?

Nahum is working hard at the military hospital in Alexandria. I received a brief note from him last week through an officer friend. He says that he thinks he's got a big surprise for us all, but he doesn't say what. Best regards to *los* Amarillos. Limitless love and kisses to you all.

The censor had lingered over such words as "sidewalks" and "code" but hadn't crossed anything out. He was a well-known author who had been made a censor in the desert because no one knew what else to do with him.

His transfer papers in his pocket, Matti drives up to the lathe shop in someone's commercial van and finds Sara delivering milk.

"Get in."

"Have we struck it rich?"

"That's just what we've done. Let's have a ball."

The car is already moving when he says:

"Sari, I hope you don't have any plans for the next hour and a half, because I'm kidnapping you out of town."

"That's a disaster," says Sara, delighted. "I still have three homes on my list."

"Can they wait?"

"If they couldn't, I wouldn't be here, Matti. I'll manage. Thérèse will help out."

He locks the door on her side so that she won't fall out.

"Are you cold?"

"No."

The village of Ein-Karem disappears with its valley, the last of the fogbound, castlelike, grace-given city, pierced by tall cypresses, smoky with winter.

"Where to, Matti?"

"To paradise." And he adds: "You Jerusalemites have forgotten what it means just to go for a ride."

"With good reason."

"Uh-uh," he overrules her. "One mustn't be penned up, no matter what. You should know that if anyone does." He stops the car in a wash of fog. On one side is a stone wall, on the other an embankment. At least let this last time be a good one.

"Come, Sari."

"Is there a path here?"

"A porcupine trail. "

A long hard climb. Matti leads the way up the slope, limping a little, reaching back his hand to her at the hard parts. An occasional arbutus tree flashes red on the hillside. Trampled porcupine quills, already well muddied. Sara gasps for breath. Tiny flakes of snow are mixed among the wettish drops that fall in a ceaseless gray mass. A cold smell, a smell of wool. Matti halts.

"Once in a squad-leader course we saw two deer cross the trail right here. Thirty meters in front of us. They disappeared over there, in that thicket."

"Weren't they cold?"

"Soon we won't be either," he promises, hugging her. This is our home. He could feel as never before his two arms and hers. This is our home, our four walls. He doesn't begin to have the strength to tell her it is finished.

Sara spreads her nurse's robe beneath a large, wet carob tree. The rock is covered with moss and rotted leaves. The cliff drops off ahead in one plunge against a background of dreaming hills that glitter silver-wet with large stones. Veiled peaks, the dark growth of winter, more black than green. A grayish fog.

"What a ball," Sara says.

"Wasn't it worth the climb?" he asks gently. He searches for a crack in the monolith of her love through which to tell her, but she is too of one piece, too bewitched to let reality in. She'll never listen to me now, it's hopeless, he tells himself, despairing and joyous at once, delinquent, a coward, but happy, swept along.

"Don't yet," she whispers.

"Can you still?"

"Forever."

"You're mine." He looks into her eyes. "Don't ever forget it. Mine." He keeps finding new levels in them, of years, paths, light, all his.

"Mine."

Something large and invisible, perhaps a blackbird, calls musically from the tangled branches of a nearby oak. It seems to Sara that she had never seen such white mountain light before, as of water before its fall, as of branches, birds, snow.

Risen on one elbow, brushing something from her brow, flesh of her flesh.

They drive home in silence. A gust of rain meets them at the entrance to the city. Sara hugs herself. Her robe is wet and smells of pine needles, and of something else too that suggests hoary lichen in chinked rock. Matti feels a total failure for not being able to tell her and withdraws inside himself, not looking at her. Sara lays a hand on his arm, but he stiffens and does not respond. Guess, Sara, he begs inwardly, guess, my clear-eyed one, so that I don't have to tell you. But Sara is adream, spindrift, and spellbound; his new mood still says nothing to her. She has lost all sense of time and can feel him still inside her. Him and the white light. The rain mixed with sleet beats fiercely against the tin body of the car.

"Drop me off here, Matti," she says. He nods and brakes.

"Next week?"

He mumbles something and slams the door shut. He doesn't like himself just then. Neither does he like the face that smiles at him through the wet windshield or the sleet that falls on her uncovered hair and robe. He cannot for the life of him imagine what there is to smile about. What a lousy deal it all is.

"Mother, do you hear me?" Hillel burst flushed with excitement into the house. "They found an arms cache in our school last night! What do you say about that? It was there all the time and nobody knew!"

"I should think that somebody must have known."

"The highest grades knew. One of the boys was standing lookout, and the others were training inside, and suddenly a C.I.D. car drove up, and one of the ceedies jumped out, and before he could press the button the ceedy said to him in Hebrew, 'No, boy, don't you do it,' but he pressed it anyway, and they got away through the field, but the ceedies found a crate with five grenades in it, right in our school, Mother! And now they want to shut it down, and they let us out early today because the principal's at the police station, but everyone says he'll get out quick because he really doesn't know anything, he's such a jerk that he wasn't even in on it. No one trusts him."

"It's too bad about the grenades," said Sara. "What kind were they, Mills?"

"What do you know about grenades?"

"What does it sound like I know?"

He was crestfallen:

"Mills."

He went off to play in his room but a few minutes later reappeared in the kitchen.

"You know what I think, they should never have left those grenades there. You can bet I'd never have left them."

"What would you have done with them?"

"You can bet I'd have done something. I can think of all kinds of things."

"What, for example?"

"I just told you, all kinds of things. Maybe I'll talk it over with Father. Maybe, I'll have to think." He left, then stuck his head back through the door: "There's going to be a student demonstration tomorrow."

On the corner of Prophets Street military policemen are busy unloading a truck full of thin, swarthy Italian prisoners of war. A deafening chorus of wolf whistles descends on her. Their war is over. They sniff their new surroundings, a hungry swarm of men, cordoned off from the street by the wall of MPs.

"Bear, where's Matti?"

"He's gone. But consider me at your service."

"Bear, please don't clown around. Where's Matti? Is he down below?"

"I just told you, but you wouldn't believe me. He's gone. Vanished. Taken a powder."

"His transfer came through?"

"To his great pleasure." He watches as he presses the tack into her, cruelly. Then he feels sorry. "As far as I know, he's already at sea."

Already.

"Bear, think hard, he didn't leave me any message?"

"I don't think so."

"Try to think, it's important."

"Well, Matti said this: 'If Sara comes tell her that . . . no, don't tell her anything.' So do you call that leaving you a message or not leaving you a message? Sit down for a minute." He graciously offers her a chair.

"No, thanks."

"I take it that now that Matti's gone, the fighting proletariat won't be getting its milk anymore," says Bear. It is impossible to tell if he is teasing her again or being serious.

"You'll get your milk," says Sara as she leaves.

Her bus comes and Sara boards it, but soon it is forced to take a detour, for a student demonstration is blocking the main street. A nervous policeman stabs the air with frantic, pointless blasts of his whistle, which only add to the general tension. Girls are screaming. Overly livid faces, overly loud voices. The bus inches its way through the commotion.

Free im-mi-gra-tion
For the He-brew nation,
Down with the Union Jack,
We want our home-land back,
Bo-o-o-o!
Ya-a-ayy!

The rally is just getting under way, but already its cadences are having their effect. Sara covers her eyes with her hands. Everything hurts her. Perhaps, it occurs to her, Hillel is somewhere in the crowd too. He is almost sure to be, though no one is wearing his own face today anyway.

To the High Commissioner's,
Break the windows, smash the chairs,
Throw the British down the stairs!

The hysterical whirlpool churns slowly away from them through the square. Deflected from its route, the bus now makes its way through a section that neither Sara nor the driver knows well. The driver loses his way and begins to curse, then cautiously backs up. The motor coughs and backfires. Around the corner is an Arab neighborhood that does not have the best of reputations. They will probably be pelted with stones now. Already young toughs can be seen beginning to gather.

Sara cannot stand the journey anymore. She pushes her way to the door and bangs on it until the driver opens. Outside she fills her bursting lungs with clean winter air. She isn't sure where she is. A long, high, seemingly endless wall rises to her right, and she follows it without any idea where it is taking her, feeling worse and worse. She can hardly make out the street anymore, and she clings to it as though it were her salvation, groping her way along the rows of damp stone. Even the stone doesn't feel the way it should: her senses have gone awry. A huge, barred iron gate looms suddenly out of the wall; by its side hangs a large iron bell with a clapper. Sara pulls the bellrope as hard as she can. The heavy clang of it makes her shudder. No one answers. A few minutes more pass when a young priest stops by her as he comes down the street.

"Sister Sara, what's the matter? Don't you feel well?"

"I had a spell of faintness," says Sara, uncertain who he is. "I think I must be sick."

"It's no wonder in times like these." He pulls a large key from his pocket and opens the gate. "There is no one to come to the gate here, Sister Sara. This is the cemetery of our Scottish Monastery, and the guard hasn't come to work for several days. He's too frightened. Sit down, I'll bring you something to drink."

He sits her on a bench in the garden and soon returns with an aluminum cup of clear water. The well-tended garden is thick with silvery frankincense. A most unsorrowful cemetery. Why on earth a cemetery? And what is there to guard?

"You don't remember me, Sister Sara, but I visited your hospital once when our principal had a heart attack. That was many years ago. No doubt you've forgotten, and little wonder, you take care of so many people in the course of a day. Once everyone in Jerusalem knew everyone else, but today we've becomes strangers. An estrangement of the heart. But look at me chatting away like this when you're not feeling well! Shall I call a taxi for you? Would you like to be taken to the hospital or to your home?"

"Home, please," says Sara. "Please, to my home."

"What times, *ya sitt,*" says the driver. The demonstration has moved on but can still be heard in the distance, echoing through the city.

Body will not protect body, Matti. Voice will not protect voice. So fare thee well, Matti-earth, Matti-childhood, warm-mouthed, hard-nosed Matti-all-mine.

Lately many cases concerning the Haganah are being referred to Elias. Word has got around that he is good at getting people out of trouble. He is approached at all hours, sometimes in the middle of the night, by men in workshirts who look a little like those who used to be called in Sara's old neighborhood *los halutsim,* pioneers, but who are calmer, more solid, less prone to interrupt and wave their hands when they talk. They do drink a lot of tea, though, and have begun to call Elias Comrade Amir. Their hands rest before them on his desk without moving, like the hands of peasants.

Elias no longer hesitates. More and more he throws himself into their affairs. All the energy that had been dammed up in him while he had struggled to make up his mind now bursts loose. Even his movements have changed: his stride is taller now, quicker, firmer. No longer does he amble lazily along on tall legs. His long mouth is not the brown wound it used to be, having lost much of its sadness. Like that of any new convert, his zeal outdoes itself.

He is a bug on safety now. By his own request he has been granted the authority to call off any underground activity in the city that is not properly protected, for which purpose he has even been given a small auxiliary of adolescent boys and girls. Sometimes, managing to pass the guard outside without being stopped for identification, he enters a room where a group is in the middle of learning to clean a revolver, or the Haganah Code, and orders it to disperse for lack of sufficient security. Generally he meets with no argument. And yet he is not even an official Haganah member, having never sworn it allegiance, and hasn't the foggiest notion of how to pull a pin from a grenade. He is the legal specialist.

Once one of the men who used to call him Comrade Amir says to him: "When the state comes close, you and some of the other comrades will have to sit down and work out a constitution for us." Elias does not see how the state is close to being close, but from then on he begins to think differently. On his own request he is hurriedly sworn in one night in a darkened room in the building of the Takhkemoni School. He does not see the faces of his inductors.

He is given a code name: Ya'akovi. Young boys are sent to him with slips of paper on which strange messages are written:

To: Ya'akovi
From: C.J.S.
Re: I-ent 2 m w s.a.

which means in ordinary language that the commander of the Jerusalem sector wishes to see him about the imprisonment of two members who had been caught by the British in possession of small arms, in other words, a pistol.

Sometimes Elias would stare at these letters and forget what they stood for, until they became mere meaningless lines. They reminded him of the rabbinic abbreviations in the texts he had studied as a schoolboy in Tiberias. People, he thought, worked their will with letters and forced them to combine in all kinds of unlikely ways, so that they could burn for a few years with an unearthly fire and then flicker and die out. His lips parched like a man's with fever, his dark cheeks flushed, he would open a new file on the 2 m w s.a. It was simple and it wasn't. If only Elias had known, he could have compared these stripped words to a certain junkyard in the city beneath which flourished a whole underground armaments plant. But he did not know. He lived in a world of words, which being generally quite stirring, gave him the strength to do a great deal.

Little by little. Step by step. How hard it was for Sara to return from that other world. She inhabited her own house as though it were a place that she wasn't yet familiar with, like a waiting room, or a hotel, where you had to learn what every object, each detail was for. She moved gingerly. Her day consisted of concentric circles, one within the other, starting with her circular walk each morning to the shops and back home again through the park. Much patience went into the folding of the laundry, cleaning a closet, preparing meals. Since she was not yet entirely over her long bout with the flu, she extended her sick leave from the Health Bureau. Thérèse came at least once a day, piled high with folders, to consult with her. Sara began to be overconcerned for the children, to give them too many sweaters and too much unsolicited love. She lived from one day to the next and not a step outside it, lying low. A wick trimmed all the way down.

"You've become an overprotective mother, Sara," Elias remarked to her. "You're more like Hulda these days than you are like yourself."

After Matti, it had simply become easier for her to love, or to express her love. She would close the shutters when she put the boys to sleep, to shut out the drumming of the rain, or get up to cover them several times during the night. She could feel the rampaging blackness very near; it was visible through each crack in the walls, which might suddenly open to admit it—and the boys were so helpless. She no longer sought fortune-tellers, but relied on herself, on her own two arms, as if she had only now discovered their true strength to support. To sustain.

With time the circles widened. One evening Tony Crowther persuaded the two of them to come to a special concert at the YMCA; throughout the performance a light machine projected its shifting patterns on a silvery blue screen at the front of the hall. Things grew less strange to her: she reaccustomed herself to the space between blanket and sheet, to Elias's breath, to the angles of the furniture. Weary of her exile, she no longer thought about it, not even in those moments before total waking when one sometimes feels impaled on the sword point of a remembered whisper. The way home was a long one, and she wanted to walk it thoroughly, without cheating. That other land had been so different—one could not even ask how.

"The further back you look, the smaller everything seems to get," mused Elias one evening to Professor Barzel, who had dropped in to visit.

It was Hulda who had urged her husband to pay a call on their friends to inform them of a letter she had received from Amatsia, from a weather station in the desert. He had written to tell her that he would be home soon, and that he was bringing with him a girl named Ya'el.

"Everything seems to have been smaller once," Elias went on. "The country, the buildings, all of us. So awfully small. Even the wars were smaller. Things seem to have been on such a tiny scale then, as though we were looking at them now through an inverted telescope."

"We've traded a sense of time for a sense of space," said Professor Barzel. "Nowadays we want to grow big, to grow out. Once this was really a very small land, but with a very big history of events. Things happened here in time rather than in space. Look at the Old City: it's just one square kilometer, but think of what's packed into it. We've grown, we've spread, but we've lost our specific density. I'm not sure we have the better of the bargain."

"I'm not sure we had any choice," said Elias.

"Perhaps not. Perhaps our debts to time have been suspended until we can afford to pay them again. A moratorium."

"Still, it *is* terribly difficult to bring up children in such a world of moratoriums. With boys one somehow manages, but girls? What really is happening with Nili?"

"Nili has switched to the cello," said Hulda. "The instrument is bigger than she is. She sits there with her knees apart, pulling this big bow with all her red hair falling over her face. Tony Crowther's become her slave. He brings her rare medieval scores. She says he's not even musical, and he says she'll be a star, though it's beyond him how two perfect tone-deafs like us, or some such phrase, could have raised a musician like her. Bimbi just barely passes muster, but I never even reached the stage of *Für Elise*."

"I saw Hillel in the street the other day," said Professor Barzel. "He was running somewhere with his hair quite combed."

"That's amazing. On the whole they've managed to stay perfectly wild. Free of all the crimes of civilization."

"Hulda, you still haven't told us anything about this girlfriend of Amatsia's. Do you know any details?"

"There's a photograph," said Hulda. "Of the two of them. Nothing to rave about."

"Let's see it."

She pulled out a glossy black-and-white square from her pocketbook. There were palms and a British army barrack on it, and in the foreground a couple in uniform, grinning for the photographer. Sara's eyes met Hulda's: neither cared for Ya'el. She was too small and made-up, and had too many teeth, maybe three hundred, said Hulda, of which she felt obliged to show all, gums included. Maybe she was a dentist's daughter. And just look how she clutched Amatsia's hand as though she owned it—oof!

"I don't suppose there are too many women in the Egyptian desert," said Elias with a smile.

"Does it upset you, Hulda?"

"Listen, Sara, once I had a princess planned for him, now I don't care if he comes back with one wife or a thousand, as long as he comes back alive. I need him alive."

"Amen. It won't be long now. The Russians will be in Berlin soon."

"Bimbi, how's your cedar? I passed by it last night, but it was too dark to see."

"The cedar is fine. It's sixteen years old already, and going strong. It must be five stories high." He resavored his victory, as old people do the past. "And Hassan said it never would take! Do you remember how he said that?"

"I remember that party as though it were yesterday," Sara said. "There'll never be another like it. Can you picture Amatsia coming home now and chatting with Taleb? He's become the Mufti's right hand, Taleb has."

"Or Nahum with Husni!"

"All the men will be coming home from wars now," said Professor Barzel. "They'll all have learned to fight. The country will change again. Everything will become more professional, the fighting too. The individual won't count anymore, only the stupid plural. The plural is always stupid. What do you think, Elias? Amatsia says that the Arabs are missing out on this century because they didn't join in the fight against Hitler."

"I say they're missing out on this century for another reason. It's because they're unable to transcend their own culture. I'm beginning to think that you can only grow if you can change. I mean total personal change. Reality passes you by if you insist on always remaining yourself."

"I wonder what will happen these next few years."

"The British will pull out."

"Do you really think so? Seriously?"

"They'll leave."

"And what will be then, Elias?" asked Hulda worriedly.

"We will be," said Elias, so quietly that they couldn't be sure they had heard right. "For better or worse, we."

After the guests leave, Sara sits in front of the bedroom mirror wearily combing her hair. She still feels cropped short like a stubbly field; where on earth might she find the strength to recharge herself. Elias comes up behind her and lays his palms on her cheeks.

"You're so patient, Eli," she says. She needs the warmth of those hands. She feels cold all the time. She draws on him these days for what she herself lacks.

"What did you say?"

"Nothing important."

"You said I was patient? That's all that I am. Nothing else."

"All?"

"Almost all. When I'm dead," he smiles his long, sad smile, "you can have carved on my tombstone: 'Here lies a patient man, Elias Amir, a lawyer in Jerusalem.' "

She smiles. The way back is slow and so long. The lamp on the night table lights up their dark heads, one above the other, two tired faces in the mirror. Lately the family resemblance has begun to appear between them, not so much in their features as in the wrinkles that run from the corners of both their eyes like many gray chameleons scuttling over stone. They are growing old the same way.

"What are you thinking of doing when you're all better, Sara?"

"Work. What else is there to do?"

The conversation that evening gave Professor Barzel a jolt: if the British were really going to leave, as his friend Elias said that they were, and it did seem perfectly plausible, it was crucial to organize, organize, organize. And systematically: courses, drills, emergency room procedures, medical stocks. Stalking through the courtyard of the Jewish Agency building (lucky bastards, four cedars!) and talking himself hoarse in the offices above, he began to pester the national authorities about the need to maintain a large supply of traumatological materials in Jerusalem. No one took him seriously. Like as not no one knew what traumatology was. Ideology, of course, but *trau* . . . what? A modern form of medical witchcraft perhaps. He wasn't budgeted a cent. And perhaps there was really no money, but he grew tired of hearing the same old clichés. We will have to make do. We will never give in. There is a Power that guides. The Winds of History. Finally Professor Barzel reverted to the style of his Heidelberg student days and told a certain national authority that the only winds blowing came straight from his behind, so that the whole country stank from them already, and that what was needed was not wind but bandages, injectors, arterial clamps, antiburn ointments, morphine, and sulfa. The national authority was insulted and refused to continue the meeting. The Jewish Agency requested that future contacts with the hospital be carried on through Professor Kapulski of Odessa, who spoke the language of the national authorities and didn't press impossible demands when the larders were empty.

Amateurs, swore Professor Barzel, damned dabblers, the war will come and catch this whole city with its pants down.

In the meantime he organized courses. For that he needed no special budget. Everyone in Jerusalem, he said, should be able to give first aid. He telephoned Sara.

"Sara, come out of your shell, please, you're the best instructor we've ever had, and I'm not starting without you. And please inform the Health Bureau that you've resigned."

She came back. Like Professor Barzel several years before, she had skipped over herself. I live on the top floors now, she summed it up to herself, where there's a constant commotion, workrooms, children's rooms, the kitchen, the living room, everyday things. The cellar's locked for good, and I don't even know where the key is. Maybe one shouldn't know.

Hayyim Cordoso too must have sensed that the British were going to leave, because he began bringing various bits of information to the Jewish underground. Since he came and went freely in British circles, though not very high ones, his reports were quite accurate. He delivered them conscientiously, as though chipping out a niche for himself in the wall of some future paradise, every day a few more chips, each painstakingly recorded, dust and all. He still wasn't convinced that his precious Mandate was a thing of the past, but meanwhile he walked the streets parading his new righteousness like a man with a freshly acquired driver's license in his hand.

Miracolo proposed to Victoria again. He presented himself to her with a large bottle of perfume, a gaunt petitioner who now boasted a criminal record thanks to the demon Lilith. Victoria said no. She gave him back the bottle.

"What are you bringing me perfume for, Nissim? At my age a woman puts perfume on her belly only to go to the gynecologist. And you might as well know that I'm not Victory anymore, I'm Defeat."

But she made him mint tea this time, and hot burekas, which was perhaps all he wanted, because from then on he came to call on her at least once a week. They would sit together beneath the strings of drying peppers on the veranda, eating and drinking. Miracolo entertained her with macabre stories from the burial society and morgue about bodies that had been switched, corpses that suddenly sat up and asked for something to eat, pranks and practical jokes Jerusalemites played on their creditors by appearing to them at night dressed in shrouds to frighten them out of a debt.

Victoria listened greedily. Death, as seen through the eyes of Miracolo Orientale, made her laugh. She could no longer look at a funeral procession without chuckling to herself over one of the little man's stories and droning through her upturned nose in parody of the cantor's falsetto voice at the head of the crowd:

They shall bear thee in their hands,
Thou shalt not fear the terror at night . . .

And she didn't anymore.

At night the searchlights crisscross in the sky to form great, groping heavenly triangles, or suddenly cast their fierce beams on a silver minaret or the tipped branch of a cypress tree, like inarticulate, diligent messengers of a distant galactic storm.

In 1945, as the war was drawing to its close, Don Isaac Amarillo returned to Jerusalem. He didn't return on his own, but was found. All this time he had been living in an insane asylum in Alexandria, from which he was now sucked back by the whirlpool of war. Some thirty years ago, it appeared, soon after running off from Jerusalem with his Claudine, he had cracked from the pressure, or perhaps had been hit on the head in some opium den, so that his sense of self, which was never of the strongest, had crumbled completely. Laughing and crying to himself like an abandoned baby, he had lain with his head shaven, unkempt and uncared for, in the paupers' ward. The local Jewish community, which knew he was a Jew even though all his papers were stolen, had paid for his upkeep.

It was Dr. Nahum who found him by pure accident, which was the surprise he had written about to Amatsia. Recalling the Amarillos' sad saga, he had telegraphed Tony Crowther to send him photographs of the missing man. When they arrived, there was no doubt that it was he: Don Isaac, to whom almost nothing had happened in the intervening thirty years, was remarkably unchanged.

"It's amazing," wrote Nahum, "that he's still alive. Most men in his situation would have died long ago from general want and debilitation, given the treatment received. I'd bring him back to Jerusalem myself, but my release is still pending. So I'll see you in Kantara when you come to pick him up."

Tío Shlomo and Tío Avraham and Tío Rafael took the train to Kantara to fetch him. Gracia kneaded her handkerchief and said, "But I was in Alexandria ten years ago, I was right near the building, and I didn't feel a thing!"

Sara waited for him on the hospital stairs when he came. Tío Shlomo opened the door of the taxi, and the three brothers dragged him out, bawling aloud like a one-year-old at the indignity. He was a uniform ashen color, the skin of his thin hands a cadaverous gray.

"Take him, Sara," said Tío Shlomo, unable to get himself to say, Take your father. Zaki. Zaki Amarillo. A still-torn pillow of feathers thirty years after the rip. A gentleman well known and well loved. He wet his long smock while being carried in on the stretcher and hid his shaven head in his hands with a whimper. They must have beaten him for wetting in Alexandria.

Sara held him and helped him into a bed. A check-up revealed malnutrition and several other ailments for which a program of treatment was drawn up, but when the psychiatrist was called in, he simply gestured helplessly in the direction of Sara, who was standing silently by. Professor Barzel came too and regarded the patient without a word.

"It's sad," he finally said, "but we'll treat him as though he were a child. Parents often become the children of their children. It's just that the children don't know it, and the parents don't want to admit it. That's what makes it so difficult."

I went down into the garden of nuts to see the fruits of the valley. Down down down. To the rockbottom beauty of madness. Sara looked at him for a long while. The great question that had haunted her for so long now lay before her, a mindless, spent little answer.

Subhi and Faiza came, both terribly aged, with Suhaila, who still lived unmarried at home. They kissed Sara's head and embraced Gracia sitting by the bed, it's the will of God, Sitt Gracia, it's the will of God, Sitt Sara. Perhaps God will reveal more to him than He has revealed to us in these pitiless times. God loves madmen. Perhaps they are better off than we who are sane.

Elizabeth Marcus came and said:

"His mind is kaput. And the mind is the man. To live like this is not worth it."

And she left. Victoria sobbed silently in the corner.

Tío Yosef "The-Messiah-Is-Coming" arrived, white as a dove and barely able to walk. He had to be helped bodily up the stairs to recite psalms by his nephew's bed. The nurses jostled each other shyly in the doorway to listen to the thin, crystal-clear voice of the old man in white, chiming sweetly:

The Lord preserveth the simple of mind,
I was brought low and He helped me . . .

"That's Sara Amir's father," whispered the student nurses in the doorway, "and the old man must be her grandfather."

Return unto thy rest, O my soul,
For the Lord hath dealt bountifully with thee . . .

"It isn't the grandfather, it's the grandfather's brother."

For Thou hast delivered my soul from death,
Mine eyes from tears,
My feet from falling . . .

"Be quiet, girls, you're annoying them; why are you gawking like that? It isn't nice."

I said in my haste, all men are liars . . .
I will walk before the Lord in the land of the living.

Return unto thy rest, O my soul. Return, O my soul.

Zaki slowly regained his normal weight, but not his normal mind. He didn't take well to being moved from the asylum in Alexandria and cried all the time, day and night. In the end he quieted down and started asking for milk, much milk. He grew accustomed to the new faces around him and no longer hid his own face in his hands. Toward summer's end they began taking him out of doors on a chair, where he sat smiling in the courtyard, looking contentedly at the light that played on the stones and trying to catch its motes in his hand, beaming at the bronzed women and occasional children passing through. He would have given his soul to them. Once, when served a watermelon in the courtyard, he actually lit up with joy. Red, he said with much effort. Red. His gentle eyes filled with tears at each small happiness.

Gracia got used to the way he was. She sat by his side to feed him every day, wiping his hands and face with a perfumed handkerchief. Sometimes she just sat near him crocheting.

"He's my husband," she said. "The only one I've got. Between the two of us we're more than one hundred and twenty years old. This is no time to start quarreling with God. We'll be with Him soon anyway."

When told he would be discharged in a few weeks' time, and did she wish to place him in some home, she answered with the sweetness she had lately acquired, nobody could guess from where:

"God forbid. Zaki Amarillo will come home. I'll take care of him." And she did, freeing Sara entirely of the task.

On such evenings Sara stepped out of the building on Mount Scopus in which she taught, a silent presence, the whole city spread at her feet, and looked at the soft fleecy light out over the mountains, over the houses drowning in radiance, as if once this city, long, long ago, soon after Creation, had burst from some great rock, its truth flown molten and shiny over the hills. She could feel the moment to the quick. Now this is me, she told herself, now this is me, here on this hill, with this feeling of great peace that will never last, or standing in the street, people know me, I have three sons and so little time. Now this is me in this moment of hers. Tomorrow I'll be gone and the street will be gone, or another street and another time. And always, forever, this fleecy pile of light, that rock tumbled halfway down the hill to a lonely stop, a terraced alley, a dripping cypress tree, a caper plant in a wall. A place to walk slowly. A place to touch the sky: now it is close. To breathe in mountain and light. Now.

ABOUT THE AUTHOR

SHULAMITH HAREVEN grew up in Jerusalem, where she lives today. She has published thirteen books in Hebrew, including poetry, novels, stories, essays, a children's book in verse, and a thriller (under a pseudonym).

Though she speaks several languages, Hareven writes only in Hebrew, "the richest and most precise of languages." She has served as writer-in-residence at the Hebrew University in Jerusalem and was the first (and for twelve years the only) woman member of the Academy of the Hebrew Language.

As a teenager, Hareven participated in the Haganah underground. She was a combat medic in the siege of Jerusalem in the War of Independence, an officer in Operations in the Israeli Defense Forces, and reported from the front line in the War of Attrition and the Yom Kippur War. With the help of Palestinian friends, she spent time in Arab refugee camps at the height of the Intifada, writing eyewitness reports. Her widely read press column strongly advocates the Peace Camp position in Israel. She is married and has two children and four grandchildren.

Hareven draws a distinct line between her public activities and her literary work. She wishes her fiction to be judged for its literary merit and not for topical allusions. Her work has been translated into thirteen languages. Her other books in English are *Twilight and Other Stories, The Miracle Hater,* and *Prophet.*

HILLEL HALKIN has been translating classic and contemporary Hebrew authors—including S. Y. Agnon, Y. H. Brenner, Shalom Aleichem, and A. B. Yehoshua—for thirty years.

Cover design: SHARON SMITH

Art direction: SHARON SMITH

Text design: ZIPPORAH W. COLLINS

Compositor: STANTON PUBLICATION SERVICES

Text type: GRANJON

Editor: THOMAS CHRISTENSEN

Production coordinator: HAZEL WHITE

Copyeditor: FRAN TAYLOR

Proofreaders: JUDY WEISS, KAREN STOUGH

Printer and binder: DATA REPRODUCTIONS CORPORATION